He laughed and actually moved closer. I had never known sanding could be so much fun. He stood with his shoulder touching mine, pointing to the wall and giving out instructions in a low voice. The scent of his cologne mixed with sweat and sawdust filled the air around us and I couldn't get enough of it.

"So am I doing it right?" I asked, looking back at him, my hand moving across the wall the way he'd shown me.

"Oh, yeah." It didn't sound like John was talking about the wall. He certainly wasn't looking at it. His emerald eyes burned into my brown ones.

I stopped sanding.

"Yeah, you look good. I meant, *it*. It looks good."

John's face reddened.

LOVE OUT OF ORDER

NICOLE GREEN

Genesis Press, Inc.

INDIGO LOVE SPECTRUM

An imprint of Genesis Press, Inc.
Publishing Company

Genesis Press, Inc.
P.O. Box 101
Columbus, MS 39703

Copyright © 2009 Nicole Green

ISBN: 13 DIGIT : 978-1-58571-381-3
ISBN: 10 DIGIT : 1-58571-381-3
Manufactured in the United States of America

First Edition

Visit us at www.genesis-press.com
or call at 1-888-Indigo-1-4-0

DEDICATION

To my mother, Diane, for her encouragement and support. Without her, this book may have never gotten written.

ACKNOWLEDGMENTS

First of all, I would like to thank Deborah Schumaker, the dream-come-true executive editor at Genesis Press, for taking a chance on this book and guiding me through the publishing process. I would also like to thank my other editor, Mavis Allen, for her hard work in helping to make this book stronger. I also have to thank the amazing members of my critique group who have helped me become a better writer and who constantly help with my crazy requests for advice and feedback. Internet Writers Workshop folks, you who you are, and I hope you know how much I appreciate you. And a special thanks to those who rode the crazy terrain with me this past summer— Carol, Amanda, Judy, Lauren, Karyn, and Pepper. And most of all, thanks to the people who've made it possible for me to believe in my writing over the years—God, my mother, my cousin Lori, my sister Ashley, and my amazing English teachers and professors.

CHAPTER 1
DOWNHILL SLALOM

Wal-Mart on Saturdays. It is something I try to avoid at all costs, but sometimes it's a necessary evil. I plotted my way down the aisles, darting around the many obstacles in my white sneakers. I wanted to spend as little time in that place as I possibly could. Plus, I was genuinely in a hurry. Another good reason to avoid Wal-Mart on Saturdays.

I was on a mission. Astoria Banks is not the kind of person you keep waiting. Have you ever had a good friend you really love, but who scares you sometimes? Well, that's how I feel about Astoria Banks. Her beauty, lack of inhibition and ability to captivate even the people who disliked her were imposing. I remember when she first cut her hair short and texturized it. When I told her I wished my head wasn't so big so that I could do something like that, she laughed at me and told me to do it if I wanted to. Astoria wore her personality on the outside. I was in awe of her.

Anyway, as I headed through the store in some sort of impossible, frantic, downhill slalom, I was of course derailed. I know, inevitable, right? "Excuse me," I muttered to a woman blocking my path with her cart, chatting to her friend while her kids ran in circles around them screaming. "Excuse me," I said a little louder as I looked for any hole through which I might be able to maneuver my cart. "Excuse me." That last one had a little more force in it. I no longer cared about being rude.

Then, when I pushed past her, she had the nerve to give me a dirty look.

"You should have moved out of my way one of the first forty-five times I asked you to," I muttered as I charged down the aisle, racking my brain for the solution to my problem.

I never knew what to get Astoria. She was so picky. Yet, she never wanted to tell anyone what she wanted. Whenever I asked what she wanted as a gift, she would ask me what the point was. She would say that if she told me what to get, she might as well buy the thing herself.

"Crap," I muttered, pulling my ringing cellphone out of my purse. I had forgotten that I was supposed to meet Suse at her house before going to the restaurant until the moment I saw her number displayed on my caller ID. I put the phone to my ear. "Hey."

"Denise, where are you? It's five. You said you'd be here by four-thirty," Suse said with a sigh. Suse was big into punctuality. Me, not so much.

"Wal-Mart. I kind of forgot all about Astoria's present," I said, grabbing a packet of stationery from a shelf and wincing at how lame a gift that would probably be. I had never even seen Astoria use stationery. Maybe because she didn't have any to use? Nah. Probably not.

"Denise! Where has your mind been lately?" Suse asked. I could almost see her small nose scrunched the way it always was when she was frustrated.

I got to know Suse through trial team try-outs during my first year. Suse is from a small town in southwest Virginia, and it shows from her accent to her mannerisms to her strange obsession with four-wheelers. She has quite a range of interests, though. She and my friend Melissa are in the same sorority. She is petite, has short, blonde hair, brown eyes and a pudgy face with a pug-like nose.

"Uhm. Lot going on. Interviews. Journal. Trial team. And on and on and it never ends," I said as I grabbed a gift set containing scented body gels and lotions. That and stationery? Was that good enough? Eh, it would have to be. Plus, Astoria knew how horrible I was at giving gifts. She should have stopped trusting me to surprise her by now. So it really was her fault.

"Okay, well, are you still coming over here first?"

"Sure thing. I'm headed to the checkout line now. Which means I should be out of here by sometime tomorrow."

"Good. Try to get here soon. We need time to decorate before Astoria gets there."

"Yep," I answered before flipping my phone shut and stuffing it back into my laptop bag. I had come to the store straight from the library and hadn't had time to switch to my normal purse.

I looked up with a glimmer of hope as the number for one of the express check out lines lit up—number three. I gripped the handle on my shopping cart, focused on the end goal. The illuminated number three. Out of the corner of my eye, I saw a middle-aged couple and a mother and her two bad kids headed toward number three, attempting to steal my glory. I couldn't let that happen. Victory had to be mine. These glory stealers clearly did not know Astoria Banks.

I charged forward, slipping past both sets of startled shoppers. I mumbled an apology when the woman of the middle-aged couple gave me a look of consternation and her hand fluttered to her heart. I skidded to a halt before the cashier. Her dark brown eyes grew wide in her burnt almond face, but she didn't say anything. She just started ringing up my items. I was actually out of breath. Luckily, I was too frazzled to be embarrassed.

Finally, I walked out of Wal-Mart, relieved and victorious with my crappy present for my best friend swinging at my side in a white plastic bag. I shielded my eyes from the late afternoon sun's rays and looked around the general vicinity of the rows of cars where mine should be.

Spotting it, I walked over to my car. My whip. My ride. My . . . well, at least it had four wheels and a motor. Yeah, with a rusted-out tail pipe, a busted rear door, paint missing in large patches over the trunk, the roof more rust than paint, half a faded Dartmouth sticker left over from a previous owner, and of course my college and law school stickers, my Sentra that had been gray at some point in its life wasn't going to win any prizes at the car show. But it got me where I needed to go—most of the time. And the rest of the time, well, the auto club needed someone to keep them in business, right?

Unfortunately, that evening was not to be one of the times my car wanted to get me where I wanted to go. The traitor left me there in the Wal-Mart parking lot alternating between heated threats and cajoling murmurs in an attempt to get my engine to turn over. Stupid Dad just had to be right about replacing the battery. Well, I just hadn't had time. But sitting in that parking lot, I was wasting plenty of time trying fruitlessly to get the car to do something I knew it wasn't going to do.

Just as I was about to scream, I heard a voice that made me freeze in mid-curse. "Denise?"

I didn't want to look up because I knew I would see John Archer's face. Sitting there in my stupid jalopy, I would see John Archer standing by the driver's side door.

"Denise, are you okay?"

Okay, maybe more embarrassing not to look up. I slowly turned my head and looked up at John Archer. John, make my palms sweat, make me smile like a moron, make me have a crush for the first time since high school Archer. He stood there in a black T-shirt and khaki shorts, his hands in his pockets.

Somehow, I managed to find part of my voice. "Hi."

"Car trouble?"

"I think it's the battery."

"I have jumper cables," he said, jerking his head in the direction of his black Mercedes Kompressor. "I could give you a jump."

Damn. Why, why, why did it have to be him? "Sure. That would be great. I'd really appreciate it," I blubbered.

"No problem," he said, already walking back in the direction of his car.

I watched him walk back, thinking about the first time I'd seen him—the first day of classes three weeks earlier.

The first thing I'd noticed about him was his teeth.

I know it's weird, but I have this thing about perfect, straight white teeth. He was laughing at some corny joke our Evidence professor had made. Dark hair cut close. Bright green eyes. The kind of guy you look at and look at yourself and say, yeah, like that's gonna happen. But he caught my eye—probably because I was burning a hole in the side of his head—as his laughter died away and smiled. I gave a half smile, unsure he was looking at me, and turned to my laptop, suddenly fascinated by my screen saver.

I hadn't been able to keep him out of my mind since.

I watched him drive around to the row of cars in front of me. The spot directly in front of me was empty. I had that going for me at least. John walked me through the process while I tried not to be too obvious about appreciating his arms. The sleeves were ripped off his T-shirt and his biceps were giving me quite a staring problem.

He told me to try to start the car and it started. He gave me a thumbs-up, put the cables away and walked back over to my driver's-side door.

"Thank you so much. I know you have way more important things to do than help me start my stupid car," I gushed. "I owe you big time."

"I didn't mind at all. I went to Virginia Beach for the day with some friends. Just getting back into town. No hurry to get anywhere," he said, leaning on the driver's side door. I wanted to be that door. "But you know, there is a favor I'd like to ask."

"Sure."

"Well, I was wondering if you would mind getting together with me sometime tomorrow," John said.

I had no idea how to respond. What could he possibly mean? I knew he couldn't mean what I wanted him to mean. I was afraid to even ask what he had in mind. Instead, I sat there gaping at him. Not a good look.

"Wait, that didn't come out right. If you wouldn't mind—I mean, I didn't get that Evidence reading at all last week and class just made it worse . . . and—if you don't want to it's fine, but I was thinking maybe we could meet at Barnes and Noble tomorrow or something," John said, running his words together, grinning the cutest embarrassed grin I had ever seen. He was bright red and adorable.

I realized I was still staring at him and making an already uncomfortable situation even worse. He looked like he wanted to run away.

"Sure," I said with an awkward smile.

"Great. Uh . . . four good?" he asked.

I nodded. I didn't want to ruin the moment with one of my corny remarks.

He smiled and then waved to some guys standing near the front entrance to the store. "I gotta go. I'll see you later."

"Okay," I said weakly. My phone vibrated and I took it out of my bag and ignored Suse's call. I didn't have time to reflect on the horror-turned-serendipity moment I'd just had. I'd never make it to Barnes & Noble the next day if Suse and Astoria killed me first.

I never made it inside of Suse's parents' house. She lived with her parents, who had moved to Richmond when she started law school. She was sitting in her car with the engine running when I pulled onto her street. I parked behind her, grabbed my laptop bag, shoulder bag and the shopping bag containing the pitiful present, slammed my door shut and ran to her car.

"Look at you," Suse groaned, burying her face in her hands.

She was right. I was a mess. I still wore navy blue cotton shorts with "Central Virginia Law School" printed on them and a gray T-shirt; my favorite studying outfit. My brown hair was swept up in a messy ponytail. Sweat glistened on my nutmeg brown skin. It was hot out, being mid-September in Virginia, and I'd done a lot of running around in the last hour or so.

"Suse, it's going to be okay. Don't freak," I said, adding to myself, *as you have a tendency to.*

"You're not even dressed. The reservation is for seven-thirty and we have to decorate and pick up the cake before she gets there. It's almost six now. And you tell me not to freak?" Suse said, racing down the secondary road that led to the interstate entrance nearest to her house. I cringed as she flung her little Nissan Versa around one curve after another.

"We can fix it. Don't panic. I'll change in the restroom at the restaurant. We'll work it out," I muttered. "Hey, my flight just got in this morning. I just got back from that job interview in New York, remember? It's been craziness all weekend. I've been in overdrive trying to get everything done and still do this birthday thing for her."

"Oh, yeah, how did that go?"

I relaxed in my seat, thankful for the subject change. "Okay. But I'm going to hold out for that downtown firm I have a callback interview with next week." I had interviewed for a summer associate position with Dettweiler, a firm I'd had my eye on ever since I had done an externship there as an undergrad.

"Oh, you'll get it. For sure."

"Hope so."

"Oh, of course you will, I was just telling . . ." Suse started.

Satisfied that she was no longer in attack mode, my attention drifted away from her. I knew she was telling me something about her boyfriend, Charles, making her crazy yet again. She's been with him since high school. They're practically married. He's a total jerk, but she thinks she's in love.

Really, I guess I should have been happy that Suse was so anxious to do something nice for Astoria. If it hadn't been for me, Astoria and Suse would not have ever looked at each other. I was truly the middle ground between them. My temper was not as volatile as Astoria's, but I was not as passive as Suse. I liked to go out and have a good time, but Astoria liked it a little too much and Suse didn't like to go out nearly enough.

Even in physical appearance, I was not as extreme as either of them. My brown skin made stark contrasts to their opposite ends of the spectrum. The only thing that they had in common and left me out on was thin. I have been trying to get over my freshman fifteen-plus-a-few since before I even started as an undergrad at the University of Virginia.

I wouldn't call myself fat, and most of the time I like the way I look. But it's hard not having body issues standing next to Suse and Astoria. Astoria especially got on my nerves with the way she ate anything she wanted and got away with it. We both went to the gym. She, Suse and I were in a roller derby league. But Astoria ate whatever and whenever she wanted and didn't gain an inch. Did it work that way for me? Not so much.

Oh, the sacrifices I've made for Astoria Banks. I sat in a too-cold restaurant pretending to enjoy sushi and trying to force enthusiasm, which was hard when I was going on a few hours' sleep and depleted caffeine levels. And especially since my mind kept drifting back to John Archer. Luckily, Astoria didn't notice too much, since she was wrapped up in conversation with two of her other friends, Erich and Sharon. She and Erich had gone to SUNY together undergrad and both ended up at Central Virginia University's Brennan School of Law for law school. Sharon was a first-year law student Astoria mentored and had become fast friends with. Brennan was a small school with only a little over three hundred students total. It wasn't a bad place for law school, though. The school was just outside of Richmond, only a few minutes' drive from the city limits.

Suse, who really had nobody there to talk to but me, kept trying to draw me into conversation.

". . . Denise? You listening?"

I looked up, realizing Suse had been trying to get my attention. "Uh . . . sorry. I was just thinking about that um . . . brief we have due," I said.

Suse rolled her eyes, nodding. "Yeah. Can you believe it? We just got back. Anyway, you coming to the thing we're having for the first years Monday night?" Suse was heading up a new mentor program for the first-year students and was constantly planning events for them. I'm sure it annoyed the few that showed up more than it helped them.

"I can't. I told Stori that I'd help her pick up some stuff for the fundraiser she's doing next Friday." I hadn't been looking forward to helping Astoria until that moment. Astoria was involved in a community group that she was hosting a fundraiser for at the law school.

"Eh. Sometimes I feel so left out with you two."

"You know you wouldn't want to come," I said with a laugh.

Suse shrugged and looked away. I knew she knew it was true.

11

We turned to watch the other end of the table explode in laughter. Erich had gotten up from the table and was demonstrating some ridiculous new dance move. Astoria was telling him he had to be exaggerating; that the dance couldn't be that stupid. He was adamant that it was. I smiled and agreed with Astoria when my opinion was asked. That was the quickest way to get out of any question involving Astoria's opinion, I knew.

Suse and I turned away from them again. I stifled a yawn.

Suse picked at her pale pink nail polish and looked up at me with chocolate brown eyes. "You know, you never told me what happened to you earlier. You told me you were leaving the store around five and you didn't get to my place until six. I don't live that far from where you were."

I stared at her for a moment, wondering how she would handle the truth. Some things just didn't happen to come up in conversation. But I had my ideas about how she would react. I decided to keep it vague for the moment. I told her about my idiot car and getting both a jump and a study date from a fellow second-year.

"Wow, a date? Denise, you haven't even talked about dating anyone since I met you. This is huge!" Suse was clearly enjoying this knowledge.

"Not a date. People study together all the time." Yeah, obviously I wanted to think it was. Even though I knew it wasn't. He wanted some help with Evidence. That was all. But still . . .

"Anyway, I'm coming over tomorrow to help you get ready."

I didn't object. I knew I could use the help.

As Suse continued to squeal and throw a fit about my study "date", I threw nervous glances at Astoria, hoping she wouldn't pick up on our conversation. I wanted Astoria to know the full story even less than I wanted Suse to know. Luckily, Sharon and Erich had her attention. They were laughing over stories about their summer jobs.

Eventually, the conversation returned to Suse going on and on about how all the first years loved her and hinting to me that I was really missing out by not coming to the function Monday night. I let her. I contented myself by thinking about John's emerald eyes and imagining something funny and unforgettable I could say the next afternoon when we met up.

Annoyed with myself for even thinking it, I still couldn't help but wonder if John really had a girlfriend. The rumor around school was this alleged girlfriend, Sasha, had already put in her early decision application to our law school. She was apparently a senior at Boston College. I liked to pretend she didn't exist and hope hard proof of her existence would never come.

Hey. Even if I had no chance, it was nice to dream.

The star of the show demanded my attention, announcing that she was ready to open presents and cut the cake. I turned to face her and attempted to push John to the back of my mind. It wasn't hard to do once I started to worry about Astoria's reaction to her present again.

CHAPTER 2
STUDY BUDDY

The next day, I replied to Astoria's text as I left the library because she'd asked where I was. Still not really feeling like telling her about John, I gave her a vague reply.

I got into my car, dumped my books and laptop in the passenger seat and started the engine. To my surprise, it sputtered to life on the first try. I took that as a good sign. I did a little happy dance in the driver's seat as I buckled my seatbelt while still holding my phone in one hand.

Just as I was about to put my phone in the cup holder, my text message alert tone sounded. I flipped open my phone and found a new message from Astoria.

Who you studyin' with? You hate studyin' with people. Astoria's message was right to the point, as always.

A guy. From our evidence class, I again left my return text vague.

What guy? TELL ME NOW!!! she responded.

After a hesitant moment, my fingers poised above the keypad, I decided that there was no point in trying to hide it. I typed in my reply, *John.*

Archer? The transfer?

Yeap.
Oh. Really.
I decided not to answer her last text.

Suse was waiting for me when I pulled into my parking lot. She looked more excited than I was. She was almost bouncing up and down in front of my apartment door.

I found Suse's enthusiasm contagious. "We don't have much time!"

I opened the door to my apartment. For once, I barely saw Tia's mess. Tia was my roommate. She was light skinned and had curly, light brown hair and light brown eyes. She couldn't have been much over five feet tall.

It was amazing to me that such a small girl could create such a huge frustration. She left her dirty underwear in the bathroom after taking a shower. She left her clean underwear hanging over the shower rod to dry. She piled oatmeal- and pasta-encrusted bowls in the kitchen sink. And I was sick of seeing her books and clothes sprawled all over the living room. She talked too loudly on the phone. Her boyfriend, Terry, was practically a third roommate. And the two of them had the most obnoxiously loud sex. Astoria sometimes referred to them as "the porno stars."

"So . . . smells like your roommate's been trying to cook again," Suse said, wrinkling her nose. It did, and it made my stomach hurt.

"Yeah, I know. Come on, let's go to my room," I said, hurrying her into my room. I didn't know if Tia was there or not—her not answering the door for Suse was no indication. She could have been in her room, passed out. If I didn't answer the door, there was a very good chance it would never get answered. The main reason I hadn't fought Terry having his own key was so I wouldn't have to answer the door for him all the time.

The apartment always smelled like old cheese except for my room, which constantly had a scented candle burning in it. I had given up on all efforts to keep the apartment clean. As soon as I had cleaned it—back when I was foolish enough to waste my time doing such a thing—she had made a mess again. Sometimes she made a mess while I was cleaning.

In addition to giving up on keeping the apartment clean, I had given up on discussing any and all issues with Tia that I had with Tia. She would nod and smile, her eyes glazed over the whole time, not listening to a word I said. That glassy stare made me angrier than her mess; just knowing she wasn't taking me seriously. And after our one-sided conversations, the place would be just as nasty as before, if not more so. And so I just lived and let live. And bided my time until May.

"Who is this guy? You never even gave me a name," Suse said, grinning.

"John. He's one of the transfers." I hoped my tone came off airy, as intended, and not insanely hopeful, like I felt. "So, what should I wear?"

Suse was already in my closet. "So, tell me more about John." She held up a skirt, frowned and then put it back in the closet.

"Well, he's tall. He's got dark hair. He's hot. He seems really funny from his comments in class. I've never had a real conversation with him before yesterday, though," I said, deliberately leaving out any racially descriptive words.

"Sounds like a catch," Suse said, grinning.

"Well, it's just coffee at B and N. And Evidence. I don't want to build it up too much and then get disappointed."

Suse nodded, scrutinizing a pair of jeans before tossing them back on the closet floor. "Denise, you either need to start hanging things up or start ironing."

"Eh." I shrugged and went to find my makeup bag. I knew it was buried in one of the plastic containers stacked in the corner of my room.

"It's a miracle. I think I found something," Suse said. She handed me a striped button-down shirt and a camisole. She then took my make-up bag away from me. "We have to make you a sexy study buddy."

I laughed.

"You know, you really should wear makeup more. At least eye makeup. You have such gorgeous eyes." Suse handed me the eyeliner pencil because she knew I had this huge fear of being blinded by one and had to do that part myself.

I looked into the mirror, holding the pencil off to the side. People always said that about my eyes. They're wide-set and brown and complemented my high cheek-bones. At least that's what the lady at the makeup counter at Macy's told me once when I let Suse drag me over to her.

After Suse and I primped me for my study date, she wished me luck and left. My heart started slamming against my rib cage as soon as she drove away from my apartment complex and reality sank in. I was about to meet John Archer outside of class. Just the two of us. I hoped. I would feel like such a fool if a whole group of people were there. And if I didn't hurry, I would be late.

I jumped into my car and started the ignition. Success again. At least my car was on my side that afternoon. My palms were sweating like I was about to give an opening statement. I couldn't stop shaking even though I had the heat on full blast. The weather was a lot colder than it had been the day before, but not cold enough to have me shivering like I was. I sat there, thinking of all the horrible things that could go wrong as my car warmed up. Man, I needed a new car. I had too much time to think on my hands. And I was really torturing myself.

What if John didn't show up? What if he forgot? What if he never intended to show up? What if he showed up with his hot girlfriend? Somewhere inside, I knew that was unlikely since I'd heard she lived in Boston and it was Sunday afternoon, but rationality wasn't my strong suit at that moment.

Finally, mercifully, my car warmed up and I was off. The drive was not a long one, but I felt like was driving to Fredericksburg instead of just a few miles down the road. I sang along with the radio at the top of my lungs to a song I didn't know the lyrics to. I did a quick mental review of what we had covered in our last Evidence class. I tried counting the number of black cars on the road, the number of cars with tint, the number of cars with luggage racks, the number of SUVs; but nothing would suppress the dominant thought flashing in neon lights in the center of my brain. I was meeting John Archer. To study. Just to study. Why wasn't that last part resonating with me?

When I got there, it took me forever to get out of the car. I dropped everything I was trying to carry several times. Except, thankfully, for my laptop. As I finally closed my car door, I caught sight of a Kompressor parked in the row of cars in front me. It had a Connecticut license plate. I stared at the blue and white license plate, clutching my Evidence book to my chest. It had to be John's. How I happened to park in the row behind him, I had no idea. All of a sudden, I really had to pee.

I spotted him as soon as I walked into the café area. My eyes went straight to him whenever he was in a room. He sat back in a leather armchair, his ankle crossed over the opposite knee. He was on his cellphone, laughing at something. His light blue sweater fit him in a way that made my already embarrassing and irrational perspiring worse.

Someone bumped me from behind, muttering an apology, bringing me back to earth. I took a deep breath and walked over to him.

". . . Love you, too. All right. Bye," I heard him say as I started setting down my things. My heart sank and I tried to convince myself that he had been talking to one of his parents while really believing it had been his supposedly model-gorgeous girlfriend.

I sat down and opened my laptop. I averted my eyes, keeping them trained on my computer screen. I had never felt more awkward in my life. I knew it was only a matter of time before I made a giant fool of myself.

"Hey," John said.

I made the mistake of looking up. Right into those gorgeous green eyes. And that perfect smile. He looked like one of those guys on a poster in the window of a clothing store. Of course his girlfriend looked like a model. What was wrong with me? I had to get it together so John wouldn't think I was some weirdo stalker groupie girl. Evidence. Right. That's what I was there for. That's all I was there for. I had to get my mind right.

"Hi," I said, but no sound came out. *C'mon!* I cleared my throat and tried again. "Hi, John." I concentrated on the moose logo on his sweater so that I wouldn't have to look at his distracting, heart-stopping face.

"I forgot my Evidence book. I thought I had it in my trunk, but realized I didn't once I got here. I guess I left it in my locker. I hope you don't mind sharing," John said.

I had to force myself to focus on his words and not on his . . . the rest of him. "Not at all." I held out my Evidence book, willing my arm not to shake. He took it and his fingers brushed the tips of mine. Okay, so now I *really* had to pee.

He moved his chair closer to mine. He smelled so good. Like one of those men's colognes I sniffed wistfully at the department store sometimes, wishing I had someone to smell. I jumped up, grabbing my laptop at the last moment before it fell off of my lap. How had I forgotten it was there?

"You okay?" John asked, poised as if he'd been about to grab my laptop, too.

I nodded. "I'll be right back," I said weakly, setting my laptop down in the chair I had occupied a moment before. I hurried toward the restrooms before John had a chance to respond.

I felt a lot better when I came out of the stall. I washed my hands and dried them, happy that there were paper towels. Hand driers annoyed me. I had never come across one that actually dried my hands. I wet a second paper towel and held it to my forehead. I wished I had deodorant in my purse. I usually kept some in there for after the gym since I didn't want it to sit in my gym bag in the car all day. It was my kind of luck that I had taken it out at some point between my last gym trip and heading over to meet John.

"Are you okay, honey?" A woman's voice jarred me back to the present.

My eyes flew open to the sight of an older, brown-skinned woman with kind eyes and a warm smile. Her smile made me feel a little better.

"Yeah. I'm just a little overheated. I need to take this jacket off," I rambled, nodding.

She nodded back. "Just makin' sure. You look like you might need to lie down."

"I'm fine. Thanks." That was a big, fat lie. But standing in the bathroom talking to her was even more awkward than being out there talking to John. I thanked her again and hurried out of the restroom.

"You okay?" John asked.

I sat down next to him and placed my laptop on the small table in front of us. I didn't trust it back on my lap at that moment, so soon after my close call. "Yeah," I said, getting sick of that question. Then again, I reminded myself, I wouldn't keep getting that question if I didn't keep acting crazy. "So, what is it about the reading you didn't get?"

It had to be my imagination. When I looked up, John looked away, suddenly very interested in my Evidence book. Had he been staring at me?

"Why don't we just start by going over what happened in class? Because I think just about everything went over my head today," John said with that disarming smile.

My mouth went dry. How was I supposed to concentrate on anything with him looking at me like that? Sitting so close to me? How was I supposed to remember anything except his name?

Somehow, I made it through the evening without making too much more of a fool of myself. And I actually had fun once I got over my nerves. John was great. Cute. Smart. Just perfect. With the perfect girlfriend to match or so the rumors went. He didn't bring her up that evening and neither did I. I was still trying to pretend she didn't exist. Still, knowing all of that, I shouldn't have had so much trouble talking myself out of the possibility of him liking me.

John walked me to my car. We laughed about something that happened in class Friday. When we got to my car, he put my books and laptop inside for me.

"That was really helpful. I think we should get together once a week. If you wouldn't mind," John said.

Mind? I had never had a study partner before or been in a study group. I studied better on my own. But there was no way I was turning down a chance to spend more time with John.

"Yeah. That'd be good," I said. I wanted to be funny, witty, charming. But I felt all I'd done the whole time was laugh too hard and make limited, stiff responses like the one I just had. Man, I could have written the book on how to be lame. Being around him just stole my ability to be articulate.

"Okay. Well, I'll see you around," John said.

I nodded. *Don't go!* "Yeah. See you at school," I said. I watched John walk to his car, trying not to feel disappointment that he was leaving. He was just my new study buddy. That was all.

Somehow I always ended up on the losing side. And the last time I'd ended up there had been enough for me. Too much, actually. I was done with all of that.

Even though I had been devastated by my one breakup, I knew I should have seen it coming. Joe had beat all the hope out of me relationship-wise, but I was finally okay again. Relationships just didn't work out for me. And I tried to avoid thinking about them for that reason.

CHAPTER 3

BUILDING ROMANCE—
OR DAYDREAMING
ABOUT IT, ANYWAY

After an intense, blurred week of a lot of school, a little bit of sleep, and much insanity since I apparently was in a contest with myself to see how many organizations I could join without dying from exhaustion, I was happy to be free. Well, sort of free. I might have been working, but at least I was outside on a warm, sunny Saturday afternoon in late September. And I was having a good time wedged between Suse and Astoria on the roof of a house. We volunteered with Habitat for Humanity a few times a semester through an organization on the undergrad campus. The group was called The Community Project. Suse had been a member of it as an undergrad and told us about it. She chose Central Virginia University for undergrad as well as law school.

"It is too hot to be up here much longer," Astoria said, sitting back on her calves and swiping her hand across her forehead.

"We just got up here," I said, tucking a stray bit of hair back into my ponytail.

"Hmph. We been up here all day. And you know I don't like outside."

"Well, how about we go down and get some water or something then?"

"Finally, you're talking sense."

The three of us climbed down the ladder.

"How's the play stuff coming?" I asked as we moved toward a table set up with pitchers and paper cups for us. Astoria had joined a community theater group. They met just a few miles from campus and so the group contained a good mix of locals and college kids.

"Pretty good. We finally decided on a play for the spring. We're casting now, which is a mess," Astoria said. "Remember that one girl I told you about? Wannabe diva?"

"Yeah." I took a sip of water.

"Well, she is a mess. You know she wants to be the lead. How's she going to be the lead when it's a musical and the girl can't sing?" Astoria then went on a tirade about the diva. Suse and I listened, laughing occasionally.

I was about to ask her what play they'd decided on when I caught something from the corner of my eye that nearly made me drop my cup. John was walking toward us, again with a sleeveless shirt. He had to stop doing that to me.

I watched him approach, unaware of the fact that Astoria was still talking.

"Hi," he said, stopping in front of me.

"Hey." My hand strayed up to my ponytail and I realized that he was seeing me in paint-stained baggy jeans and a crumpled red T-shirt splashed with bleach stains that Suse had warned me not to wear, but there was nothing I could do about any of that now. "What are you doing here? I mean, I'm sorry, that didn't come out right, but I mean I didn't know you volunteered with us. I mean them. I mean the group."

For a moment, John, Suse and Astoria all just stared at me. I couldn't blame them. I wasn't even sure what I'd just said.

Eventually, John cleared his throat and his smile reappeared. "Uh, I talked to Suse yesterday. She said you guys would be out here today." His eyes flickered to Suse and so did mine. I seriously loved that girl.

I turned back to John. "So, I guess we should uh, start building something."

"Yeah, what are we working on?"

I smiled, tuning out the rest of the world. He'd said "we".

"Let's go find Darren. He's allegedly in charge around here," I said. I was surprised when I caught myself linking my arm through John's, like he was Astoria or Suse or somebody it was normal for me touch. Then, he surprised me by not pulling away. I caught a sliver of Astoria's glare before pulling John inside of the house— well, the foundation with lumber wall supports framing what would be the house.

Darren gave us the job of sanding down the few walls that had been installed and priming them for painting. Astoria and Suse transferred themselves to this job as well. For Astoria, I didn't know if it was more about getting off of the roof or more about keeping an eye on me.

Not far into the sanding, John laughed and put his hand over my sanding hand. Heat flooded from that hand and over the rest of my body.

"Denise," he said, placing his hand on my back, "have you ever sanded before?"

"No," I said, too busy being aware of how close his body was to mine to have time to feel embarrassed.

"It shows."

"Oh, and you have?"

"Yeah. My uncle owns a bunch of construction companies." He said this as if everyone's uncles did and it wasn't a big deal. "I used to help out sometimes in the summers. Back in high school."

"Okay." I realized we were still in a strange embrace, one of his hands still on my back and the other still over mine, holding the sander to the wall.

His eyes moved over my face for a moment and I was frozen in his gaze. Somebody shouted about needing more nails and broke the trance. I realized somebody should say something before the awkwardness became any more stifling.

"Fine. You think you're so great? Show me how to sand a stupid wall then," I said, grinning.

He laughed and actually moved closer. I had never known sanding could be so much fun. He stood with his shoulder touching mine, pointing to the wall and giving out instructions in a low voice. The scent of his cologne, mixed with sweat and sawdust, filled the air around us and I couldn't get enough of it.

"So am I doing it right?" I asked, looking back at him, my hand moving across the wall the way he'd shown me.

"Oh yeah." It didn't sound like John was talking about the wall. He certainly wasn't looking at it. His emerald eyes burned into my brown ones.

I stopped sanding.

"Yeah, you look good. I mean, it. It looks good." John's face reddened.

At that moment, I caught Astoria's eye; I'd been feeling her stare in my back and finally turned to face it. Her eyes were blazing with anger. Before I could react, a guy called out for help bringing in a load of sheetrock. John hurried off to help, mumbling something about coming right back.

"What was that about?" Astoria asked, dropping the level she'd been holding onto the workhorse next to her.

"What was what about?" I dusted my hands off against the front of my jeans and tried to walk around her.

She blocked my path. "You and your study partner, there. What was that about?"

"He was showing me how to use the sander." I looked at her as if she were crazy and I had no idea what she was talking about. I knew she knew me too well for me to get away with that, but it was worth a try.

"Right," Astoria said.

"I have to get something out of my car." When had I become so bad at this?

Astoria smirked at me, clearly not buying my excuse, and she let me walk away, but I could hear her continuing to grumble behind me.

I wandered away from the house, my hand drifting to my shoulder, to the spot where John's shoulder had been pressed against mine. I knew it was stupid to think about something that couldn't have meant to John what it meant to me. Wait, it shouldn't have meant anything to me, anyway. But still. It was nice to remember him leaning in close, his voice low in my ear.

John spent most of the rest of the afternoon outside, but we did exchange smiles every time we crossed paths. Astoria, Suse and I stayed inside, sanding and priming. Astoria sanded so roughly that I was surprised there was any wood left when she was done. Suse and I kept exchanging glances and looking toward Astoria, but her mood put a damper on the afternoon for all three of us.

After we were done for the day, Astoria and I went to my cousin Apryl's to clean up and have dinner. Suse had dinner plans with Charles. He was meeting her halfway so she wouldn't have to drive all the way up to Louisa.

Apryl, her husband, and four-year-old son lived in a townhouse near downtown Richmond, so not far from the school at all. I went to her place whenever I wanted a real meal or just to hang out and get away from school.

Apryl was round and brown. She reminded me of a russet potato, but not in a lumpy, warty way or anything. She was a bubbly, cute potato. And her son, Taye, was too adorable. He followed me around the house whenever I came over, anxious to show me his new toys—he even called the ones I'd seen a hundred times new as if that would entice me to want to see them more. Like I needed coaxing anyway. I enjoyed following him while he hopped around the house, shouting and laughing.

"Denise. Please call your mama. That woman is driving me crazy," Apryl said. She stood by the stove, oven mitts in her hand, preparing to check her meatloaf. "She calls me almost every day, complaining about how she never hears from you anymore."

I was chopping vegetables for the salad. "I will."

"When?"

"Soon. She can call me, too."

"You know how she is. She worries she's bothering you. That you're too busy."

"I'm never too busy to talk to her," I said, the guilt settling in around me. I didn't like avoiding her, but I didn't want to talk about the things she wanted to talk about, either. Most of the time when we did talk, we eventually ended up at that one subject I tried to stay away from. My avoidance issues. Imagine that.

"I dunno, Denise. You spend an awful lot of time studying. You're busy a lot of the time with that," Astoria said, looking up from the lattice work she was laying in doughy strips across the top of the pie. "Real busy."

I swallowed hard and sliced a cucumber so quickly it was a miracle I didn't chop off a finger.

Apryl glanced back and forth between us, her eyes filled with confusion. Leave it to Astoria to say too much; way more than anybody had asked her.

"Yeah, who told me to take fifteen credits this semester? With journal and everything else, it's insane," I said, trying to laugh off Astoria's comment. I didn't know what she was trying to pull, or why she'd been glaring at me off and on ever since John showed up at the Habitat thing, but she wasn't going to drag me through any nonsense in that kitchen with Apryl. Apryl, who reported to my mom almost every day.

Astoria didn't say much else that evening—well, unless you counted all the heated murmuring under her breath. Apryl and I talked about my school and her job with occasional, way off-topic quips thrown in by Taye, creating most of the conversation. Apryl's husband wasn't there to join in because he was at work.

A little while after dinner, we got ready to leave after helping Apryl clean up the kitchen. Usually, I stayed at Apryl's house for hours when I came over to visit, but I needed to get back to my cite checks, which meant I would be spending the rest of my evening with the footnotes to journal articles, making sure they were accurate. I also didn't feel like sitting around with Astoria much longer was going to be a good idea that evening.

Taye held my hand all the way to the front door, babbling about some cartoon character he was infatuated with. I wished I had that much energy.

"See you later," Taye said in a high-pitched voice, his "r's" still sounding like "w's". He waved manically to us until his mother closed the door.

"What was that about? In there?" I asked Astoria. We walked toward the end of the sidewalk.

"Hm?" Astoria shot me a glance that would have shut me right up if I hadn't been so angry.

"All through dinner, the whole time we were in there, you were making cracks at me."

"I just don't understand you, Denise. That's all."

"Huh?"

"Why are you setting yourself up to get hurt?"

"What?"

"Look, I don't have time for you to play dumb. Can you just take me home?"

I stared at her, still trying to figure out what had gotten into her.

"Just—let's go." She walked down to my car, stood by the door and crossed her arms over her chest.

I decided to let it go because there wasn't much else I could do. She wasn't making any sense. It's hard to reason with a person who's already made up her mind about something, especially when you don't know what it is she's made up her mind about.

CHAPTER 4

ASTORIA ("JUST CALL ME ANGELA DAVIS") BANKS

Tuesday at the gym, I found out what had been bothering Astoria so much. I wished I hadn't. We always took an aerobics class together on that night of the week. And afterward, in the locker room, I confronted her.

"Okay, I'm tired of all the dirty looks and snide comments from you the past few days," I said with an angry sigh. "What?" Astoria had been mumbling under her breath again. The only words I caught were "white boy."

"What is with you lately?" She was notorious for answering a question with a question.

"I'm the same person I've always been. Wish I could say the same for you," I said, slinging my towel around my shoulders.

"Whatever. What was that on Saturday? I've never seen you act like that before. And over some stupid boy who has a girlfriend?"

"I thought this was about John."

"What are you doing, Denise?"

"Nothing. I know he has a girlfriend. We're just friends."

"Really? I'm sure he thinks that. But you were all over him when he was 'teaching' you how to use a sander. Which isn't all that hard to do, by the way. Are you sure that's all you think is going on?"

"Yeah. I'm sure." I turned to my locker and pretended to look through my gym bag. I didn't want Astoria to see my face. She knew me too well.

"I don't want to see you get hurt, Denise. I don't want you to get your hopes up over this guy."

I yanked my bag out of my locker and set it down on the bench behind me. "There's nothing to get my hopes up over. I know I'm not on his level."

"No. He's not on yours. But anyway, be careful how seriously you take this 'friendship' thing. Because John Archer is the kind of guy we make fun of, Denise. The spoiled, white frat boy who doesn't live in the real world and will never have to. He wants you, all right, but not the way you want him to. Please don't catch feelings for this pretty boy."

"Astoria, I don't need a lecture," I said, yanking the zipper on my bag closed.

"I'm just trying to be a good friend."

"Then stop trying to tell me what to do." I threw my bag over my shoulder. She looked put out by my attitude. I didn't care.

"Fine. You know what, do what you want. I'll just have to be there to pick up the pieces."

"You are the last one who should be counseling me on guys anyway." I knew I had dug too deeply. I did it on purpose, angry she was so dead on about my feelings for

John. Keith, Astoria's boyfriend from high school and college, was off limits. All I knew about him was that she'd had to let him go because he kept doing all the wrong things, and him stealing from her friends and family had been the last straw. And he was now married to a stripper. We never talked about him and I knew how Astoria got when the conversation so much as leaned that way.

"You know what? You know everything there is to know, Denise. Having a boyfriend for a few months once in your life made you an expert on everything relationships, love, and male. Sorry for trying to help. Obviously, I was out of line," Astoria said. She pushed past me and huffed out of the locker room.

That wasn't very smart. Now I would have to walk home. I didn't admit to myself the real reason I shouldn't have done what I did; that it was just plain wrong.

I took the walk home as an opportunity to think about Astoria's words. I knew Astoria had strong views on the race issue, and that's probably where a lot of her hostility was coming from. There was no way to be friends with her and avoid knowing. I agreed with her in some respects, but in other ways I thought she was a little too militant, and maybe even off-base.

I never realized how large a divide there is before I started law school. Even at my huge undergrad school, when I was the only black person in some of my classes. Here, in this small place, it's probably the way it was in high school, but I didn't have a high enough level of awareness to process it back then. I was still living in my safe, adolescent, self-centered bubble. I think I believed then what Suse still believes. I thought that since my friends were so diverse, everyone's friends must have been. However, law school brought me crashing back down into reality. A lot of self-segregation happened on both sides. I thought part of the problem was huge amounts of misunderstanding. Astoria had her own theories.

I remembered one conversation I had with Astoria on the subject. It happened after a racially charged incident that headlined every news broadcast and newspaper in the country during our first year of law school. That conversation made me more aware of how rotten things really were in the state of Denmark, so to speak. And of the true extent of Astoria's bitterness.

The night of the conversation was right after a special report on the news about a rash of lynchings in the preceding two weeks. We were at Astoria's place. I sat on the floor and Astoria was on her bed. There wasn't much furniture in her apartment our first year.

"I just don't get it. When will this ignorant shit change?" Astoria snapped, flipping the television off with the remote.

"Will it ever? To a lot of them, we will always be less. We will always be these inferior wastes of space, encroaching on their land, taking their jobs and threatening their way of life," I said.

"Yeah, when their way of life wouldn't exist without us. The damned slaves built this shit up from the ground while they sat on their asses in the big houses. And it was built up on land they stole from the Native Americans."

"Some people will never see it that way."

"Obviously. With people riding around, swinging nooses out of their car windows and our government over-prosecuting, over-incarcerating, over-condemning our men," Astoria said, her face clouded with anger.

This was an issue we both felt strongly about, but I don't think anyone felt more passionately about it than Astoria. Her brother was wrongly convicted and still served a stretch for manslaughter. Wrong place at the wrong time. And wrong color.

"Yeah, it's messed up."

"See, that's why I can't understand why you like Suse so much. She's so oblivious and not even trying to get schooled."

"She's a good person," I said stiffly. I didn't like to get into to it about Suse with Astoria.

"Hm. She always takes up for those ignorant, opinionated bigots. I bet her family is like that."

"Astoria."

"What? You know they are."

"I'm not gonna listen to any more of that."

"I'm just sayin'. That girl volunteered just a little too quickly in Con Law to take the dissent's position on *Grutter v. Bollinger* for me." Astoria sat up straighter on the bed and narrowed her eyes at me. "Yeah, she would think that case came out the wrong way. She probably doesn't even think you or I should be in law school. And no way we could get into the same school she got into without a little extra help, right?"

"It's not people like Suse you need to be angry at."

"She's ignorant. What? I shouldn't be angry at ignorant people?"

"She's not. She just . . . she has her own way of seeing things."

"What is that supposed to mean?" Astoria said with a snort.

I sighed, shook my head, and picked up the magazine I had brought over. We sat there in silence for a while.

"A few rich, old, white men own everything in this country when you really get down to it. And until that changes, nothing's gonna change," Astoria broke the silence when she realized I wasn't going to say anything else about Suse.

"Astoria, you're such a cynic."

"But say I'm wrong, though. Say I'm wrong."

"I'm saying I hope you're wrong. Look at all the good things in the world. All the world aid organizations that have really stepped it up in the past few years. And people are discussing race in a serious way. Especially after what just happened. Some—a lot—of people realize it's still a valid issue and that something needs to be done."

"But for every one of those, there's a discount department store that begrudges its employees minimum wage and basically tells them to not even think about health care. And the products sold in those stores? Made in some sweatshop where children are dying. Brown children. While those greedy old bastards are steadily trying to increase profits."

"Well, see, now you're getting more into a class issue than a race issue."

"Maybe. But what 'class' are most of us in? Forced into?"

"Well, I still think there's hope for a country that elected a black president."

"Yeah, well, let's hope he doesn't get assassinated somewhere along the way. You heard about those crazy people in Tennessee."

"I can never win with you, Astoria."

"This country can never win with me. I don't know how you can be so complacent in a place where hate is constantly running just under the surface."

"You can't give the ignorance any legitimacy."

"I can't have any legitimacy because of the ignorance."

"Astoria, it has to start somewhere. Why can't you just open your heart and mind to the possibility that love can kill ignorance?"

"That possibility is taking too long to become a reality. That's what King died for, and the noose is still a symbol of hatred toward our people. Our women are still being degraded. Our men emasculated."

"Well, our 'emasculated' men are doing a lot of the degrading."

"That's the only thing they feel like they have left, I guess. I can't blame a man when the system's set up against him. Do you blame my brother, an innocent man, for ending up in prison?"

"That's different."

"Like hell it is."

It always depressed me to have that conversation. I felt like there was so much that needed changing and so little we could do in comparison. The easier thing to do was not to think about it. But that was obviously not a solution. And every senseless act of hate was a stabbing reminder of how real the problem was.

But at the end of the day, all you can do is your part. Anger, while understandable, isn't going to get anyone very far. Closed-mindedness is exactly what's caused this mess, so it isn't going to help to mimic that basic reasoning flaw. Understanding and open-mindedness are much more effective than ignorance and hate.

It is important to always strive for that elusive line between realism and pessimism. Crossing over can easily throw you into loss.

I walked down the street that my apartment complex was on, still thinking about Astoria while searching through my bag for my keys.

CHAPTER 5
CAN I GET A RIDE?

Thursday, after we finished studying at the library, John was nice enough to walk me home even though he lived in the complete opposite direction. Again, I was reminded of one of the million good reasons he was not available. And like it would matter if he was. Dating wasn't for me. Not my scene.

We were talking about Halloween, which was only a few weeks away, as could be seen in the red and brown leaves scattering across the sidewalk and the fact that it wasn't even dinnertime and the sun was almost gone. We turned into the parking lot of my apartment complex. We slipped between two cars parked a little too close to each other and I was awkwardly aware of the lengths we'd gone through not to touch each other since Saturday. Not that we'd said a word about any of it. Mostly because I was insisting to myself that there was nothing to say a word about. I had the feeling John was telling himself something similar. If he even thought about it at all. Maybe I was just creating fantasies in my head. I was good at that.

John said, "So have you ever been to that haunted hayride thing in Hanover?" We continued to pick our way through rows of parked cars, cutting across the parking lot to reach my place.

"Please." I laughed. That thing was a joke.

John shrugged, grinning that melty grin at me. "I've never been on a hay ride. I think it'd be fun."

"What? Sitting on stinky hay while some lame-o comes out of the woods with a plastic ax and makes a pathetic attempt at acting like he's going to kill you? You think that's fun?"

"Sure. I think it'd be a good time. If nothing else, hilarious. We should go."

"We?" My heart leapt for all of a moment.

Until he said, "Yeah, and oh, um, you should invite whoever, you know?" He scratched the back of his head and his eyes moved across the parking lot. "I'll ask my friend Ral. You should invite your friends. Uh, and Erich. You should invite him, too. He's a fun guy and you should—yeah."

"Erich?" What did he know about Erich? "You know Erich?"

"Yeah, we play racquetball together sometimes. Aren't you guys . . . friends? Or something?"

"Yeah." Or something. Astoria had started dropping not-so-subtle hints about Erich ever since Tuesday. "I guess."

Erich was good looking enough. He was light skinned and tall. He had an adorable baby face with dimples. He had black, wavy hair. I couldn't understand why he was single anyway. I kept intimating he was gay. Astoria kept insisting he was trying to get at me.

"Well . . . how 'bout it? Hay ride? Halloween night?"

"Um, I'll check my calendar. Let you know. I think I might have something for BLSA that night," I said. BLSA, the Black Law Students Association, was doing something, but I wasn't going to it. I didn't have anything planned for Halloween since it fell on a Thursday. I just didn't know how to respond to John yet. I didn't know if I wanted to go sit on hay between Erich and John. And I was still reeling from this new info about John and Erich hanging out. Weird. The guy I had a crush on and the guy Astoria wanted me to have a crush on. I should have picked a bigger school.

"Sure," John said.

We reached my front door and I stood there. My mood had crashed from where it'd been leaving the library. And it kept getting worse. Thinking about Erich led to thinking about how little John mentioned Sasha and wondering if he'd mentioned me to her. I didn't want to have any of these thoughts.

"See you in class tomorrow," I said, pulling my keys out of my pocket.

"Yeah." John looked surprised by the suddenness of my goodbye.

We said good-bye and he walked back toward the parking lot. I turned the key in the lock and slumped against the door, pushing it open. For some reason, my mind chose that moment to fill itself with images of John and I sanding the wall together. Traitorous mind.

I sat across from Astoria and next to Suse at a diner downtown Friday afternoon, waiting for my salad and wishing I had ordered country-fried steak. I wasn't in the mood to listen to them pick at each other. My mind was firmly on John Archer and riding . . . hay.

It was frustrating not to even be able to whine to Suse, though. There were not many people who could put up with my constant complaining without rolling their eyes and telling me to shut up. Especially not Astoria. I'd never met anyone in the world before like Astoria Banks. And I don't think I ever will again. Most of the time, I thought that was a good thing.

"This food is never coming. Imma starve to death," Astoria grumbled, pushing a salt shaker around the table.

I barked a short laugh, shaking my head. That just about summed Astoria up. Impatient and always having something to say.

"Astoria, must you complain about everything?" Suse asked, raising her eyebrows.

Astoria snorted, sat back in the booth and crossed her arms over her chest.

"Are you really this angry about the food? I thought you said you weren't even that hungry," I said, slowly bringing myself back to the table, noticing the conversation had nearly died.

"I'm angry I have to go to that stupid training tomorrow. I'm angry I didn't get that job I interviewed for last week with that civil rights group. I'm angry Yeardley is the worst faculty advisor alive. I'm angry about a lot of things." Astoria tapped a long, manicured nail against her fork. Her lips scrunched up in irritation.

Suse muttered something under her breath about not knowing why Astoria had come. I looked over at Astoria, worried, hoping she hadn't heard. If she had, she was ignoring the comment. I breathed a sigh of relief and went back to my reverie.

I didn't really want to participate in their conversation. I wanted to think thoughts about John Archer. And I didn't dare tell them that, especially Astoria. So I wallowed alone in my uncertainty about the John situation.

What was wrong with me? Even if John was single and interested, he wouldn't have been an option.

I'd already had my brush with death—okay, love, but were they really all that different? I could have done quite fine without another, thank you very much. I had the single thing down. I had plenty to keep me busy. And whenever I did get lonely, Astoria and Suse were there for me.

Single was easier. Less to think about. Less to agonize over. I didn't have time, energy or heart left for relationships. Romance was the furthest thing from my mind, and I would thank John Archer very much not to confuse me.

Law school protected me. I enjoyed the challenge. Thrived on the stress. I was able to hide behind casebooks and journal articles. In a way, I resented John for transferring. As irrational as it was, I felt as if he had intruded on my life by coming to Richmond. My crush was a little scary. John stood for so many of the things I had tried to block out of my life.

I had a plan to avoid all things too emotional and too real and things started to get a lot better. Emotion was dangerous. Emotion had almost cost me my bachelor's degree. Joe had ripped everything out of me that I needed to love a man.

I thrived. And a lot of it came from avoidance. I didn't want to acknowledge a lot of the ugly feelings I had inside. A lot of the disappointments life had rained down on me in the past. I managed to trick myself into thinking everything was fine. That my life was great. And from the outside, what wasn't to love? Law review. Good grades. Trial team. Friends that loved me. It was easy to not think about the missing pieces.

After graduating law school, I'd be able to support myself and I'd be too busy being a lawyer to miss the companionship much. And I could always get a dog. Or a fish. Or a Chia pet.

After our food came, I picked at it, but I suddenly didn't want it. I made myself participate in a miserable conversation about something a Republican had said on CNN that morning. That quickly turned into an argument between Suse and Astoria. Overall, I was pretty successful in keeping the conversation away from myself. Which only caused me to feel even more twisted and wrong inside.

But through all of those thoughts about not thinking about John and not wanting him came the ugly truth. I had made my decision about the hayride. I shifted in my seat, realizing I couldn't put off bringing it up any longer. During a lull in the conversation in which everyone had fallen into their plates, I said, "So, any Halloween plans yet?"

They both shook their heads no.

I looked down at the half-wilted romaine lettuce leaves on my plate. "What do you think about a hayride?"

Astoria looked up at me, resting her fork on top of the pile of pasta on her plate. "A hayride?" I could have just suggested a walk on the moon, judging by the look on her face.

"Yeah, sure, you know the one they do on that old farm up the road. They advertise it on the radio all the time." I returned to staring at my salad as I said this. I could feel their eyes on me.

"You really want to do that?"

"Well, John—"

"I should have known." Astoria pushed her plate away and threw her hands up.

I watched them both. Suse had become a lot less enthusiastic about the John thing since she'd heard about Sasha. Or so the story went.

"Well, it's going to be a group of us. We're all going," I said defensively. I almost mentioned that he'd told me to invite Erich, but I was afraid that if I did, Astoria would insist he come along.

"I guess we better go then. Keep an eye on you if nothing else," Astoria said. She and Suse laughed. Like that was actually funny.

Halloween night, it was freezing out. The day before, the high had been almost eighty degrees, which made the cold even worse. Cruel, cruel. Virginia and its schizophrenic weather. I wore jeans, boots, two shirts under my sweater and a jacket over it all and I still couldn't stop shivering. Astoria, who hates the cold, outside, anything that has to do with nature, grumbled all the way to the farm. Of course, we were amongst only a handful of fools who had actually showed up for the thing. Our breath puffed out around us as we headed for the hay-filled truck. I almost expected it to freeze in front of our faces.

"I hope you know nobody else could have gotten me out here," Astoria said.

"I know, I know," I said, wiggling my nose to make sure it was still there and hadn't frozen off my face.

A few minutes later, John and Ral jogged up to us. They stopped, breathing on their hands and stomping their feet against the cold. Ral had short blond hair and blue eyes. He'd been an All-American on his college football team, and he still looked the part.

"Hi," John said to me, his eyes making my stomach drop. They locked on me in a way they hadn't since that day of the house building. Or maybe I was imagining things. Or maybe it was the moon. Or my poor, frozen brain malfunctioning. He then said hi to Astoria and Suse. Ral went over to Suse to talk about something journal-related; they were both on the Technology and Law Journal.

"I don't see Erich." John seemed a little too happy about it, but I couldn't be sure. I didn't want to be sure.

I was about to brush that comment off and try to change the subject when Astoria said, "I asked you about him and I thought you said you were going to ask him to come. You didn't, did you?" She narrowed her eyes at me.

Just then, I was saved by a bat. I think.

There was a fluttering of wings and an animal swooped down near Astoria's face and then flew away. Astoria screamed and ran several yards away from the truck.

"What are you doing?" I called after her.

"What was that?" she said, her loud voice carrying across the distance between us with ease.

"I dunno. A bird?"

"What? No birds out this late, are there?"

"What, a bat, then?"

"A bat? Are there even bats in Virginia? I don't want to be out here anymore. I hate the country, man."

She hadn't wanted to be out there to begin with. I had to laugh.

"What you laughing at? This ain't funny. You know I don't fool with nothing that comes out at night."

"Or during the day. Or that's outside at all," I said before walking over and putting my arm around her. "C'mon. Let's get in the truck."

She gave me a wary look.

"It's okay. The sound of the engine will scare off all the outside things," I said in a mock patronizing voice.

"Shut up, Denise," she said as we climbed into the truck, but we were both laughing.

Astoria made a point of directing Suse to sit on the other side of me. John and Ral climbed onto the bale of hay behind us. I was disappointed, but I had no right to be. Still, John kept tapping me on the shoulder and leaning close to my ear to tell me a bunch of unimportant things, and that made my frustration lessen a little.

Once, John leaned forward and placed his hand on my shoulder to ask me something about registering for spring classes. After I answered, he didn't move his hand. I turned to look at him. He motioned for me to turn around and I did. I ran my hands up and down my arms and my teeth chattered. And it wasn't all from the cold. I was a bundle of nerves and uncertainty.

"You okay, Denise? You're really shaking," he said.

"It's freezing out here."

"What? You call this cold?"

"Oh, yeah, that's right. You're from the Arctic."

He laughed. "Connecticut is not the Arctic." He shrugged out of his jacket and put it around my shoulders. I stopped shivering. I stopped everything. "Better?"

"Oh, yeah," I said. His hands slipped from my shoulders to my elbows. I was sorry there were so many layers of fabric between his hands and my skin. I suddenly wondered what it would be like to feel his hands on my skin. Sliding over my arms, down to my waist. Well, one good thing about the cold and the dark was that nobody could see me blushing.

"John," Astoria said. John and I both jumped at the sound of her voice. "How's your girlfriend? Sasha?"

John removed his hands from my arms. "She's good."

I wanted to kill Astoria. I tried to send her death threats with my eyes. She kept her attention turned toward John. I knew what she was doing. And I hadn't been doing anything wrong. Nothing illegal. No reason to bring up Sasha.

"Oh. Don't you miss her? She's all the way up in Boston. She ever coming to visit?"

I didn't listen to John's reply. I cast a sullen gaze out over the field, looking for the next tired farmer to jump out of the woods or something so I could pretend to be scared. That would give me something to do at least.

After the hay ride, I turned to say goodbye to John, but before I could, he asked, "Did you drive here?"

I shook my head, wondering what he was getting at. I wasn't going to dare get my hopes up and make any assumptions.

"You want a ride?"

"She came with me. I can take her home," Astoria said.

"It's out of your way," I said, fighting the grin off of my face.

"Out of his, too," Astoria said.

"Not really. I have to go back to the school to pick up my laptop. Denise's apartment is right around the corner," John said.

Astoria glared at both of us, but I said goodbye to her and Suse and they got into Astoria's car. I could only imagine what was being said about me in that car. And I didn't have to imagine too hard, watching shadows of Astoria's hands fly while they sat in the car, waiting for it to warm up.

I stumbled into John's car and lay my head back against the leather headrest, wondering how I would keep myself from grinning like a fool.

John climbed in and started the engine. "Have fun?"

"Yeah. Great time," I said, concentrating on his hand as he pushed the scan button, flipping through radio stations. I was afraid to look into his eyes any more that night. Even if I didn't see that confusing thing in them, he might see the guilt and desire I was fighting against in mine.

We sat in the parking lot, watching it clear out and talked about the hayride, school, his brother, and other things I can't even remember now for a long time. It was the longest talk we'd ever had. And if I had to try to pinpoint a moment now, I'd say it was that night I fell in love with him.

"So you and Erich? A thing? Not a thing?" He put those awkward, conversation-killing questions to me.

I shrugged. "I don't really know. Dating is a lot of hard work. But he's a nice guy."

He laughed. "You'd make a great politician, answering questions like that. Dating's hard work? I guess you're right about that. I was wondering why you're single, though. Maybe that explains it."

"Huh?"

"You're beautiful. You're a genius. I heard you're eighth in our class. I mean, I couldn't believe some great guy hadn't taken you off the market yet. I guess I just assumed . . . I mean, I was surprised when Erich said you're single."

There was silence in the car while I tried to get over the shock of John calling me beautiful. Didn't work. Finally, I pulled enough words together to respond, but my voice was shaky. "Yeah, well, I'm really busy right now. I don't have time for all that. After graduation, there'll be plenty of time for that kind of thing." I didn't believe that, but I didn't want to tell John I'd given up on ever finding someone. I looked down at my chipped burgundy nail polish, but I could feel him looking at me.

I didn't want to talk about it anymore. He was confusing me, and I was making me sad. "So you seem pretty laid back. Every other second year is going crazy over jobs," I said.

He nodded. "You're not going crazy, either."

"Yeah, I already have one." I told him about my job offer from Dettweiler, a firm downtown.

"Congratulations."

"Thank you. So what about you?"

"Yeah, well, I've had my job since before I was born."

"Really?"

"Dad owns me. When people ask when I decided I wanted to go to law school, I tell them when I was conceived," John said with a grin. We laughed.

I finally felt it was safe to look at him. I was wrong, and so after getting stuck in his eyes again for a moment, I concentrated on his shoulder. "Is it what you want to do?"

John took a while to answer. "I guess. I mean, I've never really thought about anything else."

I wasn't so sure, but I also wasn't so sure I wanted to push the issue.

The nearly bare trees bowed in the late October wind gusts. The moon was so bright, I could see clear across the empty parking lot.

"Yeah, I dunno. Everything's just been kinda force-fed to me up 'til this point," John said.

I looked up, startled. I hadn't expected him to say anything else.

He leaned forward in his seat. "You ever feel trapped? Like no matter what you do, it's gonna be wrong? You're gonna make the wrong decision either way and disappoint a lot of people?"

"I dunno." John's proximity was disorienting. I could have reached out and brushed my fingertips along his cheek by moving only my arm. I could barely concentrate on what he said.

"You've never been afraid to go after what you want, I bet." John sat back in his seat.

"At the end of the day, you have to live with the decisions you make. No one else can live your life for you. So I guess it's good to try to go for what you really want," I said, parroting—well, paraphrasing anyway—words to him that my mother had put in my ears for years. I didn't believe them at the time, but they seemed to fit with the rambling path John had set our conversation on.

"I'm glad I have you to talk to. You're a good friend."

John put his arms around me without warning and I froze. I was barely aware he was hugging me and it didn't fully sink in until he'd already pulled back. I shrugged out of his jacket, no longer needing it to keep warm. Instead,

I wished I could shed more layers. I handed it to him and he tossed it in the back.

"I guess we should get going." John pulled out of the parking lot without waiting for a response from me.

All I could think of on the way home was how I wanted to be back in John's arms. That and how much trouble that desire could create.

CHAPTER 6
HOW BIZARRE

After the hay ride, I seemed to have a dirty dream about John every other night. Something strange happened the night of the hay ride. We didn't mention anything about whatever it was, but neither of us minded when the other would find excuses to break study dates. And the hay ride was the beginning and end of our attempts to be see each other outside of studying.

The SBA, or Student Bar Association, and the Elder Law Society decided to co-sponsor a karaoke competition in November. It was the last big event of the semester before everyone went into hiding to prep for finals. By the Saturday night of the competition, John and I barely saw each other outside of class.

Suse and I had to go. We were signed up to be judges. As SBA officers, I guess there was no real way around it for us. But it wasn't for lack of trying on my part. I just wanted to work on my student note for law review and sleep—which would have probably turned into just sleeping—but Suse wouldn't let me back out of it. Astoria was out of town so I didn't even have her to bail me out. Astoria was at a weekend retreat. That turned out to be a good thing.

I picked up my phone, and ignored the urge to send the call to voice mail. "Suse, I'm getting in the shower right now," I said, lying on my bed and staring up at the ceiling.

"We're not going to be late," Suse said. "If you have to go funky, it'll be your own fault, but I will be there in thirty minutes and I'll drag you out if I have to."

"Yeah, yeah. In the shower. Can't you hear the water running?"

"Thirty minutes, Denise."

"Bye, Suse," I said.

She reminded me that I needed to get moving a third time before telling me she'd see me soon. I tossed my phone onto the nightstand by my bed and rolled to a sitting position. I stared at the large mountain of dirty clothes in the corner that comprised most of my wardrobe. I always put off doing my laundry way longer than I should, and I hoped there was still something clean to wear. Although, by the looks of that pile, there couldn't be anything left clean I would want to wear.

"Oh, well. It's not like I have anybody to impress," I muttered to myself, standing and stretching. "The only person I want to impress has a girlfriend." Wait, I couldn't think like that. Those stupid dreams were confusing me. Hm. Those stupid dreams . . . thirty minutes was enough time for a nap. Did I really need a shower?

"What is wrong with me? There's no chance. I don't even want there to be a chance." And with that, I slid out of my track pants, grabbed a towel, and headed to my bathroom. Without separate bathrooms, I think I would have killed Tia the day after we moved in.

The karaoke was a fundraising event co-sponsored by SBA and the Elder Law Society. It was held in a smoky bar downtown that we had a good relationship with thanks to many successful bar reviews there. That bar had made a lot of money off of serving our law students watered-down drinks over the years. I walked in, hair pulled back in a loose bun. I wore faded jeans that didn't fit right; I should have thrown them away, but it was good I hadn't since they were my only clean ones—you know, that pair. And a wrinkled Central Virginia University long-sleeved T-shirt.

Suse, as always, was the primped Southern belle. Her short, silky blonde hair lay perfectly in place. She wore a blue silk wrap dress with black pumps. And cheating, lying Charles had yet another excuse about why he couldn't come to Suse. Instead, she was going to him right after the show.

Suse and I sat next to the other three judges—members of the Elder Law Society. We all said hello to each other and they passed us pads of paper and then we started talking about our classmates who were competing.

The girl Astoria, Suse, and I called Volleyball because of her height and her undergrad athletic scholarship said, "I can't wait to see John. He's so funny. I bet his act is going to be a riot."

"Archer?" I said, my voice a few octaves higher than normal.

Everyone turned to look at me.

Then, Volleyball's blonde friend nodded. "Yeah. He just signed up a few days ago."

"Should be interesting." Suse threw me a scrutinizing look when she said the word "interesting".

"So you guys start writing your papers yet?" I said to Volleyball and the blonde. We were taking a short course together that had ended the day before. Luckily, conversation turned to that.

Some of the acts were boring, some funny, some sad, and one almost good. I felt sorry for the DJ, who looked miserable. He kept glaring at the owner, and I was pretty sure he'd been tricked into manning the karaoke machine that night.

John was the last contestant. He walked out on stage in some eighties-inspired get-up, complete with the awful, plastic Ray-Ban knock-off sunglasses, frames in neon green. So many bright colors. I couldn't imagine finding those pants, even at a consignment shop, without the aid of a time machine. Suse and I looked at each other and broke the tension between us with a laugh.

He perched the glasses on top of his head, and introduced himself to the crowd in a way that earned him waves of laughter. Then, the DJ started the song "Bizarre Love Triangle" by New Order. During the opening bars, he did this odd shuffling dance that was somehow very eighties reminiscent. Then, he started singing. Wild, loud and purposefully off-key as he bounced from one side of the stage to the other, somehow managing to keep the beat despite his manic moves.

I laughed, caught up in the momentum of watching him. So much so that I didn't notice everyone watching me. I realized at that moment how much I'd missed seeing him almost every day. Just seeing him in class wasn't nearly enough. I got lost in the memory of his arms around me.

I sat up straighter in my chair, wondering if I was imagining things. It seemed that every time John reached the chorus, he looked into my eyes, singing directly to me. I sat on the edge of my chair, my pencil clutched in my fist, trying to determine whether or not he was singing to me.

Then, for the last refrain, he came down from the makeshift "stage" area and sat sideways on the judge's table, facing me. There was no mistaking his eyes holding mine then. I put my hands under the table, afraid I would try to drag him across the table otherwise. He then went to the other judges, singing it to them, turning to a different one for each line, although the song had neared the end and was purely instrumental by that point.

After the winner was announced—John by a landslide—Suse and I headed out with Volleyball and her blonde friend. We stood in the parking lot, talking about the contest. It had been one of those freakishly warm days we sometimes get in early November and so the night wasn't all that bad. A slight chill hung on the air, but that was it.

I heard John calling my name and I froze to the spot. Looking up, I saw him jogging toward us. I watched him approach and so I couldn't catch the others' reactions.

"Some people are coming over to my house. You should come with," John said.

I was stupefied by the invitation. John had never invited me to his house. He hadn't invited me anywhere since the awkward hug and the hayride and all that.

Suse put her hand on my arm, breaking me out of the trance. "Denise, can you come with me for a minute?" She looked at John. "We'll just be gone a second."

"I'll be right back," I said in a voice so faint I wasn't sure if he heard it or not.

When we were out of earshot of John, she said, "Denise, what do you think you're doing?"

"Walking to your car."

"I'm serious, Denise. People are talking. They have been ever since y'all started spending all that time together earlier this semester. And after what just happened? You should have seen the look Volleyball and her friend gave each other back there."

"I didn't do anything."

"Yeah, but it doesn't look good. Him singing to you. That song? And now you going to his house? You should think seriously about coming home with me."

"What are you trying to say? I'm not doing anything. Like I could break up their relationship if I wanted to. Haven't you heard about Sasha?"

"Denise, it just doesn't look good."

"Suse, can you pop the trunk so I can get my stuff?" I knew I shouldn't have been getting angry with Suse, but she was getting too close to something I didn't even want to admit to myself.

"Think about it, Denise. Be smart. No, he's not going to leave Sasha. But that doesn't mean you can't get hurt." Suse popped the trunk.

I grabbed my tote and threw it over the shoulder, already holding my purse. "He's not Charles and I'm not skank of the week." As soon as I said the words, I felt sorry for saying them. Suse's eyes dropped to the side and her shoulders sagged. "Suse, that was wrong. I'm sorry." I reached out toward her and she pulled back.

"No, it's fine. Go ahead. You might miss your ride," Suse said. She stomped around to the driver's side, got in and drove off without letting me say another word.

I walked back over to John, still feeling badly about what I'd said. She'd only been trying to help and my not wanting to hear it, because she was right, was no excuse for saying something so ugly.

John and I started in the direction of his car. "What was that about?" he asked, taking my tote from my shoulder. I started to feel better right away.

"Nothing," I said.

"You sure? It looked kind of serious."

"Yeah. Let me see your trophy." I reached for the cheap plastic object in his hand I had helped pick out and knew well. I turned the conversation back to the contest and successfully avoided talking about the oddness of our relationship. For the moment, anyway.

When we got to John's place, a guy threw the door open before John could. He had short blond hair and hazel eyes. His muscled, perfect arms rested against the door frame. He stared at me in a drunkenly quizzical way. Then he held his hand up to John for a high-five. "Bud! Where have you been? Missing out on all the fun, that's where."

John turned to me. "Denise, this is my roommate, Shawn. Shawn, Denise."

"Hey." Shawn barely glanced at me.

"I thought it was just going to be a few people. Where's Tyler?" John said as we walked in. Tyler was his other roommate. I'd known them both only by name until that night.

Shawn pointed into the living room. Tyler was on the couch, talking to a brunette with an orange tan. He was tall and lanky and had shaggy brown hair.

John didn't look too happy about what was going on. He pulled Shawn aside for a minute and they had a conversation involving a lot of gestures, a few of them rude. Then, John came back over to me.

"What's going on?" I asked.

"Nothing." So it was his turn to be evasive. "It's too loud down here. Wanna come upstairs with me?"

I hesitated, staring at the hand he held out to me.

"I'll behave. I promise," he said. He waved to some girls across the room who kept trying to wave him over.

I put my hand in his and he led me up the stairs. We stopped at his room for a jacket, which he put under his arm and then we continued up the stairs.

"Where are we going?" I asked as he opened the door to the attic.

"The roof." He said that like it was a normal thing.

I stopped by the window he opened, refusing to go through. "What do you mean, the roof?"

"It's safe. It's a lot quieter. I like it out here. C'mon. You will, too." He put his hands around my waist to help me outside and onto the roof. Even though I didn't need the help, I wasn't about to push his hands away.

"You were right. It is nice out here." I looked up at the cloudless sky, admiring the stars I could actually see since we were far enough away from the city.

"Yeah. Beautiful," he said. When I glanced over at him, he wasn't looking up at the stars. He was looking at me. I fiddled with the zipper on my jacket, my tongue tied.

I shivered slightly. Even though it was still not that chilly, it was cool enough to be uncomfortable wearing just my light jacket. I was hardly aware that I had shivered until John put the jacket he'd brought from his room around my shoulders. I closed my eyes, relishing the sudden rush of warmth that had come with the jacket wrapped around my shoulders. He hugged me to him and I tried to feel like it was wrong to feel so good being pressed against him, but all I could feel was comfortable and warm.

The next morning, I leaned back against John. We'd spent the whole night out on the roof. I watched the sunrise with a faint smile across my lips. At that moment, I pretended he didn't have a girlfriend. I pretended that we never had to leave that roof.

The sky was filled with rich hues of purple, red, and pink illuminated by the golden rays of the sun. The purple was a little darker than lavender. The red, crimson. And the pink, a delicate contrast to the purple and red. There was an orange tint to the collage that gave the entire sky an ethereal beauty.

The gold warmed me inside even though there was no external warmth emanating from it. It was the most beautiful sunrise I had ever seen. That probably had something to do with the fact that I was hardly ever up early enough to see the sunrise and the fact that everything was more beautiful when I was around John.

I sighed and settled further back into his jacket.

"You okay?" he murmured.

I nodded. I was afraid to speak. I didn't want anything to ruin that moment.

John and I had talked for hours. Mostly about me. He wouldn't say very much about most of his family, though I felt like I knew his brother, Thomas—who went by Thom—personally by the end of that night. I told him about college and my parents and Apryl. The one subject I steered way clear of was Joe.

It felt so easy and natural and right to talk to him; to be around him. And that was scary because no matter how perfect the night had been, I knew there was still a Sasha out there in the world. Of course that was my luck. Fall in love with a guy who has a gorgeous girlfriend. Great job, Denise.

"What are you thinking about? You're so quiet," John murmured. He ran his hands up and down my arms as if trying to warm me up. Little did he know, he was increasing my temperature to a dangerous level.

"Just how beautiful the sunrise is," I said, coming as close to the whole truth as I dared.

"Oh," John said.

I turned to face him. He brushed the backs of his fingers along my cheek and I had to ask. The look in his eyes, a look not lust, not adoration for a friend, but something else, made me ask. "You sang that song to me last night, didn't you?"

He removed his hand from my cheek and shrugged, looking out across the rooftops of his neighbor's houses.

"John, I just don't know what to think about you," I sighed. It was the closest I'd ever come to addressing any of the weirdness that always seemed to happen between us.

"Neither do I," he murmured. "I've been trying to stay away from you, Denise. I have to."

I pulled away from him and moved from between his legs to sit next to him a safe distance away. "Yeah, I noticed. I'm not really even sure why you asked me here."

"Honestly, neither am I." He was still staring away from me.

I laughed. The absurdity of it all.

"I mean, you're cool. Really cool." He paused for a moment, wetting his lips in the interim. "And I really want to be friends. But, I mean—well, I guess it's like this. I want to hang out and stuff. But lately I've been talking myself out of asking you to. I mean, 'cause I know it's gonna be great at first. But then it's going to get to this awkward part. It's getting there right now. Well, it's gotten there already, I guess."

"I still really don't understand," I said.

He turned to face me. I immediately wished he hadn't. His eyes locked on mine with such an intensity that it knocked the air out of my lungs. I couldn't look away, but I felt as if I would melt and die on that roof if I didn't. There was more than passion between us at that moment. His eyes were so intense. It was as if he was trying to swallow me whole with them. And I wanted him to. I wanted to devour him devouring me. I'd gotten sex looks before, but this wasn't one. It was as if he wanted me to open to him; to become exposed so that he could read my entire story. And I wanted him to.

He slid over so close that our legs were touching. He pressed his hand to my cheek and I think I stopped breathing. I grabbed the back of his neck and at the same time, he pulled me to him. John kissed me. His tongue moved slowly over mine. I wasn't aware of anything in the world besides his tongue moving slowly against mine. A warmth washed over me that I had never felt before, but I liked it. I hadn't been kissed much in my life, and I never felt such heat from a kiss before.

"I want to be friends. But it's hard. For that reason." He whispered the words over my lips before pulling away from me.

I muttered something nasty under my breath that I guess he heard.

"I'm serious, Denise. I'm going through some crazy stuff right now. And I shouldn't be involving you in it. But I can't—" he stopped himself with a groan of frustration.

I turned to him, wondering if I had heard him right. "Can't what?" I drew his jacket closer to me, wishing I was drawing him close instead.

John didn't answer me.

"I dunno. It seems a pretty simple concept to me. Why is it so hard for you to be around me and just be friends if she's the one you want to be with?" I couldn't bring myself to say her name. I could still feel his lips on mine, and thinking straight was impossible. I was just saying whatever words floated to the top of my mind.

He still didn't say anything.

"Well, what are you trying to say here? We just stay out of each other's way from now on?"

He just shrugged. He could be so maddeningly frustrating. We sat there in silence for a while, just staring out over the rooftops.

For one fleeting moment, I thought about putting my hand in his again. But instead, I pulled myself to my feet with an exaggerated sigh. "I'm going home now."

"I'll drive you." He stood and walked over to the window we had climbed out of earlier. I climbed over the sill in front of him, pushing away the hand he offered to help me.

"I don't need you to," I said, but he still followed me as I crossed the attic floor.

We silently walked through the hall and down the stairs. I breathed in a mixture of stale beer and vomit. But there was no breathing in John. He held the front door open for me. I stopped in the doorway and stared at his profile, since he wouldn't turn to me.

"What you did up there was just bullshit," I said, my breath catching in my throat. I hurried down the steps and out to the sidewalk.

His voice was barely above a whisper. "You really should let me drive you."

I was walking in the opposite direction from where he was parked. I stopped, but didn't turn to face him. "No," I called over my shoulder.

I continued down the sidewalk. I ignored him trying to call me back. I let the tears fall. The wind stung my face where they cut tracks down my cheeks. I tasted salt at the corners of my lips and I was glad. I deserved to cry. I deserved to be sad. Who was I to think I had a chance with John? Who was I to think I could ever be more than I was to him? And that that could ever be enough?

Astoria could not know. Ever. I couldn't tell Suse for fear it would slip out to Astoria. That was one I-told-you-so I could not bear. Not under any circumstances. It was a pain I wanted to bear alone. And I hoped that bearing it alone would make it go away faster.

I was determined not to think about the way the previous night had felt so right. Watching the sunrise with him. The tingle I still felt from his kiss. No. Such thoughts were off limits. Permanently.

Rumors flew after the karaoke contest. Suse was right about people talking, and the night of the contest had only made it worse. I wasn't surprised that John avoided me, and I was too angry at him to care much about it.

I sat across from Astoria in the library. I stared at the stacks behind her head, mostly. My administrative law casebook lay open, the first page of that night's reading assignment glaring up at me. I couldn't concentrate on the law. With Astoria IMing me every few minutes and the fact that my mind was far away from everything it was supposed to be on, I hadn't gotten much done at all that evening.

Astoria kept sending me messages about Erich, which wasn't doing much to improve my mood. I kept giving her one-word answers. She purposefully wasn't getting the hint.

My phone vibrated on the table and I lifted it off and flipped it open. John had texted me, telling me he wanted to talk to me.

I held my phone under the table and typed a reply with shaky hands. I asked him why and where he was. His response told me only that he was in his carrel, which I couldn't see from where I sat.

I turned back to my laptop with a heavy sigh. What to tell Astoria?

I typed in several messages and deleted them before deciding on, *I have to go.*

Go? Go where? was her reply.

I'm not getting anything done here. I need to go home, I typed, purposefully avoiding her eyes.

*Hm . . . Yeah, you gonna get so much more done around
loud Tia and cable television. Who just texted you?*

Nobody.

Was it John?

I have to go.

WAS it JOHN?

I closed my laptop without replying and stuffed it
into its bag. I finally met the stare I had felt boring into
the side of my head. Astoria's eyebrows were raised and
her lips were twisted to the side. She gave me a burning
look of disapproval as if I had just told her I was going to
rob a bank or something. Strangely, I think she would
have preferred that to the inference I let her make.

So it wasn't smart. I didn't need to hear that from
Astoria. What I needed was an answer. An answer that
only John had. At least that was what I told myself.

Since I was apparently hard headed and still hadn't
learned my lesson, I agreed to meet John in the law
school parking lot. He walked up in black sweatpants and
a long-sleeve gray T-shirt. I stood there shivering in my
jacket and wondering where his was.

He rubbed his hands together and then rubbed them
over his arms before saying, "Hey. I've missed you."

He smiled at me, but when my face remained a block
of stone, his smile faded. He hit a button on the remote on
his key chain and unlocked the car doors. We got in for a
silent and tense ride to a nearly empty mall parking lot.

John killed the engine and turned to face me. "So . . .
for someone who wants to talk for a living, you're being
pretty quiet."

I continued to glare at him, shrugging. We had been sitting there for a while, and that's all he could think of to say.

"What am I supposed to say to you after that?" I said finally. "You miss me. Right."

He actually had the nerve to look surprised. "Well—"

"I haven't heard from you since the party. You act like you don't know me in the law school. Then you go and make some asinine comment like that. You miss me. What do you want me to do? What do you want me to say?"

"We talked about this at the party. And you said you understood. Anyway, I invited you out here because I want to talk to you about this. I don't want things to be weird like this."

"Then you shouldn't act like a freak," I muttered under my breath.

"I know I've been acting strangely, but I'm trying to explain," John said.

"You're not trying to explain. You're just sitting there."

"I'm trying to think of how to put this."

"Well, why don't you just say it? If you're trying to spare my feelings, I think we're way past that point," I said dryly. "You've already rejected me once."

"I didn't reject you. I have a girlfriend. You know that. You knew that before."

"Well, I'm not the one who kissed you and then freaked out."

"I'm trying to explain that now."

"So explain."

"I would if you would shut up long enough."

"Go right ahead. Nobody's stopping you. Please explain to me why you've been a jackass for the past few weeks," I snapped.

John looked annoyed. I didn't care. I turned my back to him, staring out of the passenger side window. I watched my breath fog up the window while we both fumed in silence.

"I don't even know what your deal is, Denise."

"Oh, you're one to talk. You with the girlfriend. At least I'm single."

"It's complicated."

"How?"

"I mean, I want to be with her, but—"

"Glad to hear it."

"Would you let me finish?"

"Go on," I snarled.

Dead silence again. I wanted to put my fist through the glass.

"Whatever. Never mind. You wouldn't even get it."

"Yeah. You don't get it yourself."

"Okay," he said shortly.

I whipped my head around to look at him. He was staring straight ahead, his jaw set stonily. He didn't even start to turn his head in my direction. I knew he could feel me glaring at him.

"So I guess you've decided not to explain it."

"You just said I don't know how," he said.

I was too angry to speak. His smart ass seemed to know it all anyway. I sat there, trying to figure out why he had drug me out in the freezing cold just to play mind games with me. Not only was I angry at him, I was also angry with myself for not being strong enough to turn away and leave him alone.

I needed to get my head right. To take Astoria's advice and go about my business. Instead, I'd been all too happy to go with him when he'd texted me earlier. Some foolish, idiotic part of me had thought that would be the moment. For some unknown reason, I thought I had been about to hear that he legitimately wanted to be with me. The fact that I had even contemplated it made me angriest of all. John was an idiot. And I was one to even want him, let alone want him to want to be with me.

I suddenly wished I was outside of that car and away. I just wanted everything to stop. My life was moving too fast in a direction I did not want it to go in. When had I decided to go after the impossible? And that it was okay to think about a guy that way, and one with a girlfriend at that?

I hadn't realized I was crying until I felt John's hand on my back. I jumped away from his touch even though, deep down, I wanted to leap into his arms.

"Don't you touch me!" I backed myself up as far as I could against the passenger side door.

"Stop freaking out. I was just—"

"Just drive me home. Now!"

"Fine." He muttered angrily under his breath as he turned the key in the ignition.

"Evil jerk," I muttered.

"Whatever," he sneered.

That was the best he could come up with? I wondered what I saw in him while carefully not allowing myself to answer that question.

He took his BlackBerry Storm out of his pocket, hit a button on the screen and put it in the cup holder.

"Who's that? Sasha?" I sneered.

"Well, she is my girlfriend. I guess it would make sense that she calls me sometimes," John said. Apparently, she texted him because he picked the phone up again, read something, typed onto the screen for a moment, and then put it back.

"What did Sasha have to say?" I sneered.

"I don't think you really want to know."

"Take me home."

"Be glad to." He muttered something under his breath.

"What was that?"

"I said this was a mistake."

"Yeah. Whatever."

"I'm sorry."

"Yeah. Whatever."

He didn't say anything else after that. He just started the engine and turned the radio up.

CHAPTER 7
AN UNEXPECTED TRUTH

Astoria and I had dinner together the day after I left her in the library under shady pretenses. We went to the dining hall on the undergrad campus. Astoria had a meal plan, and the food was surprisingly good, so we often went there and I sponged off her guest meals.

Suse didn't come with us. She'd been scarce over the past few days. She was more than a little pissed about what I'd said to her after the karaoke thing. I'd tried apologizing, but she wasn't ready to hear it yet.

That day, Astoria wasn't much about eating. Her salad lay untouched on the plate in front of her and she kept twirling her apple by its stem between her index finger and thumb. "I just don't understand you sometimes. Why would you spend the night at his house? You know what people are already saying about you." She stared at me like I was a calculus problem and she was an English major.

"We didn't do anything, and people should mind their business."

"You didn't do anything. You spent the night, Denise. I don't know who's crazier, you or him."

I told him mostly everything, heavily editing what had happened on the roof. And I didn't mention the kiss at all. I told Astoria most of the truth. The truth I thought she could handle anyway.

"Yeah. If everything was so great, how come he practically runs away when he sees you coming?"

I said nothing, but my smile faded. I loved Astoria for her bluntness. But I also hated her bluntness.

It was true that John avoided me, with the exception of the past night, which I wasn't going to tell Astoria about and give her more ammunition.

I shrugged and pushed the spiral-shaped pasta around on my plate. I wasn't hungry any longer.

"I don't see why you can't just find a strong, black man," Astoria said.

I rolled my eyes.

"Please tell me what's wrong with Erich."

"I already have."

"I don't want to hear all those weak excuses. He's cute. He's nice. He's smart. He's funny. I've known him for years and I just know you and him would be perfect together. I mean, do you even like black guys?"

"What kind of question is that?" That thing about black guys always got to me. I'd heard it way too much. I was attracted to them. The ones I was interested in were never interested back. And I got really annoyed that everything had to be broken down like that. What did it matter who I was attracted to? Whose business was it?

Sure Erich was attractive, but Astoria had only been shoving him in my face since I'd first shown interest in John. When I pointed that out to her, she had an answer for it. Apparently, he'd been dating some undergrad from VUU for a while.

Astoria didn't get that it was my business who I was attracted to. And John was not an option anyway, so she didn't have to worry about it.

Astoria shrugged. "Just a question. I've never heard you talking about going out on a date with one."

"I haven't been on a date since I was in college. You know that."

"Your only boyfriend was white. I only ever hear you talking about white guys like that."

"That's not true. I talk about a lot of different types of guys."

Astoria kept it up. "You have so much going for you, Denise. I don't want to see you ruin everything. Especially because of some white boy who doesn't even deserve your tears."

So I had two racist best friends. Well, actually, Suse was ambiguous on the issue. I did remember her saying she was "relieved" when Burke left *Grey's Anatomy* because "the whole situation with Christina was just too weird." Of course she didn't have a problem with the gay slur issue.

Suse always put things in the infidelity context when it came to John. She asked me why I was even interested in a guy who would cheat on his girlfriend. She asked if I wanted to be the next one cheated on. This from the girl who had been cheated on three times (and counting, Astoria and I always said when she wasn't around) by her "soul mate". That was part of the reason I'd opened my big mouth too wide Saturday night in the parking lot when I pissed her off.

I sat back in my chair. We were two of only a handful of people left in the dining hall. It was pretty late. There were a few giggling undergrads scattered around at some of the other tables, clad in variations on the same theme. They wore sweats, pajama bottoms, Central Virginia University hoodies and flip-flops. Dining hall workers had come out of the kitchen and were cleaning up in hopes of giving us the hint to get moving. One of them looked like she wanted to start prodding us out of the door with her mop.

Astoria attempted to bring my attention back to the conversation by obnoxiously clearing her throat.

"Astoria, there's nothing I can say to change your mind. And there's nothing you can say to change mine. So can we please just talk about something else?" I said, picking at my pasta again.

"Okay, well, if you're not going to answer my question—"

"No—"

"Which means you've basically answered it, how are things with Lindie?"

I groaned. The evil, horrible, snotty third year who just knew she was running things at law review. I guess technically, she did. She was editor-in-chief. A position she had basically stolen from my friend, Melissa. No, not a nice girl, that Lindie.

"Worse now that she's gotten her offer for next year from Harris and Brown."

"Hm. Well, I hope she gets deferred. Everybody else is, anyway. That girl is nuts. You know she was arguing with Jones in class Friday? Apparently, Jones is the faculty advisor for some group she's in and she took something he did personally. So in class, she wanted to argue with him about the First Amendment for, like, five minutes. Until Jones finally told her very rudely they would have to continue the conversation after class." Astoria's eyes lit up as she relayed her story. Astoria loved gossip even more than she loved to be self-righteous.

"Really? I know Jones was pissed," I said, happy to be off the subject of John.

I was having enough trouble with John on my own without the different preachings and teachings of Astoria and Suse. The little things kept me wondering about his real feelings for me. Like the way he had found something to call me for at least three times a week every since that first meeting at Barnes & Noble. Yes, I had been keeping count. Of course, he'd stopped calling even before the party and the rooftop disaster. But I still could not get John Archer out of my head. I knew it wasn't healthy, but I couldn't help it.

And it was infuriating how he kept giving me hope. But I also couldn't imagine how I would have felt if he had stopped. Even though he had a gorgeous girlfriend, his parents were loaded, and he was the frat boy antithesis of any guy I could ever see myself with, I couldn't stop thinking about how great it would have been if we were together.

After Astoria and I finished our meal, I decided to walk home even though her car was right there in the dining hall parking lot. I really did want the time to think, but Astoria was right, even though I denied it vehemently. I hadn't wanted to spend any more time around her after our dinner conversation.

I thought that maybe the fresh, crisp air would help me clear my head a little. Or at least give me something different to think about. The air was a little too crisp. The cold was biting through my thin coat. I picked up my pace, shivering.

I walked past the strip of shops and restaurants between campus and my apartment complex. I looked at the storefronts under the lonely, bright streetlights. A few joggers passed by; some in running tights and shorts and some in track pants. I narrowed my eyes at their backs. They were making me feel bad, remembering my fatty, cheesy pasta. And considering I was about to catch fire just from a brisk walk home. I hadn't been to the gym in a while.

As I reached the entrance to my apartment complex, my phone vibrated against my hip. I took it out of the belt clip. It stopped vibrating before I could even read the caller ID. I stopped dead in the middle of the street. A middle-aged lady huffed angrily and stomped around me and continued down the street. I rolled my eyes, thinking it was her fault for walking so close.

My heart jumped as I checked the name on my missed call. John had tried to call me. I called his number back without even thinking. My heart pounded as the phone rang. And it sank down to my feet when his voice mail came on. That boy was trying to give me heart failure.

"He's crazy and he's driving me crazy," I muttered under my breath. I shoved my phone back into its holder. I needed to leave him alone. I hoped I could find the strength to do that.

CHAPTER 8
LAPTOP SNOOPING

I couldn't concentrate on the article I was supposed to be reading on tort liability. The law review office was the last place in the world I wanted to be. I couldn't stand myself. Every thought in my head turned to John. Obsession. Damn. Not again. I had been down this road before and it had almost cost me everything.

I couldn't stop thinking about how angry and sad he'd made me on that rooftop. Then there was the simple message I'd read on his computer screen. He hadn't closed his Gchat message box before wandering away from his computer one day in the library. Walking past, I hadn't been able to resist taking a peek. He'd been chatting with Ral and one of the last messages from John read: I thought I knew. I know what I should want.

I looked around and no one was watching. I sat down at John's carrel and scrolled up the Gchat screen. John's previous message read: Sasha's the one for me, right? She just fits. And you don't just date someone for three years and decide it's not working. By three years, you should know. And his message before that: I've been attracted to other girls since Sasha and I started dating, but it doesn't last and I've never acted on it. Never really had any desire to. Until now. The way I feel around her. I've never felt this for Sasha or—anyone else.

Someone walked past and my guilty conscience made me jump. I'd gotten up and walked out of the library, my brain on fire. I forgot what I'd even come in there for.

As I sat in the law review office, a full week after karaoke and the trouble it had caused, staring at that journal article, those two memories kept me from retaining a single word I read.

I looked at my laptop screen, relieved, as an instant message box popped up. I grinned. Astoria. She knew I was supposed to be working on law review crap.

What's up? I typed back.

I'm bored. Blow off your law review stuff, she typed back.

Can't. But what do you have in mind? I typed. I was already mentally halfway out of that office.

I dunno. That movie we wanted to see is at the Byrd, she typed.

I sighed. *If we go to the later show. But I really have to get something done.* I compromised with myself. Maybe the promise of a night out would motivate me. And I did need to be around people. I had gotten into my nobody-likes-me-so-I'll-keep-to-myself danger zone thanks to Mr. Archer.

I'm holding you to that.

Okay, I typed back. I wasn't backing out. I needed to put John out of my mind.

What I didn't need was for Astoria to bring Erich to the Byrd with her. I couldn't hide my annoyance and I didn't want to try.

"Denise, you remember Erich," Astoria said.

How could I not when his name was every other word out of her mouth? "Sure." I didn't crack a hint of a smile. The only movement I made was to pull my scarf tighter around my neck.

"Hi, Denise," Erich said, smiling.

I felt kind of bad for him. He was a nice guy. He didn't need to get pulled into all this. But I was more mad at Astoria than anything.

"The movie doesn't start for a while. You said something about coffee first on the phone a few minutes ago," Astoria said to me.

I shrugged. "Sure." I tried to keep the venom out of my voice, but I wasn't sure I had succeeded from the look that passed over Astoria's face.

"Erich, can you grab us a table at that place down the street?" Astoria asked.

Erich nodded, smiled a confused but polite smile, and started off down the street.

Astoria turned to me and had the nerve to look at me like I had done something wrong. "I'm just trying to help out here."

"I don't need your help with this," I said, starting off down the street after Erich.

Astoria put a restraining hand on my shoulder. I looked at the hand and then up at her, and repeated these actions, looking at her like she was crazy.

"What you got for this white boy—"

"John."

"Whatever, it ain't healthy—"

"And I don't have anything for him now—"

"Yeah, right, you can't keep your eyes off him in Evidence."

"And when did I become so pathetic you feel like you have to pimp me out to Erich?"

"I'm doing this because I'm tired of seeing you upset. I'm just trying to be a good friend."

"No. You just want to act like you know what's best for me. And you don't. You know I'm not interested in him."

"I know you've never even considered giving him a chance."

"And that's my choice."

"Fine," Astoria said, rolling her eyes.

I shook my head with frustration and headed down the street toward the coffee shop. Astoria followed at a distance.

Coffee was tense and awkward. The movie was slightly better because no talking was expected. But it was still uncomfortable to have Erich between us. The whole time, I wanted to reach across, grab Astoria and scream at her to stay out of my love life. I couldn't even concentrate on the story line. I don't remember what the movie was about now. It was funny how everybody else always thought they knew what was best for me. Especially when those people couldn't even get their own lives on track.

After the movie, Erich couldn't get away from us fast enough. But he was polite about it. He gave us some excuse about having a lot of reading to do and hurried off.

Astoria turned to face me. "Give me a ride home?"

I nodded, my eyes focused across the street. I couldn't leave her stranded.

We got to the car, got in, and pulled onto the road before either of us said a thing. I took the long way back to Astoria's apartment. I knew we both wanted to talk about it, but neither one of us wanted to be first.

Finally Astoria let out an exaggerated sigh. "Are we really not grown enough to talk about this?"

"I don't want to fight about this, either, but we need to set some rules or something. 'Cause all we do is fight about it," I said, braking for a red light. I turned to Astoria. "I know he's a mistake, Stori. But he's my mistake. And he's a mistake I wanted to make, and maybe still do." I didn't mention the messages I'd read on John's computer. I didn't want to hear her theories on them.

"This doesn't make any sense. He's going to hurt you."

"He already has. And I don't know what's going to happen, but you can't protect me from life. I don't always need saving. Sometimes I need you to let me fall and fail."

Astoria slouched down in her seat and studied the gold bracelet on her slim wrist. "You know what we need to do. I need to stop talking about Erich, and you need to stop talking about John."

"We both know that ain't gonna happen," I said. We laughed.

"Yeah. It's not," Astoria said. "I'm gonna keep trying to get you with Erich and you gonna keep trying to mess up with John Archer."

"Yeah."

She muttered something and all I caught of it was Sasha's name.

I glared at her, keeping one eye on the road.

"You still sayin' this is a mistake you might wanna keep making."

"Look, you can be a supportive friend or you can be an ass. But either way, it's not going to make me go out with Erich Conners," I said, turning the car onto Astoria's street with a jerk of the steering wheel.

"I'm just sayin'." Astoria grabbed the dash, steadying herself for my wild turn.

I slammed on the brakes in front of her building.

"Coming in?"

I shook my head.

"I don't want this jackass to come between us."

"I just need some time to cool off. And you do, too."

"So no brunch tomorrow?"

"I don't think so," I said.

Astoria and I usually had brunch together on Sundays after church. We went to different churches, so at least we didn't have to worry about running into each other there.

Astoria nodded. She reached over to hug me. I half hugged back, leaving one of my hands on the steering wheel.

"See you in class Monday," she said.

I nodded. I didn't even look at her. When I heard the car door shut, I took off. I knew I was mad because she was so right about so many things. But at least out of the two of us, she was trying to be realistic.

At my apartment complex, I pulled into my parking space and killed my lights.

"Perfect end to a perfect night," I muttered under my breath as I got out of the car. Tia's boyfriend's car was parked in a nearby visitor's spot. They were really open with their sexuality. Too open. I hoped they wouldn't be on the dining room table again. I hadn't eaten on that table since the time I'd found them on top of it. "J-u-u-u-st perfect."

CHAPTER 9

SASHA THE BITCH FROM HELL

From the moment I first saw her, I knew my life would never be the same. But in a very different way from how I knew it when I first saw John. She had legs that just wouldn't end. Her thin lips were curved in a smile that did not reach her pale blue eyes. Long blonde hair. Great ass. Hell, great body, period. She was every guy's wet dream.

"I heard she did some amateur modeling before college, and Victoria's Secret wanted to pick her up, but she wanted to concentrate on school," I heard a girl say as she walked past, staring at Sasha. Everyone within staring distance was staring at Sasha.

My stomach sank to my knees. I wanted to throw up. I wanted to disappear. I wanted to erase John from my memory because I should have never had the nerve to even think about him. I should have known. I was an idiot. Obviously, John only wanted to be friends. He was dating perfection. Who was I? I had misread those messages on his computer. Or maybe I'd gotten his name confused with Ral's or something or maybe someone else had typed those messages to play a joke on Ral. There was some explanation, I guessed. All I knew was Sasha was perfection.

She wore knee-high boots that I could have never gotten one of my huge calves into even if I put both boots together. She had on a denim mini, and I could have never gotten my fat ass into it. A sweater that showed off perfect cleavage. Surgically perfect. They had to be fake. Probably a high school graduation present from Daddy to go with her Range Rover. Her dad was a neurosurgeon. He had probably gotten one of his buddies to give him a discount on Sasha's boobs.

"Close your mouth, honey. Come on," Astoria said, pulling me away from the horror.

I shook my head to bring myself back to reality. I turned around mechanically. I caught Astoria muttering something under her breath.

"Stori, I love you, but I don't want an 'I told you so' right now," I said through clenched teeth, pulling away from her.

"I know."

I stopped in my tracks and raised my eyes. This wasn't my Stori.

"No smart remark?"

"Nah, girl. She got you good. Even I feel sorry for you. I saw your face when she got out of that Range."

I didn't say a word. I just stared at Astoria. She made me mad when she was dead on like that.

"I'm taking you to the Bottom tonight. And I don't wanna hear about no law review, gotta read, gotta make a meeting agenda. It's Friday night. And we're gonna have some fun," Astoria said.

"Okay, but I'm inviting Suse and Tia." I hoped Suse would come.

"Suse, okay, but *Tia?*"

"Hey. She made me a cake after that law review disaster with Lindie last week. I'd feel bad." I grinned, taking out my phone.

"Was it even edible?"

"Stori."

"Okay, okay. I gotta go do some stuff in the library for the interview initiative. I'll see you tonight." She was part of a group that helped minorities in the Richmond area gain skills they needed to get various types of jobs. She gave me a hug and then she was off.

I walked toward my car. I had get out of that parking lot. It was beyond necessary. I couldn't stand another moment of Sasha's blonde perfection.

"Denise." No, I didn't just hear John call my name. I kept walking. "Denise."

This was not happening. I stopped, plastered a fake-as-hell smile on my face, and turned around. There was John and his Heidi Klum knock-off. The first time John had spoken to me in over a week. And look at the moment he'd chosen.

"Hey, John." I forced the words out of my mouth in a voice I didn't recognize.

"Sasha, this is my friend, Denise. Denise, this is my girlfriend, Sasha," John said.

I couldn't believe it. He didn't look like he thought he'd done anything wrong. He was acting like I was just some random girl he knew from class.

"Denise, I haven't really seen you around lately."

"Yeah, well, you know, finals coming up. And— journal stuff and all," I said, forcing that smile to stay on my face while thinking that he hadn't really tried to see me lately. It was hard for me to believe the person standing before me was the same person from the rooftop. I began to wonder if he had split personalities.

"Hey, Sasha. It's nice to finally meet you," I said, sticking out my hand. I thought my cheeks would burst if I had to hold that plastic smile much longer. Sasha smiled her cold, barely civil smile. Or maybe she was baring her teeth at me. I couldn't really tell. I pulled my hand back since she obviously had no desire to take it.

"Yeah," she said. She started pawing through her leather Coach bag. "John, honey, aren't you taking me to get a manicure before all the shops close up in this pathetic excuse for a city?"

"Okay, well, later, Denise," John said, smiling as if we were really cool.

"Yeah," I mimicked Sasha's greeting to me earlier. She had to be naturally nasty. There was no way she could know anything.

I thought I saw a frown on his face as they turned away. I watched them walk off together. He leaned in close and said something to her. Her response to him didn't seem friendly. His body tensed and he said something else. I turned away with the hope that they were fighting. I couldn't watch them any longer, though. I couldn't stand the sight of Sasha.

I forced myself not to storm to my car. I refused to look fazed. Inside, I was boiling. Inside, I pictured myself ripping Boston College Barbie's head off, reattaching it and ripping it off again. I needed to get downtown. I needed some drinks.

Shockoe Slip and the Bottom are great places for people-watching on Friday night. Central, Richmond, VCU and VUU undergrads dressed to impress. Drunks stumbling around. Music blaring out of pubs, clubs and bars. People just generally having the times of their lives. I don't get there often enough.

I love Richmond at night. Richmond has a good blend of cosmopolitan flavor and rural charm. Bright city lights and a hometown feel.

We went to a club in the Bottom we frequent because Astoria knows a couple of the bartenders and so we always get generously poured drinks there. It's a good spot. The DJ is usually decent. And the clientele is a little less violent there than in some places in the area. I'm not interested in seeing a bunch of fighting and posturing. I just want to dance.

Astoria was her usual crazy self. She was off dancing with some trying-to-be-gangsta. Tia sat next to me, feeling the beat to whatever smack-a-ho, kill-a-snitch nonsense was playing that I can only tolerate because of the beat.

Suse was on my other side, swirling the stirrer around in her mixed drink. She had gotten over what I said enough to come out with me that night. Plus, I think she knew I really needed her that night. She's a better friend than I deserve.

"Not again," Suse muttered, rolling her eyes and putting her drink down. She took her cellphone out of her brown leather clutch. I saw a message notification as she flipped open the phone.

"Charles?" I asked.

She sighed, nodding as she started texting him back. "Yeah. I'm going up to Louisa to spend the rest of the weekend with him starting tomorrow morning. And he's pissed I'm not coming tonight even though he has to go to Charlottesville to take his mom to work tonight anyway."

"I'm sorry." I added to myself, *What's new?*

"It's not your fault he's being a baby," Suse said, closing her phone. "I don't know why I'm putting it back in my purse. He's gonna text me right back."

I nodded, staring across the bar. I had a sour look on my face. I knew I looked too scary for anyone to ask to dance or to even come near with that expression on my face. And I was glad about that.

"You want to talk about it?" Suse smoothed out the cotton fabric of the skirt of her orange dress.

"Not unless we can talk about what horrible skanky skeeze Sasha is," I said. I knew Suse didn't like it when I talked like that, but I had enough vodka in me not to care.

"Now you know what I have to say about that," Suse said, taking her phone out of her purse. She hadn't been kidding about Charles.

"She couldn't even bring herself to say hi to me," I said, glowering at no one and nothing in particular. I couldn't even enjoy the sexy I'd created for myself that night. My makeup was perfect—smoky eyes, dark lipstick and a gold eye shadow, all of which highlighted the angular features of my face. I wore a V-neck, knee-length black cotton dress with cap sleeves. And on my feet were my most recent splurge—black Italian leather pumps.

Suse slumped forward and twisted her promise ring around her finger like she always did when she was getting fed up. "She probably knows. She can probably tell."

"She doesn't know," Tia chimed in. "All she knows is how to be a skank. I know her kind."

"Exactly," I said. Was I agreeing with Tia? Wow.

"Hm. Okay," Suse said.

I didn't need to see her face to know her lips had gone tight, her face muscles clenched and she was turning bright red. That's how Suse dealt with disapproval, dislike, and disagreement. She was not confrontational. She was so passive-aggressive that she could annoy the crap out of me with it as much as Astoria could by getting in my face. And speaking of Astoria . . .

"She never gives up," I said.

"What . . ." Tia started. Her voice trailed off as I pointed to Erich just walking through the entrance to the dance floor. ". . . in the world does Astoria think she's doing?"

"Having good sense," Suse said snippily. That was her way of feeling justified. She had gotten back at me. And someone else believed she was right. At least in her mind.

"Hey," Erich said, greeting us all, but he zoned in on me. Suse and Tia said hi to him. The look he gave me let me know all the time I'd spent getting ready that night hadn't gone completely to waste.

I nodded a greeting to him. Then I downed the rest of my screwdriver.

"Can I get you another?"

I shrugged and Erich stepped up to the bar.

Hadn't we had talk after talk after talk about Erich? I was so mad, I couldn't speak. Besides, anything that would have come out of my mouth would have been unfair to Erich. He hadn't done anything.

"I saw your editorial in the paper last week. It really moved me. I don't think Central does enough to reach out to underprivileged kids with an interest in higher education, either," Erich said.

I shrugged. I had written an editorial for the law school's newspaper the previous week. It hadn't been a big deal. It was based on some research I'd been doing for my student note for law review anyway. I dashed it off one night when I hadn't been able to sleep. Because of Mr. Sasha, of course.

"Thank you," I managed when Erich handed me my drink. Astoria was making her way over with Mr. Hood Gangsta. My eyes narrowed to slits and I could barely see out of them.

"Erich. I'm so glad to see you!" Astoria exclaimed, hugging Erich. "Is Denise playing nice?"

"Nicer than you," I said.

Erich looked confused. I almost felt sorry for him. Eventually, he would stop coming around if for no other reason than he thought I was a big freak. I was looking forward to that day.

"Erich. Isn't this the song you were talking about the other day?" Astoria said, dancing up on Hood Gangsta. "Oh, I'm sorry, y'all. This is Terrell."

We all greeted him. Terrell mumbled a return greeting. Hood Gangsta had a name.

"Denise. You haven't danced since we got here."

"Come on, Erich. She's not going to leave us alone unless we get out there." I threw my screwdriver back, downing it like a straight shot. I grabbed poor Erich's arm and headed for the dance floor.

"What's up with your girl?" Erich asked me as we fell in with the beat.

"She's out of her mind. I dunno."

"I need to ask you something about you and John."

"There's no me and John. He has a girlfriend."

"That's what Stori said, and what he says even, but I have to ask if there's something there. 'Cause I like you and I just want to know before I make a fool of myself." Erich rushed his words, like he was almost afraid to speak them.

I stopped, my arms still in mid-air. This was the moment I'd dreaded. And the moment Astoria's ignorance had been pushing on me for months.

I leaned toward his ear so he could hear me. "Erich, it's . . . complicated. You're a nice guy and all. And I don't want to pull you into all the confusion. I think you're cool as a friend. But—it's just—really complicated."

Erich nodded. "Well, it's good to know where I stand."

I was going to kill Astoria. Bring her back to life. And kill her again. And rinse and repeat until satisfied with the results.

"I hate this song," I said, grateful for a change in song to give me an excuse to get out of the most tense situation I'd been in since—well, earlier that afternoon when I'd met Sasha. What a day I was having.

Erich nodded. He looked like he wanted to leave as badly as I did. I felt like such an ass. And it was all Astoria's fault.

I rushed over to Suse and Tia. Erich went over to Astoria and Terrell.

"Erich just asked me if I had something going on with John because he wants to ask me out. See what Astoria and her meddling have gotten me into?" I said.

"Well, I think you should give Erich a chance. Forget about John," Suse said.

I knew her frustration at Charles combined with her sense of self-righteousness was making her worse than usual, but my frustration combined with alcohol was a bad answer to Suse's attitude.

"Suse, please. I don't know what your real deal is about me liking John—"

"What is that supposed to mean?"

"Oh please. I think you know." I grabbed my purse from the stool next to Suse. "But anyway, I can't be here anymore right now."

Her eyes widened and she pinched her lips together. Even though I couldn't see the color in the dark club, I knew her face was habañero red as well. "Denise, don't try to turn this into something it's not. I have never done anything to make you think—"

"I don't want to hear it!"

Suse's mouth dropped open.

I turned to Tia, who looked bewildered. Her eyes had been moving back and forth between us. "Tia? Can you take me home?"

"Sure." Tia jumped up, looking glad to go.

"Good. Tell Erich and Astoria I left," were my parting words to Suse. Without giving her a chance to reply, I turned on my heel and headed for the exit, Tia behind me.

"You okay, Denise?" Tia asked once we were outside.

"No," I said as we headed for the pay parking lot where Tia's car was.

"Do you want to talk about it?" she asked.

I flipped off a group of guys who were cat-calling us and drew my jacket closer around my shoulders. "No." I knew Tia had to think I was crazy. Maybe she was attributing it to my drunkenness. Maybe not. I didn't care. I just wanted to go home and sleep.

Seeing her slammed it home for me—ripped my ability to lie to myself about John right out of my hands. Sasha fit right in. I was a far cry from the perfect fit. I didn't have a surgeon dad and a socialite mom. I hadn't gone to some private boarding school in upstate New York for high school. I wouldn't know the first thing about a debutante ball. I was pretty sure coming out parties had something to do with sexual orientation.

I knew I'd been rotten to every single person I'd come across that night, but it was hard to put on a pleasant front after having my inkling of hope snatched away from me.

CHAPTER 10

WTF?

After the weekend of Sasha, I reached a low point. Lindie James, the leader of the law review, made my miserable life even less bearable. What a horrible little cretin. I don't think she liked the idea of me being on the journal at all. I had been spending a lot of time in the journal office, which was making the situation with Lindie progressively worse.

I thought that Lindie had something personal against me even though I had never done anything to her that I knew of. She pushed me harder than anyone else on the journal. Harder than my note or articles editors. Whenever there was some tedious task that no one wanted to do, I found myself doing it. She hated every idea I had come up with for a student note, even when my note editor said my topic was fine. Finally, she vetoed both me and my note editor and gave me a topic.

Most of the time, I did my best to keep her from getting to me. I tried to tell myself that was how it would be in the "real world", at any rate. But on top of everything else going on in my life, Lindie was more than I could take.

One afternoon, Lindie and I ended up screaming at each other so loudly in the law review office that several students and a professor came running to see what was happening. I was so embarrassed that I started planning my time in the office around when I knew Lindie wouldn't be there. Lindie hadn't seemed to mind. We had been communicating via emails and post-its ever since.

My episode with Lindie was very indicative of the way things had been going for me. I had been stalking around the law school, becoming increasingly unkempt. By the end of November, I had almost made a uniform out of sweats, a ratty baseball cap, and old running shoes that hadn't been run in for many years and had definitely seen better days. People were beginning to talk. Of course, that was doing nothing for my "sunny disposition."

Then, the *pièce de résistance* came the day before Thanksgiving break.

When I saw John standing just inside the journal office, the only thought in my head concerned wondering why he was there. I stopped in the hallway, trying to balance a painfully heavy stack of books, my lunch and my shoulder bag while my laptop bag was slipping down my shoulder. He took the books with my lunch perched on top from me. I walked inside. The office was empty, which was rare.

"What do you want?" I asked with acid in my voice.

John drew me to him and kissed me hard. So furiously it almost hurt. My shoulder bag dropped out of my hands. The strap of my laptop bag hit the crook of my elbow. I wrapped my arms around him without thinking. He tightened his hold on me and I suddenly snapped back into myself and pushed him away.

"Denise—"

"No. We've been here before."

"Let me explain—"

"There's nothing to explain. We've been here before and you were an ass before. And when I was willing to listen to what you had to say—"

"I broke up with Sasha," John said.

Okay, he finally had me speechless. Until he reached out to touch me again.

I backed away. "What?"

"We need to have a long talk. I know you're busy, but it's important."

I was still having trouble processing his words. Sasha had been there not a week before. Okay, this had to be good. Maybe I had to take time out to hear this.

"After Evidence. I have some free time then if you do," I said. Man, I was good. That hadn't sounded at all like I was talking around a heart beating in my throat.

He nodded, gave me a weak smile, and walked out. No time for law review. I had things to do. I was in sweats! How did these things always happen to me? I needed a consultation, and quick. Astoria hated John. Suse wouldn't understand. And anyway things had been tense between the three of us since the night of the club incident. There was only one option left.

I ran to my car and tore out of the school parking lot. Was I really about to ask Tia for advice? I didn't have to worry over whether she was home or not. Tia didn't have Tuesday classes and she didn't leave the apartment if she didn't have to.

I careened into my parking space, grabbed my laptop and shoulder bags, and sprinted up the two steps leading to our front door. I burst in and Tia looked at me with narrowed and concerned eyes.

"What are you doing home?" She looked worried as I fell onto the sofa next to her.

"I need some advice," I said, jumping back up. I darted to my bathroom to plug in my flat iron and ripped the baseball cap off my head.

Tia followed, no doubt curious.

"John kissed me."

"What?" Tia had the same reaction that I had had.

"Yeah, and he told me he broke up with Sasha and we have to talk," I said, hurrying to my room with Tia on my heels.

"So . . . you're gonna meet him."

"I have to, right? I have to find out what this is all about," I said, pushing jeans out of the way, trying to find the pair I wanted in my closet.

"Well . . ."

"Don't be Astoria. Or Suse," I said, shooting an accusatory glance at her before heading to my chest of drawers.

"Just don't expect too much. And be cool. Don't let him see you like this," Tia said. "And don't wear that."

I sighed, tossing an orange sweater aside. I looked up at Tia, who was handing me a pair of jeans. Hm. Better than the ones I couldn't find.

"So, what should I do?" I asked, taking a pair of earrings and a necklace from Tia.

"Just act pissed off no matter what. Let him know he's been a fool. Be an ass to him like he's been to you," Tia said, coming over with my makeup kit. This was good. Makeup was one of the few things she didn't screw up.

"Okay," I said, closing my eyes so she could apply eye shadow. "I do hate him, so that should be easy."

"No, you don't."

I laughed. "No, I don't. But I should."

"You definitely should. So did you tell Astoria and Suse?"

"Are you kidding?"

"I didn't think so. All done," Tia said, handing my lip gloss to me. I went over to my full-length mirror to apply it while she went to find me a sweater.

"I know they're just trying to look out for me, but they're driving me crazy. I'm twenty-four. I can look out for myself, thank you," I said, heading back to the bathroom to smooth out my edges. I took a moment to admire the job Tia had done with my makeup before picking up my flat iron. She'd used the warm tones, which looked best on me.

"Yeah, I know," Tia said. She stood in the doorway. "Your sweater's on the bed."

"Okay," I said, rubbing oil onto my scalp. "You think I'm crazy?"

"Yes." She laughed.

I grinned. It didn't make sense to me, either, but I had to go talk to him. Guys didn't just grab you and kiss you every day. Guys who had broken up with their hot, near-model girlfriends for apparently no reason. *Especially* those guys.

John waited for me outside of our classroom after Evidence.

"You look nice," he said with a tentative smile.

I simply nodded even though inside I was eating up his compliment. "Where do you want to go?"

He shrugged.

"Just pick a place. I have a lot to do today."

"How about that coffee shop? The one near Carytown we went to a few times?"

I didn't say a word the whole way to his car or on the drive to the coffee shop. He kept glancing at me nervously. I wasn't giving him any encouragement to talk. He was the one who had wanted to meet. I just hoped it wouldn't be like the last time he wanted to talk. But, things were shaping up to be different this time. I was just wondering how different.

We got to the place, ordered and picked a table. John went up to get our coffee when it was ready.

"So?" I took a sip of my latté.

"I'm sorry. I've been a jackass and I know that doesn't begin to cover the explanation I owe you. But I'll start with the short answer. I was afraid of what I felt—well, feel—for you."

"Huh?" He was going to have to explain better than that.

"I know that sounds stupid. But listen. Denise, I've liked you ever since I first saw you in Evidence. You're funny. Pretty. Smart. I've never met anyone like you."

"You mean black?"

He laughed. "No, I don't mean black. I know. I don't really hang around a lot of black people. And it's one of the things that intimidated me. I'm trying to explain. Don't make that face. I know I'm doing a bad job, but just hear me out.

"At first, I made up that excuse about studying. And the more time I spent around you, the more I wanted to be with you. But I felt like it was wrong. I had a girl-friend. We're really different people. Please, just let me finish before you say anything. We are. You know we are.

"My parents have always been weird about the type of girls I bring home. I knew they'd like Sasha. I think part of the reason I was with her so long was because it was easy with her and with them—"

"You were with her because she's hot," I interrupted, rolling my eyes.

John sighed. He reached across the table and touched my arm. I hated the way he could make my heart stop with one touch.

"Yes. She's hot. To deny that would be stupid, but she's not what I wanted. I had never found what I wanted until I met you. You complicated things," John said. He paused, took a deep breath and looked up into my eyes. "I was going to propose to Sasha this Christmas. My parents would have been thrilled.

"Anyway, it was hard for me to realize that my feelings for you were not going to go away. And harder to realize I didn't want them to. At first, I tried to pretend you weren't interested. Then I couldn't pretend anymore because I could see it was mutual. Then I tried to make myself think you weren't the right type of girl for me. But the truth is, I'm just not good enough for you. I've never been.

"You don't care about what people think. You do what you want to do. You see people. You want to be around them because you see who they really are and you like them. Not for who they are and what they can do for you. Most of the people in my life before you treated me like an asset and not a person.

"You have a good personality and such a good heart. You're the type of person I want to be. The type of person I want to be with. Because you make me better, despite how hard I try to resist it.

"I have no reason to believe you'd want to be with me after how I've acted. Or even that you'd want to be my friend. But I want to be with you. I can't hide it anymore. And I don't want to."

I was speechless. I sat there with my mouth hanging open and no Astoria there to close it for me.

"But Sasha was here last week." I sounded like an idiot. Why couldn't anything witty and cutting and perfect come out of my mouth? I should have made him feel like he had me feel that night I went to his house after the karaoke competition. And then walked out, leaving him there feeling stupid. But the only part of me I could move was my mouth, and, obviously, I could barely move that.

"Yeah. Yeah, she was. And that's what made me see I couldn't do it anymore. After a weekend of her parading around and treating me like I was tradable on the stock market, I pretty much knew it was over. I kept looking at her and trying to find a good reason why I was trying to save our relationship, but I couldn't come up with one. I realized just how shallow our whole relationship had been. Nothing she did made me feel the way you make me feel.

"But I was still reluctant to call it quits. She was my first serious girlfriend. I mean, I kept thinking there had to be some reason I spent three years with her besides her being fun to hang out with and we liked to do a lot of the same stuff. I kept trying to find reasons to be in love with her, and I couldn't. It's scary to realize you don't love someone you wanted to spend the rest of your life with just a few weeks earlier.

"Then, after Sasha got back to Boston, my mom called to tell me all about how Sasha had come over and they had talked about Sasha's weekend here. Then my mom started dropping hints about how nice it would be to have her for a daughter-in-law. And telling me about this family heirloom she wanted me to give my fiancée when I picked someone. Even though I was going to propose, I got kinda pissed. I started realizing how truly sick I was of having my life planned out for me. Right down to my wife. A wife I don't love.

"So, I called Sasha after I got off the phone with my mom and ended it. She didn't take it well. She threatened to come back down here this weekend," John said.

"It's Thanksgiving break. She could see you in a day or so," I said. Why couldn't I have at least scrounged up some sarcasm?

"Yeah. I pointed that out to her and that she had just been here two days ago," John said. "But then I finally had to admit to her I wasn't coming home for Thanksgiving and she said she was coming here."

"You're not going home for Thanksgiving?"

"Nah. I don't go home a lot," John said, toying with his coffee cup. "The last time I was home was early last summer. I spent most of the summer in Bucharest, and other random places in Eastern Europe."

"Don't they miss you?"

John waved his hand in front of him in a way connoting his lack of concern. "I'll see them at Christmas."

I wondered about his answer, but I didn't push him.

"You still haven't told me what you think about any of this, Denise. Do you want to be with me? Come on, fill me in."

"John, this is too much. I mean, you've been acting so shady lately."

"I explained all of that to you. Don't make this more complicated than it is. I know you're pissed. I know you're hurt. But I can't fix it unless you let me. Tell me how you feel about me. If you don't want me, I'm gone."

I almost laughed. Yeah. Right. That was why I'd been having seven different kinds of fits daily. But could I trust him?

"Stop it. You know I want you and you're loving it," I said, breaking away from him and picking up my coffee. It was cold. I drank it anyway.

He laughed, looking relieved.

"So am I coming to meet the fam?" he asked.

I choked on my latté. "What?" I rasped, reaching for a napkin. "I'm going home tomorrow. We started dating two minutes ago."

"But we've known each other since August. We've wanted to be together since then. Oh, don't even try it. You know we have."

"I don't believe in love at first sight."

"You don't have to love someone to want to be with them."

"Whatever."

"So, is it go home with you or fast food for Thanksgiving?"

"I guess home with me. I can't let you be poisoned," I said.

He laughed.

"I'm warning you. I don't live in no mansion. And you're probably going to have to sleep on the futon in the den because my uncle has the guest room."

"Fine." John shrugged, staring at me, smiling.

I stared back, narrowing my eyes. It was impossible to figure him out. I didn't know how I felt about that. "What?"

"I just want to look at you. Is that okay? I haven't seen you look at me, smiling, in too long," he said.

I rolled my eyes and picked up my coffee cup.

CHAPTER 11

THANKSGIVING BREAK

John had Ral drop him off at my apartment Wednesday afternoon. He walked up to me as I was packing the last of my things to take home into my little Sentra. Stuffing them in, actually. There were two months worth of laundry, all my school stuff, an old desktop a friend had given me for my mom because my mom's computer had blown up, and some other stuff.

He wrapped his arms around me and pressed his cheek to my shoulder. I melted into him. I could get used to that kind of thing.

"Hi," I said.

He kissed my cheek. "Hi."

"You ready?"

He picked his bag up off the asphalt. "Let's go."

We got in, and John had many jokes about my little car. To be fair, he was pretty scrunched up in there even after pushing the seat back as far as it would go. The metal track that allowed the seat to move back and forth was warped, so it wouldn't even go back as far as Nissan originally intended.

Conversation became more and more scant as we neared Derring County. I think we were both nervous about what would happen when we got there. I don't think we thought about it much until that point. We hadn't really had a lot of time to think about it. I kept making up excuses to myself about why I hadn't told my parents John was coming home with me and ignoring the real reason—fear of their reaction. John kept glancing at me furtively. I noticed because I kept watching him out of the corner of my eye, not daring to turn and look at him. Neither of us wanted to discuss how crazy we were being.

"Okay, John, obviously they don't know you're coming, so . . . this might be awkward," I said, turning to him with a sigh as I killed the engine.

He smiled and kissed my closed lips. "That's cool. I'm with you. That's all I really want right now. I can deal with a little awkwardness."

I smiled back tensely. I'd mentioned John once, but I hadn't mentioned we were dating, or that he was white. I didn't think my parents cared about that stuff, but I wasn't sure.

"Okay. Let's go," I said, grabbing my purse and opening my door. John got out as well. We headed for the front door. He reached for my hand, but I pulled it away. I saw him give me a strange look out of the corner of my eye. I didn't turn to him.

I figured knocking would be less of a shock to my parents than me just barging in with John on my arm. So I knocked. My mother opened the door.

"Hi, Mom," I said, wrapping my arms around her in a huge hug.

"Hi, honey." I could hear the confusion in her voice. And see it in my father's eyes over her shoulder.

"Hey, Dad. Mom, Dad, this is John," I said. Time to get it over with.

I stepped inside and John followed.

"Hi," my mother said to John with a strained smile. She then gave me a look that said, Who is that white boy and why did he walk into my house with you?

"Mom, I told you about John. Remember?"

"Denise, dear, I want you to come to the kitchen with me for a minute. We'll be right back, boys," she said, still staring me down.

I followed her into the kitchen, making a point of avoiding John's eyes.

"You did not tell me about him. Who is that sitting in my living room?" Mom hissed as soon as we were in the kitchen.

"I did tell you," I insisted, but I knew it wasn't really true. "I told you about John from my class—"

"You told me one time about John you study with. Why would John you study with be in my house the day before Thanksgiving? With you?" My mom would have been screaming; I knew it. But thankfully she thought better of it with John on the other side of the door.

"It's kind of a long story. But we just started dating yesterday."

"*Yesterday?*"

"It's not as bad as it sounds. We've known each other all semester. I told you it was a long story."

"I have time. Now to start this long story, go back to you started dating yesterday and please explain to me why you brought him home for Thanksgiving."

"Mom—"

"Where is he going to sleep, Denise? You know your uncle has the guest room. And I haven't cleaned for company. I was only expecting family. And you've only been dating for a day. What has gotten into you?"

I stared at her. I didn't know how to answer. What I'd done didn't make much sense, she was right. But I couldn't help thinking that at least she didn't seem to have a problem with the race thing. She hadn't mentioned it. At least not yet.

"Denise? You better answer me," she said in that you-better-or-else tone.

"Well, he didn't have anywhere else to go. He lives in Connecticut and he didn't want to go home for Thanksgiving. I mean he just broke up with his girlfriend and he—"

"What?"

"I keep telling you it's a long story, Mom. I'll explain it all later. Just please don't kick him out?"

My mom laughed. A little confused, but very relieved, I said nothing.

"No, what kind of person would I be? Kicking him out? But you have a lot to explain. This isn't like you," Mom said.

I silently agreed with her. I'd been doing a lot of things that weren't like me in the past few months.

"We're starting dinner in a few minutes. Yes, you're going to help me cook, Denise. It's the least you can do after what you've pulled. And it'll give you time to tell me that long story of yours. But first, I'm going to go out here and properly introduce myself to that poor boy. He probably thinks I'm as crazy as you are."

We went back out to the living room. I felt sorry for poor John. He sat on the couch with my dad. The two of them had obviously been making painfully slow small talk about football. Some game was on the television.

"Hi, John. I'm sorry about that introduction earlier, but my daughter didn't tell me we were having company. I was caught off guard. I'm Lisa. Denise's mother." My mom held out her hand.

John shook it. "That's okay," John said with his melty grin as he took her hand. Hopefully it worked on parents as well as it worked on me. "I was just telling your husband what a nice place you two have. Thanks for having me on such short notice."

"Oh, no problem. I'm just sorry we don't have a room for you."

"Oh, I don't mind. This couch seems very comfortable."

"Oh, it is, John. I should know. I have spent many nights right here myself," my dad spoke up.

Everybody laughed. I felt a little more comfortable. Like maybe my parents weren't going to kill me. Or maybe they at least wouldn't kill John.

Back in the kitchen, once my mom had me chopping and boiling away, she grilled me on everything I knew about John and everything about us. She didn't quite believe me when I insisted I hadn't stolen him from any-body. But it was the truth. Mostly. I mean, he came to me. I'd been leaving him alone . . . but only because he made me? Ah, well. And of course I left out some choice tidbits. Mom didn't need to know all the raunchy details.

I told her that I hadn't wanted to leave him alone with no family and all his friends out of town. And that it'd "slipped my mind" to call her and forewarn her. She didn't buy that, and neither did I. She told me she didn't have a problem with "the race thing". She did, however, have a problem with the "my boyfriend of less than twenty-four hours spending Thanksgiving weekend at her house thing". By the time dinner was cooked, she still wasn't happy with me, but at least she no longer wanted to strangle me.

CHAPTER 12
DINNER BY FIRE

By the time dinner was served, my parents had gotten over the initial shock. My uncle was at work. He worked the evening shift at a truck stop, so we weren't going to see him until Thanksgiving Day. My mom called him at work so he wouldn't have a fit when he came in and saw a stranger on the couch that night.

My mom spread her napkin over her lap and asked, "John. What do your parents do?"

John stopped chewing. I knew he didn't want to talk about it. I didn't know whether I was more pissed at myself or at him that I didn't want him to talk about it for the same reason. Obviously, the Riches were in no league remotely near the Archers.

"Oh, well, they work in the city. New York City. Manhattan," he said, pushing potatoes around on his plate.

I watched his fork, not daring to look up.

"Really. They commute? Denise. Your Aunt Hattie lives in New York. You know. The Bronx," Mom said.

I winced inside, but I just nodded, glad John was beside me so I wouldn't have to chance looking at him as my eyes swept across the table.

"So, what do they do there?"

"They work on Wall Street. They're lawyers," he said.

Please don't make him say his dad owns the majority stake in the firm. Please don't make him say his parents went to, and met at, Harvard Law. Please don't make him say anything else about them. I tried to will my mom not to push him for more information.

Luckily, John changed the subject. "What do you two do?"

"Oh, certainly nothing that impressive. Denise will be the first lawyer in the family. She was the first to go to college. Lots of firsts in our girl Denise," my mother said, stabbing her plate with her fork. She was working hard to make things uncomfortable.

"I'm a custodian for the elementary school and Lisa's a supervisor at a factory in town," my dad said, his nostrils flaring a little.

John nodded. "That's great."

"Oh, I don't know what's so great about it," my mom said with an airy laugh; that laugh was deceptively dangerous. I knew it well.

"That's enough," my dad said. He obviously knew it well also.

"Just trying to make conversation," my mom said with a shrug, shooting me a pointed glance as she took a sip of water. Everyone stared down at their plates or off into space. Conversation had definitely been killed. I was so furious, I could barely keep the tears prickling my eyes from spilling over.

I shoved baked chicken around on my plate. Hadn't she already told me off? That wasn't enough? I glowered at my fork. John was so tense next to me, I imagined all the muscles in his body coiled into one central knot. He wasn't the only one.

"Well, John, it's really nice to have you over for dinner. And for the weekend. Denise hardly ever brings friends home," my dad said.

"Thanks, Mr. Rich," John said. I could hear the grin in his voice.

"Barry. Please. I already told you about that, John."

"Okay, Barry, thanks. And thank you guys both for having me. You have a really wonderful home," John said.

"Thanks. Lisa's always bringing home some new gadget or decoration of some kind," my dad said. Mom finally looked up with a tense smile.

"Yeah, I really love this uh—centerpiece thing. It looks like something from one of those home-decorating shows my mom watches," John said, quickly picking up on my dad's words. He was rambling a little, but my mom ate it up, which made me very happy.

"Thank you. I put it together last week." Mom's tone still had a little edge to it, but it was definitely much more relaxed. I heard relief in John's voice as he asked her more about her centerpiece. I was glad his charm worked on parents, too.

That night, as I was getting ready to go to my room, John grabbed me by the elbow, stopping me. I turned to him, surprised. He was already set up for the night. My mom had given him way too many blankets and pillows. I didn't really want to talk to him. My parents had already given me enough crap that night, most of it without saying a word to me. And the looks they'd exchanged all night. I knew they had started tearing me apart as soon as they went into their room for the night. And if they came out and found me still in the living room with John, it wouldn't make them happy.

"What?" I asked, looking at his navy blue T-shirt and thinking about the very nice chest that had to be under it. I didn't want to look at his face.

"Denise, I hope I didn't get you into trouble by coming here," he said.

I looked up at his face and smiled. "It's okay. I'd much rather you be here and me have to take a little heat from them than you be in Boston or at your parents' with Sasha," I said, sinking into the couch with relief. He smiled. He had me transfixed every time he looked at me.

"Yeah, well, I don't think *they* would. I think they pretty much hate me. I made a horrible first impression, huh?" John pulled one of the pillows into his lap.

I grinned, hugging him. "No. I think they're pretty pissed at me, but it's whatever. They'll get over it. I think it's just really a shock to them. I've only brought one other guy home, and he never even spent the night."

"Really? I've had plenty of girls stay at our house. I mean, my parents think we sleep in separate rooms, but—"

"Okay, okay, that's about all I want to hear about your sexcapades. I'm sure you have way more than I can handle hearing about," I said, laughing and pulling back from the hug. But I wasn't laughing on the inside. The last thing I needed was visuals.

"All right. I'm just a little shocked by that. One guy? Really?"

I had to change the subject. We were too close to talking about Joe. "You really want to be with me, huh?"

"Yes." John put his finger under my chin and tipped my face up toward his. "Do you know how beautiful you are, Denise? And the most important thing is that it's inside and out. Wait. Why are you looking at me like that?"

"I'm sorry. But a deep frat boy? I can't believe there's such a thing."

"Yeah. Okay, Denise," he said, rolling his eyes. "That's enough of your lame frat boy insults. I might start taking you seriously one day."

"Hm," I said, staring at him.

"What?"

"I'm just glad you're here."

"Me, too," he said, moving closer to me. I put my head on his shoulder and he put his arm around my waist.

"So have you talked to your parents since you've been here?" I asked. He tensed under me.

"No. I called 'em Monday to tell 'em I wasn't coming home for Thanksgiving. I haven't talked to them since." Something had changed in his tone. The change was almost imperceptible, but I thought his voice might have become a little icy around the edges.

"Were they upset about you not coming home?"

"I think they were more upset that I broke up with Sasha."

"Did you tell them about us?"

"Not yet," John said. His answers were getting smaller and smaller. He didn't talk about his parents much. I began to wonder what the story was there. I looked up at him, my head still on his chest. He looked down at me with those emerald eyes. How I loved those eyes . . .

"You plan on telling them any time soon?" I asked, trying to make my tone come off light and teasing.

"Yeah. When I call them tomorrow for Thanksgiving, I'll tell them," he said. He lowered his head and kissed my nose. "Don't worry. I can't wait to tell them about you."

"Okay. But why don't you talk more about them? I just realized that I really don't know much more about them other than they're lawyers who live in Connecticut."

"There's really not much more to know," John said.

I had the feeling his smile was forced. But I didn't get the opportunity to press him further at that moment.

We looked up as my parents' bedroom door opened.

"Denise, I think it's time you went to bed and let John do the same," Mom said, her patient, polite smile worn the thinnest I'd seen it all evening.

"Yeah, Mom, I was just going," I said, jumping up and heading to my room without looking back at John. And I didn't dare look at my mother.

Thanksgiving Day was interesting, to say the least. Things were tense, but better than at dinner the day before. My dad, uncle and John watched football all day. My uncle was cool with John. He had started laughing and joking with John as soon as they'd awakened that morning. I was glad at least one person didn't make me or John feel like criminals.

I spent most of the day in the kitchen with my mother. She wasn't mean and insulting anymore. She was really quiet and polite, which was even worse. That was the way she treated people she didn't like very much. And she had never acted like that with me before. She was only talking to me to ask me to pass her ingredients, check things in the oven, or stir something more briskly.

"Mom, what is the deal?" I finally asked, throwing down the oven mitts and putting my hands on my hips. I had just told her the turkey was on fire and she had replied, "That's fine. Thanks, dear."

For a minute, she just stared at me. Then she sat down at the kitchen table. "Denise, it's never been like this between us," she said, placing an elbow on the table and holding her forehead in her hand.

"Got that right," I muttered, leaning against the kitchen counter and looking down at her, feeling as tired and confused as she seemed to.

"Denise, this isn't you. I feel like I don't know my own baby. You're bringing home strange men. You hardly call home anymore. You're distant when you do." She still had her head in her hand. Her voice sounded strained, but I couldn't tell if she was crying or not.

I pushed a breath through my closed lips. "So, it's not just John that bothers you."

"Well, most of it—a large part of it—some of it; I don't know. I just want my Denise back."

I went over to the table and sat in the chair next to her. I put my hand on her back. "Mom, this year's just been difficult. I mean, the second year of law school is insanity. And I've been going through some things with Astoria and Suse. I know I could do better. And I will. But you need to tell me these things are bothering you."

"I know, Denise, I know. I just don't want to bother you. But I miss you so much. And it's just—I've never had to before. I don't like how our relationship's changing. And I especially feel left out of your life when you bring some man home," she said. I handed her a napkin. No tissues were handy. She took it and thanked me.

"I'm always going to be the same crazy, corny Denise. I'm always going to be my mother's daughter," I said with a grin, patting her back. "I know you didn't expect this John thing. To tell you the truth, neither did I. But he's amazing. I adore him. I'm sure you will, too. Once you get to know him."

"He does seem nice," Mom said somewhat grudgingly.

"He is, Mom. And I promise. We'll catch up on all the mundane things in my life that you probably tune out on when I tell you about anyway. And our relationship's not really changing. Whatever little change there may be is for the better. You'll see."

"Oh, Denise. I don't mean it that way—I don't know what I mean. I just miss you is all. You're my only baby. You're my baby girl, Denise."

"Well, you can't miss me right now. I'm all yours until Sunday."

"Sure." She rolled her eyes.

"I mean it. You know I don't really talk to any of the friends I had around here anymore. And John will probably be in there watching whatever game with dad and Uncle Jay most of the time."

"And we're still going shopping tomorrow?"

"Of course."

"You should bring John."

"I will," I said with a smile.

Thanksgiving dinner was nice. I was pleasantly surprised to see John treated like a member of the family. So was John. By dessert, the conversation had turned to embarrassing Denise-as-a-little-kid stories. John was in. Though I grimaced a little at the tales, I was able to relax for the first time since I had walked through the front door with John.

John and I went to see a movie Friday night after an exhausting day of Black Friday shopping with my mom. My dad and uncle and stayed home, but I dragged John along. I hadn't been about to suffer alone. Plus, I was excited that Mom had asked me to bring him. Mom made us get up at four that morning. So even though it was early in the evening, we were about to head home and to bed.

The movie had not been nearly as good as the previews had hyped it up to be. But somehow we'd managed to stay entertained throughout. I was enjoying finally having him to myself.

As we came out of the theater, I was laughing over some of his ridiculous spring break stories.

John took his vibrating BlackBerry out of his coat pocket.

"Who is it?" I asked, putting my arm around his waist.

"Sasha," he said with a little frown. "She's called like a million times since I've been here. I'm gonna answer it because if I don't, she'll just keep calling."

"Okay," I said, a little wary, but feeling reassured in that if he were being shady, he wouldn't have answered the phone right in front of me.

"Hello," he said in a cold, blank tone. I shuddered. John pulled me closer, probably thinking I was shuddering from the cold. I smiled. That was better.

". . . No. I haven't been answering the phone because I don't want to talk to you . . . we broke up . . . yeah, so why would I call to wish you a happy Thanksgiving? . . . No, I don't want to talk to Cindy. You put her on the phone and I'll hang up. I promise you . . . that has nothing to do with us . . . hey, you leave her out of it . . . It's no one's fault, Sasha. There's no controlling these things . . . I'm serious . . . you say—would you listen? You say her name one more time, and I'll hang up . . . because I don't want to be with you anymore . . . I'm sorry, but that's the way I feel . . . we've already talked about this. A lot . . . yes, I am . . . Okay. That's it. I warned you. I'm going now. If you call back one more time tonight, I'm cutting off my phone."

John put his phone back into his pocket and turned to me with a smile. He gave me a quick kiss.

"I'm sure she had only good things to say about me," I said.

He laughed, squeezing my shoulders. "Of course."

I stopped at the car and pulled him close to me, burying my face in the front of his jacket. He lifted my head by my chin, and lowered his face to mine.

"You okay?" he murmured before kissing my cheek.

"Yeah," I lied. Out of all the voices that could have crept into my head at that moment, Astoria's had to be the one that did.

"You know, I've really had a good time meeting your family. No, really I have. You and these looks you give me. I like them all—especially your uncle. Anyway, I hope you'll want to come meet mine over winter break," John said. He kissed my lower lip.

My mouth dropped open. "Really?"

"Yeah. I was thinking after Christmas, you could come up to Connecticut and stay through New Year's. And we could come back to Virginia afterward together," John said.

Wow. And there I was thinking I was going to be some big secret kept from the family.

"I mean, we have this boring New Year's thing we always go to, but I think it'd be much less boring to have you there for it."

"I'd love to." I had never met a boyfriend's parents before. Big step. And not just any parents. Super rich Wall Street lawyer parents. How did I feel about that? At that moment, it didn't matter. All I knew was that John wanted to take me home to meet his family.

I hugged John close and he kissed me. I couldn't imagine myself ever getting tired of John's kisses. There was always a measure of excitement in the fact that he wanted to kiss me. He wanted to be with me.

CHAPTER 13
ACROSS THE LINES

John and I got back to my place early Sunday afternoon. I was going to take him home that evening, but he'd wanted to come over for a while since we hadn't had much time completely alone over Thanksgiving break. And of course I didn't mind.

I groaned as soon as I saw Astoria's car parked in a visitor's spot as I pulled into my own spot.

"What is it?" John asked.

"That's Astoria's car back there," I said.

"Why do you sound so upset? I haven't really met any of your friends yet. This is good."

"Yeah. You won't be saying that once you meet her," I said.

"What makes you say that?"

"Oh, she hates you and she hasn't even met you. Still excited to meet her?"

"Why does she hate me?"

"Because you're white."

"You're joking, right?"

"Kind of," I said with a half smile.

He raised his eyebrows.

"C'mon. I'm sorry. I'm not trying to scare you. I'm just not happy to see her here. She's been getting on my nerves a lot lately."

"You can take me home first if you want some time alone to talk with her."

"No. The only person I want time alone with is you," I said, leaning over to kiss him.

"Good."

"And if she wants to be difficult, she can be the one to go home."

"All right. Let's go. I'll get your bags."

I kissed him again. He hugged me long and hard. He then pulled back and opened his door. Sighing longingly, I opened my own door and climbed out of the car. John got my bags and we headed to the front door. I opened the door and we were greeted by Astoria's sour smirk. She sat on the sofa, across from the front door.

"Hi, Astoria. Good to see you. How was your break?" I said.

She shrugged.

"This is John. John—"

"I know who he is," Astoria snapped.

So much for trying to be nice.

"I'm just gonna take these to your room. I'll be back," John said quietly, kissing my cheek.

I nodded, watching him go. I had just spent a crazy Thanksgiving getting John acclimated to my family. I wasn't about to go through any nonsense with Astoria. "Stori, look. I'm not going to do this. If you're not here to talk sense, I don't think we have anything to say to each other right now." I stood in the middle of the living room. The only seats in the room not cluttered with Tia's mess were on the sofa, and I had no desire to sit next to Astoria.

"Don't you call me that. My friends call me that. And you're not being much of a friend right now."

I snorted and crossed my arms over my chest. "I haven't done anything to you, *Astoria*. You're always going off on me. And for what? Because I won't let you run my life?"

"I'm not the one actin' a fool."

"Yes, you are. Look at how you just treated John. We haven't even gotten through the door good yet, and here you are. Rollin' your eyes and stampin' your feet."

"That's because I wish you would leave him alone. He is no good for you. He's rude. He's stupid. He's just another one of *them*. And all he wants is to see what it's like to have a black girl on her back."

"You don't know a thing about him."

"I know all I need to know," Astoria said. Her eyes shifted to John as he entered the room. "Worthless," she sneered.

I gave him a pleading look and he nodded before walking back into my room.

"Astoria, I don't know what your deal is. He hasn't done anything to you," I said.

"He's just playing with you. He knows he can't bring you home."

"I'm going to John's parents' for New Year's. Besides, our relationship has nothing to do with you."

"You're my best friend. When somebody's trying to hurt you, I make it my business."

I shook my head. "No. It's not. My parents don't even tell me who to date. What gives you the right?"

Astoria glared at me. "You are a fool."

"Out." I pointed to the door.

She jumped up and stormed to the door. "I tried to warn you. I don't want you to come crying to me when this blows up in your face." She slammed the door after her.

"What's her problem? I wish you'd told her we haven't even had sex yet." John had emerged from my room again.

"I warned you. And I didn't tell her because she doesn't need to know our business." I wrapped my arms around him. "Just forget about her."

"Hmph," John grumbled.

"I bet I can make you forget about her." I kissed John's chin.

"Oh, yeah?" he asked, allowing me to take his hand and lead him toward my room.

I nodded, kissing his hand. I pulled him into the room and shut the door.

John sat on my bed with my head in his lap, stroking my hair away from my face. I stared up at him.

"So, you really think being with me is worth all the work?" John grinned.

"I could ask you the same question," I said.

He laughed. "True. Well, I hope you do. Because I've been happier this weekend than I ever was with Sasha."

"Really?" I was warm all over.

"Oh yeah. But you've always had a hold over me, Denise."

"Stop lying."

"No. Really. I mean, didn't you ever notice how I always made an excuse to get closer to you when we were studying?"

"Yeah." I grinned. "I thought it would probably have been pretty hard to forget your laptop when you were coming to a study session."

"Yeah. And the way I used to always make excuses to touch you?"

"Yeah."

"And now the best part is—I don't have to make excuses anymore," he said, stroking my cheek.

"That is a definite benefit," I said, putting my hand over his.

"Yeah," he said, his perfectly green eyes moving over my face. "I just don't see how you can put up with her." He linked his fingers through mine.

"She's actually a pretty good friend when she's not being an ass," I murmured.

"When's that?" he asked with a snort. We laughed.

"So what do you like about me so much?" I was ready for a subject change.

"Hm . . . what don't I like?"

"That's a cheap way to get out of the question." I grinned.

John removed my hand from his and moved from under me. He then straddled me.

"Let's see . . . I like this," he said, kissing the bottom of my earlobe.

I giggled. "That tickles."

"And I like this," he said, pulling my sweater away from my shoulder and kissing it. He let his tongue linger on the flesh of my shoulder. "And I really like this," he murmured, gently caressing my arm as he pushed my sweater sleeve up. He tenderly kissed the skin of the crook of my arm. He then did the same with my wrist, right over my pulse point, and his eyes locked on mine. My pulse quickened even more.

"Oh yeah? What else do you like?" I whispered.

He grinned wickedly. "You sure you wanna know?" he asked, unbuttoning my jeans.

"Yeah I do," I said, turning out my bedside lamp. I plunged us into darkness and he plunged me into shivers of pleasure by running a thumb ever so slightly across my lower abdomen. I gasped as he lowered his lips to the place where his thumb had been. Then he started trailing kisses upward. Damn. I wanted him to go the other way. He pushed my sweater up as he went.

"I like this almost the most," he murmured into the flesh of my breast as I finished removing my sweater and T-shirt for him. I was impatiently waiting for him to get to the bra.

"What do you like the most?" I whispered as he flicked his tongue over my nipple through my bra before his teeth gently bit at it.

"This," he whispered the moment before his lips descended over mine.

I like this the best, too, I thought with a moan as he finally got rid of my bra without ever separating his lips from mine. I ran my hands down his back, my hands savoring every solid, muscled inch. I let my hands rest at his lower back. He groaned, pressing himself closer to me.

He kissed the top of my ear. Then, my right temple. Next, my forehead. Followed by my left temple. And finally, the top of my left ear. He sat up and pulled me up with him. I wrapped my legs around his waist and rested my head on his shoulder. I then rolled my head back, eyes closed, as he did sinfully delightful things to my body with his tongue.

I thought at that moment that he was more than worth whatever I had to go through to keep him. I was bewildered as to where that had come from all of a sudden. But if I had known what was really to come, I wonder if I would have still felt that way.

On the last day of classes for the fall semester, I was on my way to John's place so we could go out to dinner when Astoria accosted me in the law school parking lot.

"Denise, we can't keep this up. We're too good of friends for that," Astoria said. We had hardly seen each other outside of class since that Sunday at my place after Thanksgiving.

"As long as you keep attacking John, I don't have anything to say to you," I said. It hurt me to cut her out that way, but I wasn't going to take her constant, ignorant bashing of John.

"I don't trust him, Denise. I wish you didn't, either. You're only going to get hurt."

I started walking in the direction of my car.

She followed me, calling my name repeatedly. "Denise. Dating out of your race only causes trouble. Look what happened to my mom. Bethany still has never met her father."

I stopped and turned to look at her.

She held open the passenger-side door to her car. "Get in. It's too cold to stand out here."

I got in and so did she. She started the engine up and we sat there hugging ourselves, waiting for the air coming out of the vents to get warm.

"Bethany's only my half-sister. Her father's white," Astoria said.

"I thought she was just really light-skinned."

Astoria ran a hand over her face and shook her head. "No. This man and my mom were fooling around. He never meant her any good. The moment she told him she was pregnant, he said he didn't want anything to do with it. He told her to get rid of it or give it away. And that was the last she saw of him."

"Astoria, that's terrible," I said, reaching out and putting my hand on her shoulder.

"Yeah, and I don't want to see that happen to you, Denise."

"I know you're worried, and that's a terrible thing your mom had to go through, but that was a long time ago, Astoria. Things have changed."

"Twenty-eight years isn't all that long a time ago."

"It is to me, but let's just say it's not. John's not that guy. John is not Bethany's father."

"He's close enough."

"You're judging John without getting to know him, Astoria. How does that make you any better than the people you show so much anger toward?"

"John's perfect, huh? He's been so wonderful to you, right?" Astoria narrowed her eyes at me.

"He's a good guy. Nobody's perfect."

"He's a lying, manipulative white male who thinks he has all the power and the world revolves around him and he always gets what he wants. I don't have to be all up underneath him or spread my legs for him to know that."

"That's it. I'm out of here," I said, seeing that Astoria was determined to remain ignorant about this.

"You know I'm right and you don't want to hear it."

"I know you're being ignorant. You want to be small-minded and mean because of the things other people have done that nobody can control? Certainly not John? Fine. But I don't have to sit here and listen to it." I got out of the car.

"Go be his sex toy, then, 'til he gets tired of you and goes back to Sasha."

I slammed the car door behind me in response to that.

CHAPTER 14
HOME TO CONNECTICUT

I was high on love all through the first part of winter break. I was home with my family for Christmas and I was going to meet John's parents for New Year's in Connecticut. John had earned extra points with my parents by calling them for Christmas. They loved him. I loved him. Things were perfect.

And then I got to Connecticut. I took the train up and John picked me up at the train station in part of his Christmas present. His parents had given the Kompressor to Thom, John's younger brother, who was a sophomore at Princeton. John had his parents' S-Class that was only a year old. And John's parents had a new S-Class in addition to their older Mercedes SUV. So everybody traded up.

"Hey." I grinned after a nice, long, warm, make-you-forget-it's-December-in-Connecticut hello kiss.

"Hey you," he said, hugging me close to him. "How was your trip?"

"Decent. I mean, my back hurts a little," I said as he picked up my suitcase.

"I'll take care of that later," he said with a mischievous smile. I smiled back, hoping so. "You hungry?"

"Yeah."

"Good. Let's grab something on the way back."

"Okay," I said. I thought it was a little weird that we weren't going straight back to his house. But I had never met parents before. I was a little nervous. And I was in no real hurry to get to his house. However, I couldn't help observing, neither was he.

We stopped at a small diner near the train station in Stamford. John lived not too far away in Greenwich. His dad commuted to Manhattan. His firm did a lot of work with hedge funds and so they worked with all these financial heavyweights. John's mom worked at a firm that was also somewhere on Wall Street. I didn't really know all the particulars. John still had not opened up about his family. Every time I asked, he gave me an elusive reply that always concluded with something about the fact that I would meet them over winter break.

He seemed a little anxious, but I tried to ignore it. I was just happy to be with him. We hadn't gotten to spend a lot of time together since we'd started dating. We'd basically had Thanksgiving break and a few moments in between studying for finals. And most of that, we hadn't even been alone. Either my family or friends, minus Astoria, had been around. It didn't bother me any. Out of John's friends, only Ral hung out with us. The others didn't spend a lot of time around me. I think they thought I was shady because of what had gone down with Sasha.

That afternoon, I thought John was probably second-guessing himself and that made him act strangely. I couldn't stop thinking that had the roles been reversed, I would have been second-guessing myself, too. I tried to tell myself that those feelings were just related to nerves and being in a new place surrounded by strangers, but I wasn't so sure.

"So how was your Christmas?" I asked, not really knowing what to say.

"Okay. How was yours? Did you like your gift?" John fired at me rapidly. Yeah, he was being weird. Even for John. I smiled. He had gotten me a good gift, though. A gift card to Barnes & Noble with a very sweet card about that first night of studying being the best night of his life. I hadn't been able to stop smiling.

"It was great. To both. How'd you like your gift?"

"Considering I already knew what it was?" John asked. We laughed. So I hadn't been so slick at finding out what his size was and whether or not he liked the sweater I wanted to buy him. I had never bought a guy a gift before. Not a boyfriend, anyway. And I'm not a very creative gift-giver. I hadn't wanted to mess up. "I loved it. Thanks."

"Sure," I said, smiling. I jumped as my phone vibrated. I took it out of my pocket. I had a text message from Astoria.

Are you in the Whiter Wonderland yet? it read.

I closed my phone and tossed it aside. Astoria was still at it. She'd been a little hurt we wouldn't have our whole one-year-old tradition of getting drunk at yet another trashed Bottom club. And she felt I was choosing John over her and good sense. I couldn't see why she expected me to want to spend time with her when all she did was harass me about John.

"Astoria?" John asked.

I nodded.

John shook his head, looking out of the window. "Your friends don't like me very much, huh?"

"I could say the same about your friends," I said.

John didn't say anything. He didn't even defend himself like he usually did by telling me his roommates were not his friends and that Ral liked me and that I shouldn't worry about anyone else. He just kept staring out of the window.

"My family likes you. Suse likes you. Who cares what Astoria thinks? You know she's crazy, anyway."

"Denise, would it matter if they didn't?" John said, suddenly turning to me. There was an intensity in his eyes that freaked me out a little. It was almost desperation. I didn't really know what to say. I was glad our food came at that moment. I started in on my Cobb salad and then realized John hadn't even touched his fork.

"What?" I asked.

He was still staring at me. "Would it matter if your family didn't like me?" John asked, his eyes still trained on me.

I shrugged and pretended to be very interested in my salad. I mixed my salad dressing in and tried to ignore his intense gaze.

"It would matter, wouldn't it?"

"Wouldn't it matter to you?" I countered. I getting more and more edgy. I was already nervous about meeting his parents. He was only making it worse.

"Not really," John said with a shrug. He sat back in the booth and went back to staring out of the window.

"John, have you invited me up here knowing your parents have a problem with it? And you didn't tell me?" I said, suddenly losing my appetite.

"No. They're gonna love you," John said softly, still looking out of the window. I dropped my fork onto my plate with a sigh.

"Aren't you gonna eat?"

"I guess," he said with a shrug, turning his eyes directly to his plate. What was with him? He was avoiding my eyes when I looked at him, but staring at me like some kind of freak when he thought I wasn't looking.

"What is it, John? You're acting really weird about this. If your parents have a problem with me, I want to know about it. If they don't like me for some reason and they haven't even met me, I want to know about it. Is it because I'm black? Poor? What?"

John finally looked up at me. A strange look flickered in his eyes. It was gone before I was sure I'd seen it. "It's just—I think they really want me to be with Sasha."

I wasn't convinced. But I sighed, nodding. I picked up my fork. I wasn't hungry anymore, but I wanted to take my time getting to the house. I had a feeling John wasn't telling me the truth, whole truth, and nothing but the truth.

We ate the rest of our meal in relative silence. By the time the check came, my stomach was in knots. John paid and we left. I was thanking Mercedes overtime for seat warmers as we got in. It was freezing out. I already didn't like Connecticut. I didn't like John because of the way he was acting. And I didn't like Astoria because I was feeling more and more that she was right.

"What are you thinking about?" John asked as we pulled out of the parking lot.

"Oh, nothing," I said airily. If John could lie, I could lie.

I knew I was out of my league when John drove into a gated community. I knew I was in trouble when I saw the size of the houses. These things could fit three or four of my parents' house in them. And I knew I was in the shit when John pulled up in front of the biggest one I'd seen at the back of the community. I thought for a moment maybe we weren't there yet. Maybe we had stopped at the mayor's house for a minute for some reason. Then I saw that we had parked behind John's old Kompressor. My heart jumped into my throat and my stomach lurched. My Cobb salad wanted to revisit me in a really unpleasant way.

"So are we just gonna sit here all day?" John asked with an awkward grin.

No. You're going to take me back to the train station because I don't know what I was thinking by coming here, I thought, but I said with the weakest smile I'd ever given in my life, "Let's go."

"Okay. Don't worry, they'll love you as much as I do," John said, reaching over to hug me.

"John? You love me?" I said, looking up at him.

He nodded, looking down at me quizzically. "What?"

"You've never said that before."

"Really? Well, I dunno why I haven't. But I do."

"I love you, too," I said, hugging him to me. The prospect of meeting the Archers suddenly didn't seem that daunting.

John's words carried me all the way up the walkway to the front door. John opened it and we went through the foyer and into the family room. Then all the warmth faded from my body despite the merrily glowing fire in the gas fireplace.

"Mom, Dad, this is Denise," I heard John's voice coming from somewhere, but all I could see was the stern face of John Archer III and the blanched face of Elizabeth Archer. They didn't handle surprise well. John Archer III was a handsome man with a full head of silver hair. My John looked exactly like his father. Elizabeth Archer had the best face money could buy. Her porcelain skin was flawless. Her auburn hair, which didn't have a hint of gray, was pulled away from her oval face. She wore matching pearl earrings and necklace. There was no warmth in her severe, gray eyes. There was a lot in her demeanor that reminded me of Sasha.

"Denise? This is your girlfriend?" Elizabeth recovered first. Her eyes were focused intently on John. I was glad as that gaze, more of a glare, would have killed me on the spot had it been directed at me.

"Yes," John said, moving a little closer to me.

"Denise. Nice to meet you," John Archer III said tersely, reaching out for my hand. I shook his hand, trying not to wince at the firmness of his grip.

"Denise." Elizabeth said my name as if it almost physically pained her to do so. Her handshake was limp, and her hand was quickly withdrawn afterward.

"Nice to meet you both," I said, feeling as if I was barely in the room. Both of John's parents were focused on him.

"Where's Thom? I want Thom to meet Denise," John said, that weird tone in his voice that had been in it at the diner. A contradictory blend of uncertainty and determination.

"He's out. Kelly picked him up earlier," Elizabeth replied. "He'll be black—oh, oh, excuse me. I misspoke. I meant to say he'll be back by dinner."

Finally, there was some color in her face. Oh, so that was what was bothering Mrs. Archer. Hm. Thought so.

"Denise. Darling. I'm sure you're tired. Alex will show you to your room. You can have some time to freshen up or take a nap or whatever you wish to do," Elizabeth said.

She signaled an older Mexican-American gentleman into the room. He was short and his body hinted at having once been well built through his three-piece suit. His black hair was starting to gray at the sides. Alex picked up my suitcase. I followed him up a staircase and down the hall to a doorway at the end of it.

The room was nice. Mahogany furniture. Four-poster bed. Plenty of expensive-looking fixtures. The kind of stuff from those furniture stores I passed, afraid to even go in and look at the price tags, on my way to Ikea. I was tempted to take a nap on the forty million thread count sheets, but I was even more tempted to eavesdrop on John's conversation with his parents.

Alex set my suitcase down and asked me if I needed anything else. I assured him I didn't. He then hurried off. Probably afraid Elizabeth would demand something of him when he wasn't there to comply. I didn't blame Alex. I was afraid of that woman, too.

"So this is who you left Sasha for? Unacceptable, John."

"I can't believe this matters so much to you guys." John's voice was tired and strained. I felt a little sorry for him, but I was mad at him to for letting me walk into this mess.

"John, you should have told us she's—not white. Why wouldn't you tell us that?" John Archer III sounded more than a little ticked.

"Well, quite frankly, I didn't know you were racist," John said.

"Don't you take that tone with me. And I am not racist. That is a *horrible* thing to say. I have plenty of black friends. Why, Charles was just promoted to partner last week. But son—there's a difference between us. You can't just go marrying one of them."

"Dad. Pretending to like black people at work is not having black friends. Promoting someone who's deserved that promotion for years and had been overlooked again and again does not count. And nobody's saying anything about marriage, but if—"

"Stop right there. This family has an image to uphold. We are the Archers. Do you know what that means? I'll throw you out on your ass, John. I will not hesitate one moment."

"But—"

"I'll give it all to your brother, I swear. Who pays your bills? Where do you think the money in that trust comes from? And you would turn your back on your family like this? John, I am completely disappointed in you. Just when I thought you were finally beginning to get your act together. And you have that poor girl here now. What kind of New Year's will this be? It's all a disgrace. You can't be a partner like this. You can't be on the board of Randy's company like this. How would I explain your black babies to—anybody?"

"Dad, I'm tired of you trying to run everything. Your way isn't the only way. This is my choice and my life and I love her. Screw the trust fund if that's how you feel. The firm, everything!"

"I am not losing my son over this," Elizabeth Archer screamed.

"Thanks, Mom."

"Oh, don't thank me. Now what we have to do is get Sasha back, son. You're confused. Obviously this girl has—"

"Denise didn't do anything. I went after her. Yeah, your perfect lily white son went after the evil black woman. I love Denise. I do not love Sasha. I'm not going to marry an image because that's what you think is best for me. And if I marry Denise, there's nothing you can do about it."

I heard a thud. For a moment I thought it was me. But then I realized that I was still on my feet.

"Elizabeth! Look what you've done to your mother. Get Alex," John Archer III shouted, but Alex was already running into the room. "Hurry, get a wet cloth and some water. My wife has fainted. Faster, or you'll be on your way back to Mexico before dinner."

Alex hurried back out of the living room. He didn't even notice me.

"Out. We'll discuss this later. You better hope and pray you come to your senses, too. And thank your mother. If it wasn't for her protest, you'd be out of this house tonight," John Archer III said.

John burst out of the living room. He saw me. There was a furious look on his face. Of all the thoughts that could come into my head, I couldn't help thinking of how sexy he was at that moment.

"You heard all of that?" he asked quietly. His expression softened.

"Most—I just I wanted to take a shower and I couldn't find the towels and I was looking for Alex . . ." I rambled on nervously. Why did I feel guilty? Why did I feel I owed him an explanation about anything? But somehow, he had that effect on me.

"Come on." John hugged me to him and we went upstairs to the room Alex had shown me. He sat me down on the bed and closed the door. He then pulled up a chair in front of me. He turned the chair backward, sat and rested his chin on the top of the back of the chair. Those eyes. He could make me do or say anything with those eyes. I looked away. He gently took my chin between his fingers and turned me to face him again. I still avoided his eyes. "I'm sorry."

"You didn't tell them."

"You shouldn't have heard that. I wanted to protect you."

"Yeah, 'cause that turned out so well."

"Did you tell your parents I'm white before we went to your place?"

"That's different. I knew they wouldn't care." So I exaggerated a little. I had been pretty sure they didn't care about such things, and I was right. "Why didn't you tell them? Why didn't you at least warn me they didn't know?" Tears, hot and prickling, threatened to pour down my face at any moment. I couldn't stop myself from bringing my eyes back to his. They were so sad, so tired, and yet still so intense.

"I guess I didn't want to believe it would be an issue, even though deep down I knew. We never really talked about it, but I mean, I guess the signs were there. I'm sorry."

He got up from the chair and sat next to me. I moved a little further down on the bed.

"John, why would you put me in this position? You knew what would happen. You knew. That's why you were acting all strange at the train station. You knew. That's why you acted weird when I asked about them at Thanksgiving. You always knew. Why did you bring me into this? You've always known. And you knew we wouldn't be able to stay together. And now I'm in love with you and there's nothing I can do about it," I said as the tears streamed down my face. I knew it wasn't all his fault and that I had been in love with him before he even broke up with Sasha, but I wasn't about to admit that.

"Denise, I know, and I'm sorry. But I just couldn't stay away from you. There's just something about you that pulls me in. And what do you mean about us not staying together? Are you breaking up with me?" John asked in a low tone, his voice thick with emotion. I couldn't bear to look directly at him or let him touch me. I would fall apart if he did either. I wouldn't be able to march myself right out of that house with whatever little resolve I had left. I scooted back on the bed a little.

"They're going to disown you. What do you think?"

"Who cares?" John reached up to brush away my tears before I could stop him. I grabbed his arm, intending to push him away, but I froze for a moment, and that was all he needed. He gently loosened his arm from my grip, grabbed my shoulders, and pushed me back onto the bed. He lay on top of me, still holding me.

"You do," I said, trying to swallow my sobs.

He bent down and sweetly kissed both of my wet cheeks before kissing my lips. I sighed a little and then gave into him completely, kissing him back.

"I don't. And even if I did, I can't stay away from you," John whispered over my lips before kissing them again. John's kisses were undoing every bit of resolve I wanted to have about the situation. I finally forced myself to turn away from his kisses, and then he started kissing my neck, which was even worse.

"I can't believe you put me in this situation. You got me all the way up here and they hate me. You know I can't stay here. You know we can't—"

"Sh. How about we stay for dinner? I really want you to meet my brother. No, he's cool. He's not like them. And we'll take a train back to Virginia tomorrow, if they won't let me take the car. We'll spend New Year's in Richmond," John murmured before kissing me again. What was this spell he had me under? I was supposed to be mad. And here he was, telling me all the right things.

"Hmph," I snorted, still trying to put on a mad front.

"I really am sorry," he said as he sat up and told me to turn over. I did. When I asked him what for, he said, "I owe you a massage."

"I let you get away with way too much," I sighed. His hands felt really good on my back, kneading my sore muscles, though.

He laughed. "Does that mean you'll stay tonight?"

"You sure they won't try to lynch me at dinner?"

"That's not funny. And they know better than to try anything. They know I'll leave tonight if they don't behave."

"Then okay. But if we're not outta here in the morning, I'm outta here in the morning," I said, closing my eyes. I was on the edge of consciousness. I was mentally, emotionally, and physically exhausted. And I hadn't really been able to sleep on the train. And John's hands on my back were so relaxing. I decided to close my eyes for just a moment . . .

Dinner was extremely tense. The only good thing was Thom, John's brother, really was wonderful, as promised.

He had his mother's auburn hair and his father's green eyes. And the sharp Archer jaw line.

"So, Thom, how's Kelly?" Elizabeth nearly spat. John rolled his eyes exaggeratedly. Kelly was Thom's girlfriend, I had discovered.

"She's great. Her mom made me some cookies. They were awesome, but I already ate 'em all before I even got back here," Thom said, oblivious to his mother's dig.

"She's such a nice girl. She's so perfect for you, Thom," Elizabeth said. Okay. Not even a rock could have missed that one. There was silence around the table; not even a fork scraping. John squeezed my knee.

I took a huge gulp of wine.

"More wine, Denise?" John Archer III asked dryly, giving me a disapproving look.

"Yes, please," I said with a testy smile. Screw John Archer III. He signaled to Alex with a sour face.

"Oh, you know how they are with their drink, John. Excuse her," Elizabeth said.

"Mom, that's ignorant," Thom said, looking at his mom in disbelief.

"What? I meant—college students—drink a lot," Elizabeth looked a little flustered. But she still made sure to give me a pointed, nasty look.

"Sure you did, Mom," John said. "But you don't have to worry about looking at Denise anymore after tonight. I know how much you hate to do that. We're leaving in the morning."

I wanted to kiss him right then and there. But I didn't want to be responsible for any heart attacks or double murder-suicides. Or felony murder if his parents died of shock because of my grand theft white boy. Although, I wasn't quite in the clear with that last one yet.

"John. We have New Year's plans in Rochester with the DuPrees. As we do every year. Bring her if you must, but tell everyone she's a friend. We never miss this."

"Well, I'm sure you, Thom and Dad will have an excellent time. But Denise and I are spending New Year's in Richmond," John said firmly. He turned to his dad. "I've tried everything I can think of and nothing's worked. I'm tired of fighting for your approval. I shouldn't have to work so hard for the love of my parents. If you can't accept me as I am, I guess you just can't accept me. But I'm not going to be with someone I don't love just because it's a sound business decision. And I'm not going to spend the rest of my life trying to live up to some impossible standard you keep trying to hold me up to."

"What the hell are you talking about, John?" John Archer III's face turned a shade closer to purple than red.

"I'm done being unhappy for you on the slim chance of a hope that you might treat me like a son one day and not like a useless, dumb lump of clay you have to mold into something respectable and worthy of your time. You know why I got kicked out of three boarding schools? Why I almost dropped out of Boston College? Because of you. Then I tried doing it your way. For some reason, I thought that might make things better.

"When I finally thought I could do something to please you, go to law school, I still wasn't good enough because I couldn't get into your precious Harvard. Even with your help. Fine. Give it all to Thom. It's not worth it to me anymore. Your approval isn't something I'm willing to sacrifice anything for anymore. Especially being with the woman I love."

Silence followed John's shouting. John Archer III looked at John for a long moment and John stared right back. Elizabeth kept smoothing out the table cloth around her plate. Her lips were stretched into a line so thin they were barely visible.

"Come on, Elizabeth," John Archer III said. He and Elizabeth left the table.

Thom patted John on the shoulder. "Don't worry about them, bro," Thom said.

"I'm not. I meant it when I said I'm done with all that," John said. He smiled at me. I shrugged and smiled back. It wasn't what I had envisioned for New Year's. But in a lot of ways, it was much better.

John and I left the next day. John's parents gave Thom the S-Class, but agreed to let John take the Kompressor back. So he wasn't completely out of the family. Only Thom saw us off. He told John their parents would come around. And he told me that he couldn't wait to have me for a sister-in-law and thanked me for taking Sasha out of the picture.

I was never happier in my life to leave a house. I had never met people like John's parents. And it wouldn't have hurt my feelings if I never did again. I couldn't help but thinking how much I would love to give them some black grandbabies one day out of spite. Even if they never so much as looked at the kids.

CHAPTER 15
NEW YEAR'S

Once we were on our way back to Virginia, John looked at me, grinning, and then turned back to face the road several times.

"What?"

"I was just thinking of how happy you were this morning as opposed to all day yesterday."

"You were really different yesterday, too. You kind of freaked me out a little bit."

"Yeah, well, you almost got me disowned."

"You lied. A lot. To everybody."

"Okay, yeah, but you weren't so truthful yourself. Thanksgiving ring a bell? And don't give me any of your excuses about that," John said, smiling, his eyes still on the road.

I watched the white, snowy landscape ahead. "John?"

"Yes?"

"You never told me about any of that. The boarding schools. Almost failing out of undergrad or anything."

John drove in silence for a while, staring straight ahead out of the windshield. I watched the windshield wipers move back and forth, sweeping wisps of powdery snow across the glass, while I waited for him to say something.

"I don't like talking about it."

"What happened?"

"Whatever I said yesterday, that's all there is to it. I wasn't the best of students." He shrugged. "We can't all be geniuses like you." John laughed, but it sounded forced.

I could tell I wouldn't get any more than that out of him, but I was curious about what had happened. A lot had gone on between him and his family, it seemed. I wondered what could make him feel like his parents didn't love him.

I grabbed my throw blanket from the back and reclined my seat, preparing for the long ride ahead of us. I closed my eyes and thought happier thoughts, my lips curving up into a smile as my mind went back to John's massage the night before and how good his hands felt on my back. I wondered how much better they would have felt without my shirt between them and my skin.

***

We stayed overnight in Baltimore because we didn't feel like driving anymore. And we weren't in any hurry to get back. We decided on a hotel just off of Interstate 695. I shuffled up to the counter behind John. I was cold and more tired than hungry. My fingers were numb and frozen inside my thin gloves. I hoped John wouldn't say anything about dinner, because I just wanted to sleep.

A woman with badly damaged, bleached blonde hair stared up at us with her beady brown eyes.

"Hi, can we get a room tonight?" John asked, pulling his wallet from his back pocket.

The woman's eyes moved from my face to John's and then back to mine again. "Just the one room? For the two of you?" She had a faint New Jersey accent. I thought that she couldn't have been a native Marylander.

"Yeah. Just one," John said, his voice hardening.

"None of my business, I guess," the woman murmured, typing something into the keyboard on the desk in front of her. "You'll need two beds then?"

"No. We only need one," John said.

Her lips puckered. She ran a hand through her brittle hair and then scratched her forehead. I noted the spidery blue veins and age spots on the back of her hand, keeping my eyes away from her face. Her gold-plated name tag had the name "Roxy" printed on it.

"So do you have a room for us or not?" John asked. His nostrils flared and he clenched his wallet in his fist.

"I'm sorry. Looks like we're all booked up." She twisted her lips, giving us a sour look.

"Really? Is that the same answer your supervisor would give us?" John asked.

Roxy's sour faced puckered up even tighter. "He's not here."

"You have a phone number for him?"

Roxy glared at John for a moment. It looked like she was deciding whether or not she wanted to push the issue. Finally she made a sound in her throat that reminded me of the growl of a dog that feels threatened. Then, she looked at her computer screen. "Oh, well look at that. I guess I missed a room. Y'all mind a smoking room? No vacancies in the non-smoking rooms."

"Is that okay with you?" John asked, rubbing my shoulder and pulling me close. Out of the corner of my eye, I saw Roxy give a little shake of her head.

"Sure," I said. I just wanted to sleep. I could have curled up on the couch in the lobby and been fine as long as Roxy didn't kill me with her scathing looks.

John turned back to Roxy and registered us.

We were walking away from the desk when I heard her mutter, "Some people have no respect for themselves. Mixing like that."

John turned back and opened his mouth.

I grabbed his arm and shook my head. "It's not worth it."

He looked uncertain, but I tugged at his arm, pulling him in the direction of the elevator. Still looking unsure, he followed me. He set our bags on the floor of the elevator and pulled me close to him.

When we reached the room, I flopped down on the bed and closed my eyes.

"You hungry?" he asked. The bed sagged slightly under his weight.

"No," I said without opening my eyes.

He ran his hand over my back and kissed my cheek. "You sure?"

"Yeah."

"Well, I'm going to run out and get something. I'll be right back." I heard him moving around the room and then I heard a door open. "If you were hungry, what would you feel like eating?"

"Anything," I said.

The door closed and I rolled over and pulled a pillow over my head.

John came back with pad thai and prawns. I sat up on the bed and looked over to the table where he'd set the containers.

"Looks good," I said, sniffing the odor of the spices in the air.

He grinned. "There's enough for two, you know."

I went over to the table and sat across from him. He handed me a paper plate and a bottle of water. I was hungrier than I'd thought and for a while we ate in silence, too hungry to talk. I sucked down noodle and prawn so quickly that I almost didn't notice how well spiced and tasty the meal was.

Eventually I looked up and saw John toying with the top to his water bottle, the corners of his mouth tilting down in the beginnings of a frown. I lay my fork aside and pushed my chair back from the table.

"What are you thinking about?" I asked.

"Nothing," he said, still spinning the top.

I stood and paced the floor just in front of the table. "This is the dumbest thing in the world. Why are people like this? Why does it have to matter what color our skin is?"

John finally looked up at me. "It doesn't."

"What are you talking about? Your parents. That asshole downstairs. You know it does. You should see your face right now."

He stood and wrapped his arms around me, stopping me from pacing. "It doesn't matter to the only people whose opinions count. And all of those people are standing in this room right now." He pressed his forehead to mine. "Tell me you believe that. Because I have to be with you. Please don't let the inconsequential opinions of some close-minded people come between us."

"I want to believe it," I said, closing my eyes as he trailed feathery kisses down my cheek, my neck.

"Please. It's only us. Only we matter." He pulled my sweater over my head and put his hands under the hem of my T-shirt. His hands were warm against my skin, almost hot. I lay my head against his shoulder and he slipped his hands into my jeans.

I turned my face up to his and pressed my lips to his. I was only aware of his tongue against mine for a moment and the next time I was aware of anything, I lay under him on the bed in only my panties and he was shirtless. I remember vaguely turning out the light at some point before that. His kisses were deep and wet in the valley between my breasts. I pressed my fingers into his back as his mouth closed over my nipple. His hand slipped inside my panties and I reluctantly grabbed his wrist.

"No," I moaned, motioning for him to move aside. I sat up and pulled my knees to my chest.

"What? Why?" John sounded genuinely confused.

Maybe I was as well. Because part of me wanted to pull him back on top of me.

"We've only been together a little over a month," I lied. That wasn't really what bothered me. I didn't want to mess things up with sex. Sex always messed things up. The furthest I'd let him go so far was heavy petting.

John lay back on his elbows. I could see his face in the shadowy light from the street lights coming through the curtains. His features were soft. He licked his lips and a fresh wave of warmth flooded over me as I thought of better uses for that tongue.

"Well . . . I just—" I started, and finished in my head, *am afraid I'll get even more emotionally wrapped up with you. Scared I'm no good; I've only been with one other guy.*

"What?" John interrupted my internal war. He moved closer and started rubbing circles on my inner thigh with his finger.

"Uh, well, I think we should wait."

He kissed the spot where his finger had been. "For what?"

That was a good question. It was hard to think. I throbbed with desire for him, and he must have felt the dampness when he brushed his finger over my panties.

"You know how long I've been waiting for you, Denise? I haven't had sex since I met you."

"But Sasha was—"

"I haven't had sex with anyone since August." He emphasized his words with kisses. To my stomach, thigh, hip. "You really don't want to?"

"Not tonight." It took all of my willpower to say that.

"Okay," he said, kissing my side. He then kissed my shoulder before bringing his lips back to mine. Then he rolled away from me and stood.

"Where you going?" I asked, disappointed.

"I have to take a shower or I'm not going to be able to leave you alone."

"You don't have to leave me alone. We can do other stuff."

"Denise, I've been thinking about making love to you all day. I don't think it's a good idea for us to do anything right now," John said, walking toward the bathroom.

I lay back on the bed with a groan, wondering about the wisdom of stopping him.

When we got back to Richmond on New Year's Eve, it was snowing. We went to the train station to pick up my car and then he followed me home. We went straight to my place. John said he didn't even want to see his roommates, which made me exceedingly happy.

We walked in and Tia and her boyfriend were sitting on the couch, making out. They didn't bother to stop at the sound of us coming in.

"Hi, Tia," I said loudly. They reluctantly tore them-selves away from each other and looked up at us.

Tia's brow wrinkled in confusion. "I thought you weren't coming back until the day before classes start."

"Yeah, well, we had a change of plans," was all I was willing to volunteer. "You have a good break so far?"

"Yeah. Terry's been over here the whole time." Tia grinned at her boyfriend. I had to will myself not to roll my eyes. "Did you, Denise? John?"

"Yeah. It was great," John said flatly. He brushed a hand over his short, bristly black hair, knocking the snow from it. I wondered what he'd done with his hat.

"Why are you back so early, though? I thought you two had big New Year's plans at your parents', John," Tia said.

"Well, the party got canceled and my dad had an emergency work trip to take the day after New Year's anyway, so we thought we'd have more fun here," John said.

I wasn't sure it sounded convincing to me, but Tia and Terry seemed to buy it. Not that they were probably all that concerned with what we were doing. For one thing, they could barely keep their eyes off each other even though Tia was attempting to carry on a conversation with us.

"You two have plans for tonight?" I asked.

"Nope," Tia said. Her small body was nearly swallowed up by Terry's looming form.

"Well, do you want to go to dinner and make a trip by the ABC? Then we could all just come back here," I said.

"Is Astoria coming?" John and Tia asked together. I laughed. Ms. Banks was notorious.

"I hadn't planned on asking her if she wanted to. I was just gonna call Suse and see what she and Charles are doing," I said.

"Okay, sounds like fun. Anywhere special you want to go?" Tia said.

"Nah. You guys can pick. I'm gonna go call Suse," I said, taking out my phone and heading for my room. John followed me.

"Hey. Having fun in Connecticut?" Suse answered the phone. We had gotten even closer since I didn't like spending a lot of time with Astoria anymore. Suse had been cool with John and I ever since John had broken up with Sasha. I guess the sneakiness really was what she had disapproved of. Well, at least that was her story and she was sticking to it.

"Actually, I'm back in Richmond."

"Really? What happened? Where's John?"

"He's with me. Long story," I said, and quickly got to the point before she could ask more questions. "You and Charles have plans tonight?"

"No, not really." Suse sounded confused. Yeah, I didn't blame her. "Charles and I were just going to head out to Louisa."

"Well, I was wondering if you'd want to come over. It'd be me, John, you, Charles, Tia, and Terry. We could have dinner and hang out here after that."

"Okay," Suse said. "Let me run it by Charles, but I'd say count me in."

"How about you come over around . . . seven-thirty?"

"Sounds good. I'll see you then."

"Bye," I said, hanging up the phone and turning to John. "You want to go to the ABC?"

"Maybe in a little while," he said, putting his arms around me. A devious grin lit up his face.

"We might miss it," I said, not making any attempt to stop him from pushing me back onto my bed.

"Well, if we do, we do. I can find alcohol like it's my job," he said before kissing me. I laughed. I didn't doubt it.

We lay in my bed talking, kissing and touching for hours. I was seriously thinking about doing more when my eye caught the time on the alarm clock on my nightstand.

I began to untangle myself from John.

"No," he murmured, pulling me closer.

"Yes," I sighed. I rolled away from him. "It's time to get ready. I must have a shower before we go."

"We have to get up?" John asked, sounding disappointed. He moved next to me.

"Yes," I laughed, his tongue tickling my ear. "It's already close to seven."

John reached over me to turn on the lamp, and I stopped him. "What?"

"I don't want you to see . . ." I felt awkward for the first time since we'd climbed into my bed.

"Okay. What's this thing you have about me seeing you naked?"

"It's just you've been with girls like Sasha and . . ."

"So? I know I'll love your body. If you just let me *see* it," he said in that tone I hated because I couldn't say no when he used it, or when he kissed the back of my neck like that. I took my hand off of his arm. He turned on the lamp. At first, I was afraid to look at him. Until he turned me to face him. I looked into his eyes and I didn't see disgust. I didn't see laughter. I saw desire. So much desire I thought about giving him what he'd been trying to get since the night before.

"We really do have to start getting ready to get out of here," I said, but I made no attempt to move from the bed.

"I wish I hadn't turned on that light. 'Cause now that is *all* I'm gonna think about all night. As if it wasn't hard enough already to behave."

"You call what you've been doing behaving?" I teased.

"Oh, yeah. This is the best I can do. You'd have thrown me out by now if I wasn't trying," John said, reaching for me.

I shook my head, laughing as I stood. I grabbed my robe and turned to look at him one last time before heading to the bathroom. Wow. He was really in my bed.

By the time John and I finally showered, got dressed, and made it out of my room, it was a little past seven-thirty. I was surprised when the front door opened and Tia came in, followed by Terry carrying a huge cardboard box. I had assumed they were in her room.

"What's that?" I asked.

"We went by the ABC. I figured it would be too late by the time we got back from dinner," Tia said as Terry sat the box down on our dining room table.

"I was thinking the same thing, but we obviously never made it."

"Yeah . . . it didn't seem like you were leaving your room any time soon," Tia said. She and Terry laughed. All of the blood in my body seemed to rush to my face.

"So, how much do I owe you?" I avoided the awkward innuendo.

"Consider it my Christmas present to you," Tia said, smiling. Tia wasn't so bad after all. I was going to ask her what she'd gotten when there was a knock on the door. I ran to answer it. Suse and Charles were standing there.

"Suse!" I grabbed her and gave her a huge hug as she came through the door. Her pink coat was wet with snow, and I felt the cold dampness of it through my shirt before pulling back from her. "Hey, Charles."

"Hey," he said. His black hair had a few flakes of snow in it. His large frame filled most of the doorway until he came inside and closed the door behind him.

I proceeded to make introductions all the way around. Suse and I exchanged Christmas stories. She told me all about mud bogging on Christmas Day and hunting things with her dad and Charles. She seemed excited that they were starting to get along. Her parents had never really liked Charles from the beginning. Suse said realizing there was no getting rid of him must have been making them warm up to him.

After some more chatting, Charles spoke up, saying he could eat a horse.

"Well, where does everyone want to eat?" I asked.

"How about that sushi place near Short Pump we went to for the SBA thing last semester?" Tia suggested.

Charles made a face and Suse patted his shoulder. "There's that Chinese buffet near it," Suse said.

"Ugh, that place is so greasy," Tia said.

"The steak house down the street," Suse said.

Everybody agreed on that and we left for dinner.

Shortly after we ordered and had our drinks, we started talking about how we'd spent other New Year's Eves and I listened to every word out of John's mouth carefully, wondering if he'd mention Sasha. I tried to tell myself it wouldn't matter if he did.

I felt a hand on my shoulder and looked up to see Astoria standing behind me next to a guy whose grin revealed a gold tooth.

"Denise. Denise, girl! How you doin'?" she slurred, grabbing my shoulder. "And your boy, John! Hi, *John!*" She'd obviously started her celebration early.

"Hey," John said, annoyance flickering over his features.

"Everybody, this is Irvin. Irvin, these are my worthless friends who didn't invite me out with them for New Year's Eve."

We exchanged tense, awkward greetings.

"This one." Astoria glared at me. "She didn't even tell me she was back in town."

"I just got back," I said, but it was hard to defend myself when I knew she was right.

"Yeah, okay. Mind if we join you for dinner?" Without waiting for our answer, Astoria sent Irvin off to find a couple of chairs.

Dinner went okay even with Astoria there. She mostly behaved herself, but she kept making snide comments to Irvin loud enough for the rest of us to hear over our conversations, most of them about John. And her drunk ass did order a cocktail, much to the consternation of everyone else at the table.

I still had a good time. John sat next to me and he mostly ate with one hand, the arm of his free hand wrapped around me. He kept whispering things to me that made my ears burn. Occasionally, I forgot we were sharing our table with six other people.

When we got back to the apartment, everybody was ready to drink, mostly so we could bear Astoria's company. I had almost strangled her when as we were leaving the restaurant, she told John she was surprised to see him out in public with me. He handled it really well, but that didn't make it okay.

Terry started making our drinks. In his varied and interesting travels, he'd become a mixologist while living in Denver. Terry had traveled for a few years before "settling" in Richmond. He'd been there for five years—the longest he'd been anywhere since graduating high school. I didn't know where Tia had come across him, but he wasn't a law student. Really, I had no idea what Terry did.

Once everybody started drinking, Astoria came up to me, wanting to have a "serious conversation." I should have smelled the trouble. My filter was off and I was going to be too honest. But it was time for the conversation we were going to have, anyway.

She pulled me aside after John, Terry, Irvin, and Charles started a conversation about basketball.

"So, why aren't we friends anymore?" Astoria asked.

"We're friends. I just don't want to be around you too much right now. All you do is trash John and it pisses me off," I said.

"I'm just trying to look out for you."

"Well, I don't like it and I don't need it. Why do you think I'd want to hear all that about somebody I love?"

"You don't love him. You don't even know him."

"I do."

"Even if you think you do, he don't love you."

"Huh?"

"You're not white. When he's bored, he'll leave you for some white chick. Probably go back to Sasha. You never going to be anything *serious* to him," she said.

"He took me to meet his parents."

"Didn't go too well, did it? What you doin' back so early? I don't remember you sayin' . . ." Astoria pretended to look perplexed. For the first time in my life, I wanted to hit her. Right in her loud, fat mouth. I couldn't believe the words coming out of it. And I couldn't believe how deeply they were touching on the painful, ugly truth.

"You're pathetic. You're just jealous that I have a boyfriend."

"Oh, please. This isn't middle school. You don't have a boyfriend, either."

"What are you talking about?"

"All you have is a fuck buddy."

"We haven't even had sex yet!"

"Oh. That's probably why he's still around. Just wait until you do. And he gets tired of it."

"I'm tired of this conversation. I just knew you would come here starting stuff. And you've been picking with people all night. Now you're back on the same old shit you been on with me for months. I want you out. Out of my house!" I yelled at her. I could feel everybody's eyes on us, but I didn't care. I was focused on Astoria.

"Fine. Forget your real friends," she said. "C'mon, Irvin. Let's go."

"Out!" I shoved her coat at her. "If you were a real friend, you would want me to be happy."

"Don't push me," she said in a low, threatening tone. I shoved her toward the door. She pushed back. I moved forward again and someone grabbed me from behind.

"I think you better go," John said to Astoria, drawing me close to him.

"Whatever. You're dumb. All of you. I don't know why I waste my time with you people," Astoria snarled, but there were tears in her eyes. She snatched her gloves from Suse and stormed out.

I sagged against John, staring at the door. Suse went after her, muttering something about making sure Irvin was driving.

"You okay?" he murmured, hugging me.

I turned around in his arms and hugged him back, nodding. I wasn't.

"You just wanna go in your room for a while? Cool off?"

I nodded again. I followed him to my room. We sat on the edge of the bed, my head buried in his shoulder.

"You wanna talk about it?" he asked softly.

I shook my head. I looked up at him. He lowered his head, kissing me softly. I kissed him back hard. I pushed him back on the bed and started tearing at his clothes. He restrained me by gently taking my wrists in his hands. "I'm gonna take this the wrong way if you don't tell me not to."

"I want to. I want you," I said. He let go of my wrists.

"We're probably going to miss the countdown," he said as I threw his pants across the room.

"Do you really care?" I asked, throwing my sweater across the room. My jeans quickly followed.

"No way," he grinned, his eyes widening as they traveled downward. I ran my hand over his head and what little hair he hadn't shaved off.

"Good," I said. He caressed the side of my face. I put my hand over his. I grinned down at him, lost in his eyes. The only place in the world I wanted to be at that moment.

I sighed against John's lips as he removed my bra and ran his hands over my back. I closed my eyes and arched my back to his touch. He rolled over, pinning me beneath him. I watched as removed his boxers, my eyes traveling greedily over his body. It was the first time I had seen him completely naked. I reached out, running my hands lightly over his perfect abs.

"Whoa," he said, grabbing my hand. "It's really been a while. And it's gonna be all over if you do that."

I grinned lazily at him as he kissed my fingertips. He started trailing kisses down my arm. I moaned softly as he reached my shoulder. His teeth and tongue transported me to a place I'd never been before. He moved greedily over my body, trying to consume me with his mouth and hands.

"John," I whispered as I felt his fingers slip between my thighs. They rested lightly on my inner thigh, dangerously close to where I wanted them to be. I pushed my legs further apart.

"Yes?" he whispered back, his tongue tickling my earlobe.

"I love you," I said as he kissed my throat.

"I know. I love you, too, Denise. So much," John murmured into my navel, his hands in mine. My name on his tongue almost gave me more pleasure than what he put on his tongue next.

Nobody came to check on us—they seemed to know we neither needed nor wanted that. And we had no idea what was going on out in the living room. We spent the rest of the night either holding each other or making love. I was on top of him when the sky started to lighten on the other side of my curtains.

CHAPTER 16
TAU GAMMA TERRORS

The first few weeks back after winter break were a blur. Sasha decided to sic her Tau Gamma Chi sisters at Central on me. That was fun. To add to that, even though Astoria and I had technically made up, we had barely had a civil word for each other since New Year's Eve. I wondered if our friendship would survive my relationship with John. And school stress was a constant factor.

The beginning of the end came when we all ended up at some party that a bunch of the third-years threw. Me, John, Astoria, and Cindy and her Tau Gamma Chi crew. Suse refused to come. She had admonished Astoria and I against going, telling us that "nothing but trouble would come of it." Suse had lost that battle—she lost most battles with Astoria and I. Still, we should have listened to her.

I drank way too much. John was off with some of his idiot friends I avoided whenever possible. I liked Ral, but he wasn't there. I stood in a corner with Astoria. We were trashing the Tau Gammas while I wondered what they were saying about me. They'd been following me around and spreading rumors about me for weeks.

"Why is this bitch laughing at me? Look at her," I said, glaring at Cindy and the other two waifs. They were standing across the room, laughing and looking in our direction. Something about us was really funny to them.

"I can think of a few reasons," Astoria said with a snort.

I ignored her and drained my cup before setting it on the table next to me. We were standing next to the makeshift bar. A card table piled high with liquor.

"Here they come," she said.

"Of course," I said, watching them approach me.

"Denise," Cindy said. Her two cronies stood behind her, smirking. All three were blonde, tall, and thin. They were low-rent versions of Sasha.

"What?" I snapped.

"I thought I'd say hi to you for Sasha," Cindy said. And with that, she dumped an entire cup of some sort of spiked punch over my head. I saw red and it had nothing to do with the punch.

I shrieked, pushing my dripping hair away from my face.

"Oops. Did I get your sweater, honey? Don't worry, I saw plenty more on clearance at Macy's where you got that one from. Or wait, is that a Wal-Mart knock-off? I wouldn't know. I don't go into such stores," Cindy said, tapping a perfectly oval, pink fingernail against her chin, just below her frost pink lips. Her harpies thought that was the most clever thing they'd ever heard, apparently.

I lurched for her. Astoria grabbed my arm.

"Denise, no," she said. I could tell she was struggling to restrain herself as well.

"You better learn where you belong before much more gets ruined than a cheap sweater," Cindy said.

"You tell Sasha she can go fuck herself!" I shouted.

"I think you want to choose your words a little more carefully," Cindy said.

"What for?" I pushed Astoria off of me.

"Give it up. How long do you think you'll last anyway?" she asked with a glare.

At that moment, I looked up and saw John standing at the edge of the circle that had formed around us. Avoiding my eyes.

That hurt much more than anything Cindy had said. I brushed away Astoria's hand when she reached out for me again and stormed out of the house.

"Denise," I heard John calling after me. Now he could come to me. Outside. Where no one was looking. I continued down the sidewalk, pretending I hadn't heard a thing.

"Denise!" Astoria too. I didn't stop for them. But I did let them catch up to me. Big mistake.

"Denise, I'm sorry," John said.

"Damn right you are," Astoria said.

"Shut up, both of you," I said, still walking and staring straight ahead.

"You have to be freezing," John said. I pushed away his coat even though he was right. I had left my jacket back at the party, and my sweater was drenched.

"She *humiliated* me, John. And you acted like you didn't even know who I was," I seethed, still not looking, still not stopping. I bit my lip so hard that it pulsed with pain, but that did nothing to stop the tears.

"See? Told you about things like him," Astoria said.

I finally stopped and whirled around to face them. "You. With the I-told-you-so's! That's enough!" I shouted at Astoria.

"But—"

"Enough, I said!"

"He's the one—"

"Go!" I screamed.

Astoria stared at me, shockingly at a loss for words. She eventually found a few choices ones for both John and I and then stormed off.

I turned to John.

"And you. How dare you?" I screamed at him.

He said nothing.

"You don't have anything to say for yourself?"

"I'm waiting for you to finish. You finished?" he said.

"Go on. Explain yourself."

"There's nothing to explain. You ran out before I could say anything at all. Do anything. Denise, you were out of the door before I really knew what was happening."

"Liar. I saw you standing there. Avoiding my eyes."

"Denise, I was still trying to figure out what was going on. I was outside. As soon as I came in, I asked somebody what was happening. And, like, five seconds later, you're running out of the door like you're on fire, dripping and apparently trying to freeze to death or something. You really think I wouldn't care that Cindy did that to you? What, you really believe that?"

I suddenly felt a little foolish. But I didn't want to be wrong. So I just stood there, staring at him angrily from under a mop of punch-soaked hair, shivering. He sighed and shook his head. He once again moved to put his coat around my shoulders. This time, I didn't try to stop him. I let him hug me.

"So you gonna take me home?" I said.

I felt him nod against my cheek. "C'mon."

He put his arm around me and walked me back to his car. First, I wasn't great at apologies because I was horrible at ever admitting I was wrong. And second, I wasn't sure I completely believed John. The hateful cynic in me wanted to believe John wanted me to disappear at that party. It wanted me to accept that I had no place in John Archer's life; that Cindy was right.

Back at my apartment, we still weren't talking. He walked me to my room. I let him remove the ruined, dripping sweater along with my T-shirt and bra, which were in similarly shabby states. I watched him put everything in a plastic bag. I remained motionless, except for involuntary shivering. He unbuckled my belt and removed it. I glanced at him long enough to see that he was avoiding my eyes just as I had been avoiding his. I wondered what was going through his mind.

I stepped out of my punch-soaked jeans and he tossed them into the bag as well. I wrapped my arms around myself. John went over to my bed, grabbed a throw blanket, and wrapped it around me. He pulled me to him.

I wanted to say something to him, but I didn't know how. He seemed to be having a similar problem. I heard him take a deep breath as if he wanted to speak several times, but there was no other sound from him. I hugged him closer to me, resting my head on his shoulder. I closed my eyes. I just wanted John and I didn't want anything to destroy that—us.

I took a deep breath, trying hard to keep the tears away; trying to swallow them back inside of myself. But I felt it coming. My throat was raw. My eyes burned. My breathing was unsteady. I finally looked up at John. The look in his eyes—sadness and pain and love all mixed together—made me want to cry even more. He gently wiped the tears away from the corners of my eyes with his thumbs.

"You're all sticky," he said with a forced grin.

I forced myself to laugh.

"C'mon."

I followed John to the bathroom, my hand in his. He sat down on the edge of the tub and pulled me onto his lap. He turned on the faucet with one hand. The other was holding me. I rested my head on his shoulder. He brushed his chin against the side of my face before kissing my cheek.

"It's warm," he murmured in my ear. We stood together. I let the blanket fall to the floor and stepped out of my panties. John was not shy about observing. Finally, some warmth spread over me.

I smiled as he turned the knob for the shower. "You coming in?" I asked.

He had turned to leave the bathroom. His eyes widened as he turned back to me. He seemed shocked I was actually talking to him. I was kind of shocked myself.

"Only if you want me to," John said, but he was already undressing.

"Of course I want you to," I said, watching the last of John's clothing hit the floor. I stepped into the tub and he followed. I wrapped my arms around him and let my head sink into his shoulder. His wet, warm hands moved down from my shoulders. He kissed my lips and then my chin. It was almost enough to make me forget why my hair was clumped uncomfortably against my neck—almost. At the thought of that sticky hair, my back stiffened.

"What?" John whispered into my ear.

"Nothing," I said. I wanted peace with John, no matter how temporary it had to be.

"Your hair," John said softly, as if reading my mind. He lifted my head from his shoulder and tilted it back. I smiled faintly. His fingers gently kneaded against my scalp. He was pretty good for someone with practically no hair. I sighed, relaxing into his soft yet strong hands.

"That feels good," I murmured.

John murmured assent. He drew me closer to him.

"I never want anything to hurt you. I want to protect you. You have to believe that. I don't want to lose you over anything stupid. I don't want to lose you at all," John said.

I nodded, which was difficult with his hands still in my hair. "John, I love you so much. It scares me. I'm worried I won't be able to do enough to keep you. They scare me because I think they're right," I murmured, loving the feel of his fingers against my scalp. He was distracting me into telling too much of the truth.

"They're wrong. They're just bitter, stupid harpies." John's voice was hard, but his fingers were gentle, loving.

But I remained unsure. "Please, John, please . . ."

"Please what?" John whispered into my ear before kissing it. Our bodies were pressed together. His fingers were still tangled in my hair. His chest moved against mine with each frantic breath he took.

"Please don't tell me lies. I can't stand to love you this much and not know the truth," I said with my eyes closed. I felt his lips against my eyelids.

"I *am* telling the truth. I love you more than anything in this world. And anyone who tries to take you away from me will have to answer to me. That includes you."

I could hear the grin in his voice. I laughed and relaxed into his hands. I tried to push down all thoughts of panic and fear and give myself over completely to him.

John and I couldn't find our way to normal. Virtually overnight, we had become the pariahs of the law school. And our law school is a small place. Claustrophobically small. There was no escape from the hell of disapproving glares of the nosy people who were apparently incapable of minding their own business. Astoria had stopped saying so many hateful things about John, but probably only because everyone else was saying them for her. I knew she still didn't want us together, and she had that in common with everyone. In the world.

Then Cindy and the other two started causing Lindie to harass me even more. Lindie came to me one day, furious that I hadn't turned in my cite checks. I swore to her I had turned them in right at the deadline. Little did I know at the time that I had been sabotaged. And they weren't nearly done with me at that. Shortly after the cite check incident, Lindie came barreling down on me again one Wednesday in January. It was unseasonably warm, but I'll always remember that Wednesday as the coldest day of the year; possibly of my life.

I knew it was all over when Lindie came down the hall, screaming at me. She was waving papers and gesticulating wildly. She looked crazy, even for her. People stopped to stare curiously at her as she hurtled herself toward me. Lots of curious eyes darted around corners and snuck glances while pretending to pore over whatever they were supposed to be reading.

"Office. Now." That was all she could manage to get out. I had no desire to argue with her after seeing the expression on her face. I stepped into the journal office. She was right on my heels and slammed the door behind her. She then slammed those papers she had been waving around down on the desk in front of her. She looked at me like they were supposed to mean something to me.

I narrowed my eyes in confusion at her. "Lindie, what is this?"

"Don't play that game with me. It's one thing if you want to embarrass yourself. But this school—this journal has a reputation to maintain. A reputation that you should care about," Lindie said. Her mouth was still moving, but she was apparently too disgusted, furious, or whatever else to make more words come out.

"Huh?" I looked down at the papers, but none of it made any sense to me still. Most of the papers were photocopies of journal articles from schools with lesser-known law reviews. And there were some other papers mixed in as well.

"This. You didn't think I would notice? That no one would catch you?" she screamed.

My heart sank as I started to catch on to what she was ranting about.

"This is what you consider a student note?" She raked a hand through her strawberry blonde hair before gesturing to the papers again, apparently at a loss of words at that point.

I tried to swallow, but my mouth was too dry. It chose that very inopportune moment to imitate the Sahara. I peered more closely at my outline, the note that was supposedly mine, and the student notes from the other schools' law reviews before me. They all had striking similarities from what I could see. Too striking. But I had nothing to do with any of it. The only thing familiar was the general topic. I hadn't even used those notes as part of my research.

"That's not mine," I said in a very small voice that I barely recognized. That, admittedly, did not sound very convincing. Lindie gave a cry of disgust mingled with disbelief that made me jump with its intensity.

"Denise! This is from the thumb drive you put in my box," Lindie said. My heart sank further, which I hadn't thought possible. I had given Lindie my thumb drive to check my note progress because I was having computer issues, but—

"Well, it can't be my, last semester you saw my—it's just not mine," I said weakly. I sounded like such an idiot. A lying idiot. But I was in such a state of shock that I couldn't come up with anything better.

Lindie jerked something from her pocket and held it up to my face. Well, it did *look* like my thumb drive. It was pink like mine. And had a chip in the lower left corner of the casing like mine. Sighing angrily, she huffed over to the computer at the desk. After jamming the thumb drive into the USB port on the front of the computer, she looked over at me pointedly for emphasis. She tapped her finger impatiently on the desk for the few moments it took the computer to register the drive. Then after double-clicking the "My Computer" icon, she clicked on the icon for the thumb drive.

I let out a little cry of shock as I hastily read the names of the folders on the drive. They were mine. Folders for my outlines, my exam answers, and so on. I held my breath as Lindie double-clicked on the folder entitled "Law Review Stuff." I scanned the files in panic. The file for my note was gone. There was no file entitled "D's Note." Instead, there was a file that shouldn't have been there. A file I had not put there entitled "Student Note." So my note was gone. All of my work. All of my research. For a fifty-page paper. Gone. And this impostor in its place. This impostor that could get me kicked out of school in its place.

"That's just not mine. It's—it's not mine. Someone switched—someone must have switched 'em. Someone took my jump drive. And they put this thing—this thing that's not mine on it," I stammered, backing away from the computer. A pain I had never known before coursed through my stomach. I was suddenly grateful I hadn't had time for lunch. The only thing I was grateful for at that moment.

"Likely story," Lindie said with a harsh little laugh of disbelief. "We'll just see what honor council has to say about this." She looked a little too happy about that. I had the feeling that Lindie didn't care if I'd plagiarized my note or not. She just wanted to see me kicked off of law review. She hated me that much.

"But that's not mine. My note's gone. Lindie, please. Someone got my drive. Someone got to that before you." Tears welled up in my eyes. I couldn't get kicked out for something I hadn't done. I couldn't get kicked out in disgrace. I couldn't get kicked out of law school. My mother would die. I would die.

"Denise, there are large sections of these notes verbatim in your supposed note draft and outline. And no hint of a footnote. Then again, I guess your whole damned paper would be one long-ass footnote if you tried to do that, huh?"

"But—"

"No one messes with my law review!" she screamed. Her face was redder than her hair.

"I—"

"I mean it. Leave."

"Give me—"

"Now."

"I just—"

"Out!"

"You can't do this to me!" I finally found my voice. But it was too late.

"We'll just see about that, you lying, sneaking thief. I knew you weren't law review material. And now I have the proof. You probably lied your way onto this journal in the first place. Now you're finally going to get what you deserve." Lindie pushed me out of the office. And with that last syllable, she slammed the door shut in my face. I sunk down against it, wondering what I was going to do. If there was anything I could do. I didn't know who was watching and I didn't care.

Who would do such a thing? Who could hate me so much that they would want to ruin my life? What have I ever done? What horrible person—

Of course.

"Cindy." I jumped to my feet. I must have looked pretty insane in that moment. Hair sticking up all over my head. Eyeliner and mascara streaked all over my red, wet face. Sweater all twisted up and wet and wild-looking from having been my makeshift handkerchief.

"What are you looking at? Get the hell outta here!" I screamed at no one in particular, but at everyone in the hallway at once. I have never seen people scatter so fast in my life. Another new hot gossip topic. Ah, how wonderful for them. Glad my life was all the entertainment they could need and want.

I gulped, my mouth acid with fear as I took a very official-looking letter out of my mailbox from the dean's office, followed by another very official-looking letter from the honor council. It was the Friday after Lindie had contributed to the ruining of my life. I sank down on the ground next to the mailboxes for my apartment complex. The boxes were stationed outside near the parking lot. I didn't even feel the cold and wet of the concrete beneath me. I felt nothing at all. The world was rapidly falling out from under me.

I didn't have to read the letters to know my life was over. But I went through the mechanics of ripping both letters open simultaneously. I skimmed over formalities, procedures, and more formalities. I then hugged the letters to my chest and closed my eyes.

Yeah, yeah, yeah. I'm gonna be given a chance to present my side alright, I thought.

It was all going to be over very, very soon. No more law school. Nothing. Less than nothing. Left with fear, bitterness, and anger. Just when I thought life had thrown its worst at me, it was only getting started. It seemed the harder I tried to be happier, the harder life pushed me back down into darkness. I wanted to see life in a less bleak way. A less desperate one. But it wasn't happening. Man, was I a genius at screwing up my life. Ironically, it was the only thing I could get right anymore.

"What should I even care anymore?" I muttered.

"You okay?"

I jumped, startled, at the sound of a voice. How dare someone interrupt my wallowing? I glared up into the confused face of some undergrad who was always hitting my window with Frisbees. Even in the middle of winter. Especially him.

"Yeah. I'm fine. Don't mind me. My life is just falling apart here," I said.

He jumped back, raising his hands in front of him in some stupid, defensive gesture. "Hey, um, I just want my mail. That's all. So, whoa, don't freak out or anything."

"Then get it. And go away. Leave me alone. Just get your stupid mail and walk away. Don't mind the freak show. Watch your step. Don't wanna get too close. Don't let life get too real for you. I wouldn't want to force you out of fantasy land where everything's so perfect for you."

"But you're—well you're kinda in front of my box . . ." he started. His voice trailed off as I shot daggers into his eyes with mine. "Um, yeah, that's okay. You know what, you just stay where you are. I can totally come back later," he said. And he backed off, tripping over his feet. Then, he turned around and jogged back to his apartment.

I laughed bitterly. My bitter laugh turned into a sob. Astoria would have found that hilarious, if I could have found the strength to pick up my phone and press send. But even more importantly, if I could have found the strength to hear her voice. I had been carefully avoiding Astoria since having received the worst news of my life. I knew it wouldn't be long before she found out, though.

Astoria cornered me after our trial advocacy class one day before I could leave the classroom. I knew what she was going to say and I'd been trying to avoid this conversation.

"I knew he would lead to something like this. Should I kill him? Or are you going to?" Astoria said.

Astoria had been trying ever since the day Lindie threw me out of the journal office to talk to me about what was happening. I hadn't seen Suse since "the incident." And I was sure didn't want to. Suse was spending a lot of time locked away, working on her own note and going through the latest Charles drama. Which made me feel even crappier. I couldn't even be a good friend to Suse because of the nonsense that was going on in my life.

"He doesn't have anything to do with this," I said defensively, even though I was thinking the same horrible thought as Astoria.

"Like hell he doesn't. You know those bitches did this. And you know why they did it, too."

Of course I did, but I repeated to Astoria the line I constantly got from John, even though that line infuriated me. "He can't control them."

"Aw, hell. You sound just like him. He done up and brainwashed your ass now."

"I knew you would do this," I said.

"What? Talk sense?" Astoria snorted, her voice acrid with sarcasm.

"I should have known. You've been against us from the start."

"Everything's been against you two from the start. You know why? 'Cause you shouldn't be together."

I jumped at the sound of John's voice. "Here we go again. Always with this shit." I hadn't even heard him come in.

"What? I'm the only one using common sense out of anyone in this room," Astoria said.

"Sense. That's what you call this ignorant, vicious noise you're always putting in Denise's ear?"

My eyes kept darting between them as if I was watching some kind of awful, nightmarish tennis game. The words volleyed between them were becoming more brutal with every swing.

"Well, I'm tired of you leading her on. All you're going to do is crush her in the end. Leave her broke up and not even care that you did it. Why you playin' with her emotions like this? That's what I don't understand."

"Maybe that's because you never considered the fact that I'm actually in love with her. That's a possibility you would never allow your scheming mind to consider."

"Maybe I'm the only one watching out for Denise because, out of the two of us, I'm the only one who does care for her. What the hell kind of relationship do you two have where she's crying herself to sleep every night?"

"Astoria!" I gasped. It wasn't her place to say that. That wasn't something I wanted to come out to John. Not like that. With so much hurt and tension in the air.

"Maybe you should mind your own business, Astoria. Maybe that's what's wrong with our relationship. You ever think of that?" John shouted at Astoria.

"You are what's wrong with my friend. Every since you came into her life, it's gotten worse day by day."

His eyes were two green flames in his bright red face. He repeatedly clenched and unclenched his fists and did the same with his jaw.

"That's because you are always in our business. Filling her head with bullshit I'm not even doing." John said. "Just because you're bitter—"

"Don't you judge me!" Astoria cut him off, screaming. He had obviously hit a nerve. Well, to be fair, both of them were hitting nerves all over the place. "You don't know nothin' about nothin'. And you damn sure don't know enough to be passing judgment on anybody. We ain't all born with a trust fund and a silver spoon. So why don't you—"

"Stop! Just stop. Both of you," I screamed.

They both turned to me, glowering, like I was doing something wrong.

"You're talking about me like I'm not even here. And you're tearing each other down when you're two of the people I care most about. I don't wanna hear it anymore. No one's to blame for this but me," I said.

John sat down on top of the long, rectangular table at the front of the classroom and leaned forward, resting his elbows on his thighs. "I'm sorry, Denise."

"I'm not. I meant what I said and hopefully you'll see I'm right before you finish destroying your life." I watched Astoria leave, the heels of her ankle books clicking against the tile floor. I had no desire to stop her.

I went over to John and sat next to him, leaning my head against his. He put his arm around me and I let him hold me, but I left my arms by my sides. He gently stroked my arm for a few moments, saying nothing. He was willing to give me the silence we both needed.

I was the hard-headed one who broke it. "How's this ever going to work?"

I felt him shrug.

"C'mon, John. Don't you want it to work? Say something. I'm tired of all this quiet shit. All this shrugging. You tell me what you want. What you think," I said, looking up at him. I wished I hadn't. His eyes were full of unshed tears.

"I'm just sad. That's all I know to say," he said hoarsely, looking away and swiping at his eyes.

"What? I make you sad?" I asked, testing him.

He shook his head.

"John—"

"No. I just don't know how we're gonna make it. Everyone's against us. Including you." His voice sounded so tired that it broke my heart just a little bit more with every word he spoke.

"How could you say that?" I asked, tears welling up in my eyes. I started to pull away, but tightened his arm around me.

"You know it's true. I can't do anything about them. You always try to make it my fault. And then Astoria always gets in it. And she always makes it worse. And people—people hate me, Denise. I think my own parents hate me. Sometimes, I think you hate me. How are we gonna do this?" John said. Something about him saying I hated him killed me a little inside. I knew the end was coming, even though I ignored it like hell. I was losing him.

"John. I don't hate you. No one hates you," I said. I wrapped my arms around him and buried my face in his shoulder. I couldn't look into his eyes. I couldn't take the chance of seeing his love for me drain out of them. It would have killed me.

"Ral's the only person who will talk to me. Nobody else wants to come near me. My roommates make sure I hear every nasty thing anybody has to say about you and me. Sasha's uncle is threatening to pull his company's business away from my dad and—and I just feel like I've ruined so many lives—"

"Because of me?"

"Including yours. Maybe—maybe everyone's right. Maybe it's just too hard for people like us to be together."

"Black and white?" I pulled back from him. I still wouldn't look him in the eyes, though.

"Not just race. Everything, Denise. Don't you sometimes feel like the bad outweighs the good since we got together?" he asked.

My breath caught in my throat. I didn't even want to think about the answer to that question. He had just given my darkest thought voice.

"John, how could you say something like that? I can't have this conversation right now. With everything going on right now? With Astoria? With the honor council and everything? With Lindie? With Cindy and the others trying to ruin my life?"

"All that would go away if I did," John said quietly. "I don't know how else to make it stop. I don't want you to be miserable."

"You don't want you to be miserable."

"You're right. We shouldn't be having this conversation right now," John said quietly. So quietly I almost didn't hear him. With that, he kissed me hard on the lips. I pushed my needy lips back against his. Our tears mingled, hot on our faces. Instead the sighs of pleasures usually between our kisses, there were escaped sobs of fear and sadness. We held onto each other tightly, as if somehow that could save us from the hell we were in.

Then suddenly, he separated his lips from mine and turned his head away.

"Huh?" I was perplexed.

"I gotta get outta here for a bit. I'll call you later."

"Where you going?"

"I just need to think. I think I'm going for a drive. A long one. I just—I'm sorry."

"For?"

"For just—a lot of reasons."

I started to follow him.

He turned to face me, shaking his head. "Just don't, okay?"

"John," I called out after him. He stopped again, but didn't turn around.

"Hm?"

"Are we still, you know, together?"

"What kinda question is that?" He left the room, never turning to look at me.

"A good one, apparently," I muttered, watching his retreating back.

I hugged myself and tried my hardest to remember the last time we'd laughed really hard together. Or had a conversation in which we exchanged no harsh words. He couldn't be right. The bad couldn't outweigh the good. It just couldn't.

CHAPTER 17

SOMETIMES LOVE JUST AIN'T ENOUGH

"Oh, you're just angry that you can't be the popular, lovable frat boy anymore huh? I guess I've just sucked the life out of you, right? Sorry for being real. I am so sorry I brought you into the real world, John," I snarled, angrily pushing away from the table. I had invited John over for dinner to try to repair things, but it wasn't going well at all. John and I had just sat down with our salad. It was one of those pre-mixed salads in the bag. Our frozen lasagna had just finished heating up in the oven and was cooling on the stovetop.

John and I were having the same fight. I felt like we had this fight every time we so much as spoke to each other. I couldn't stand it. The only thing I could bear even less was the thought of losing him altogether. Even though we were fighting, at least he was there with me.

"Denise. We shouldn't have to try this hard. That's all I said. And that's all I meant," John said. His voice sounded so tired, it hurt my heart to hear it.

My eyes burned with tears. Tears of fatigue, frustration, anger. We were two tired, angry, jaded people.

"This was supposed to help. All it's done is bring us even closer to the edge," I said with a humorless laugh, picking at the hem of my new navy blue skirt. How naïve of me to expect dinner to fix everything.

"You accuse me of shutting you out. But you shut me out, too. You don't even want me at your hearing." He sat back in his chair and folded his arms across his gray polo.

"It's a closed hearing," I muttered emptily.

"Denise, you know you're allowed to have some friends or family present," he said in his quiet, testy tone. A tone I had grown to detest over the past few weeks.

I shrugged moodily.

"And you're always getting on me for shrugging and not talking."

"I don't want anyone there. I'm embarrassed. I'm ashamed," I said through clenched teeth.

"And you blame me for it. That's the real reason you don't want me there," he said.

"You don't even like touching me anymore," I said, standing up and walking into the living room. I was desperate to change the subject, and it was true. He'd barely touched me since the shower we'd taken together weeks before. I heard him get up and follow me.

"What are you talking about? I kissed you hello."

"Our kisses are empty and sad now. They hurt me."

"Then why are you complaining? Sounds like you don't want me to touch you."

"You know what I mean. I want you to—I want it to be like before. I want everything to be like—before," I said, clenching my fist.

"I want that, too."

"How can we fix it?"

He looked down at his hands. "Dunno."

"C'mon. You haven't even tried to make love to me since—since before. Maybe if we just—"

"Denise," John said softly, arresting my hand in its path down his chest with a single touch.

"No?" I said.

"No," he said firmly. But I still heard the almost imperceptible crack in his voice.

"It's worth a try." I didn't even attempt to wipe away my tears.

"If a kiss hurts, what do you think that would do to us?" he said as he gently wiped my tears away.

"You doin' it with someone else?" I avoided his horrible, painful question with a hateful one of my own.

"How could you even—if I didn't cheat on Sasha, how could I—Denise, you are just unbelievable." He pulled away from me.

"Then why don't you want me?" I couldn't stop. Why was I trying to make him angry?

"I do. Badly. But this isn't a good time for us to do that," he said, taking a step back from me.

"Huh? Not a good time? I inconvenience you, right, Archer? I'm just one big inconvenience to your life, aren't I?" I screamed. I wanted him to show some emotion.

"You know what? I've had enough." I got an emotion, all right. He sounded thoroughly disgusted with me. "You keep pushing me, Denise, and you're gonna get what you want. You're gonna push me too far."

"Oh, really?"

"Yeah. I gotta get outta here. This is just too much." He grabbed his jacket off of the sofa with an angry jerk. And the next thing I knew, he was out the door, slamming it behind him.

And I was about to find out, not that night but soon, that he really had.

That night, John and I had a really beautiful and very silent night together. I'll always remember that night as the night I knew that no matter what happened, nobody could destroy our love. They could break us apart, but they couldn't break that bond. I didn't always let John know I knew that, though. And therein lay a huge problem for us.

After I had thrown everything into the trash—dinner, centerpiece, and anything else I could get my furious hands on—I changed into a pair of old sweats and debated over whether I should throw away everything of Tia's not in her room while I was in a mood to throw things away. Including people, apparently.

I contemplated this over a half gallon of vanilla ice cream and half a pie I found in the refrigerator. The pie tasted a little rancid, but I didn't care. I hoped I did get food poisoning. Maybe that would dull some of the more unbearable pain I felt in my heart. I don't know how long I sat on the sofa like that, doing the thing I was becoming most expert at—feeling sorry for myself.

I don't know what time it was when I heard that knock at the door. I pushed the empty ice cream and pie containers aside, wondering who would dare intrude on my angry silence. I stared at the door, willing the persistent knocking to stop. Even if Tia was home—and I had no idea whether she was or not—I knew she would never answer that door. Even if she knew who it was. And this person was not gonna go away.

I walked to the door grumbling, ready to cuss Astoria out if she was on the other side and half hoping she was because I wanted to cuss someone out. But, no such luck. I opened the door and stood there for a moment, too shocked to move. When I finally opened my mouth to speak, John's fingers closed over it.

"Sh. Don't say anything. I just want to be with you tonight. I just want you. I only want us to be together. And we can't seem to do that if we open our mouths," he said.

I could only nod. He walked in and closed the door behind him. I silently led the way to my room. After closing the door to my room, he pulled me to him and hugged me tightly. I breathed in deeply, needing to smell the clean scent of his cologne. I wanted to breathe him in; be surrounded by him. He gently pushed me back far enough so that he could remove his jacket and polo. He kicked off his shoes and pushed off his jeans. I grabbed him again immediately and pressed our bodies together. He sighed shakily into my hair before pulling back far enough to kiss my cheek.

I took his hand in mine and we walked over to my bed. We sat on the edge for a moment, watching each other with wistful, love-torn eyes. We tried to say the things with our hands that we couldn't say out loud. Hands on faces, necks, shoulders—hands over hearts. Fingertips between lips.

We slid under the comforter and I pressed my back against his chest. His hand was still in mine. I brought it to my lips and let it rest there. He rested his chin on top of my head. I smiled faintly as I closed my eyes. My first smile in way too long.

John loved me. He wanted me and needed me near him as much as I did him. There was no sound more beautiful than John's even breathing. No better sensation than his chest moving in time with that breathing against my back. Except for maybe that of his warm breath against the back of my neck. I always wanted that. I wished his hand could stay at my lips. I wished he could hold me close in that bed forever. I knew that was the only place we were safe anymore. Oddly enough, I got the best sleep I'd gotten since we had returned to class following winter break.

When I opened my eyes the next morning to the harsh blaring of my alarm clock and the unforgiving glare of the morning sun, he was gone. I wept bitterly after I hit the snooze button. I wept harder than I had in my entire life. I surprised myself with the new heights of despair I seemed to reach daily.

The Tau Gamma Chis, my arch nemeses, continued their reign of terror, adding even more joy to my daily life. The day before my hearing, later in the morning that I had wept alone in my bed—so utterly alone—they cornered me in the restroom. That was the day it was over for me and John. Two days before Valentine's Day. Robbed of a Valentine's present again. Although that was the last thing on my mind at the moment.

I came out of the stall and there they were. Fresh from hell. Cindy, Lacey, and Jess. And they looked liked a Cindy, a Lacey and a Jess, too. They all had blonde hair of various highlighted shades. They wore matching smirks, pearls, and cashmere.

"What do you want now?" I said to the collective body. They were really all one person to me anyway.

"You still haven't gotten the message, have you?" said Cindy.

"Hm?" I said, playing dumb. I was bringing it down to their level.

"You stupid bitch. You still want to pretend like you have a chance with John and mess everything up for Sasha," another one said. That one was probably Lacey.

"I haven't done anything to Sasha. She did it all to herself," I said, beginning to put that all-too-familiar defensive front up.

"Yeah. Whatever you want to tell yourself, but we're here to let you know it's time to stop playing around," Probably Lacey said. "You can't go messing with Sasha's future. They're supposed to be together. That's just the way things work. I don't know what you think you're doing. But it has to stop."

"Yeah. This ends right here, right now," Cindy said.

"What are you going to do? Try to fight me?" I said incredulously. I turned to leave the restroom.

One of them put a hand on my shoulder.

"You've already taken all you can take. I'm about to be kicked out. Don't deny it was you who did this. And get your hands off of me."

"Oh, no. Little miss gangster wants to fight us. What is that your kind calls this? Scrapping?" Cindy said with a smirk. They all burst out laughing; the same laugh.

I was boiling inside. "You can shut your ignorant ass up right now."

"And if I don't want to?" She raised a perfectly arched eyebrow.

"I think you'll want to," I said. I wasn't about to back down from that petty thing.

"You wouldn't touch me," she said scornfully, looking at me as if I were dirty and not even worthy of the "honor" of doing so.

"Oh, I'll do more than touch you," I said.

"You better watch her. She probably has a knife," one of the other two spoke up. "You know. They all carry some kind of weapon. For when the drug deal goes bad."

"You and your groupies need to get out of my face. Right now and from now on."

"I'll press charges," Maybe Cindy said. She looked scared.

I smirked. "Whatever." I set my laptop bag down on the floor under the sink. "You feeling froggy, then c'mon. Otherwise, stay out of my face."

"You just leave Sasha alone."

"I'm not bothering her."

"You know what I mean."

"John's a grown man. He does what he wants. And obviously what he wants is to be with me."

"No, it's not. I don't know what kind of spell you put on him, but—"

"What? Now you think I know voodoo? I understand how you can be in the bottom of the class. But what I don't know is how you even got *in* to law school."

"You shut your mouth."

I laughed. "I guess the same way *your* kind gets anything. What Daddy can't get for you, you spread your legs for. So did Daddy pay your way in here? Or did you?"

"Trailer trash!"

"Hm. Trash describes you better than it does me," I said. "Guess money can't buy class."

"I'm gonna destroy you. I'm gonna show you your place since you can't find it on your own." She glowered at me and clenched her fists at her side. Her pearl necklace stood out against her red neck.

"You don't scare me. How many times do I have to tell you that? Hm. You're slower than I thought."

"And no one's denying anything. You can make this all go away, you know. You're doing this to yourself. You really want to lose everything?"

"You really think you're going to get away with this, huh?" I said with a scoff. Inside, I was beginning to care less and less whether she did or not.

"C'mon. She's not worth it. Don't worry. She'll be finished after tomorrow. Pathetic loser. Has no idea what's good for her," one of them said, tossing back her blonde hair and glaring at me.

I sneered right back.

"Yeah. You know this isn't going to last much longer anyway. John has to get bored with her soon," the other one said, looking down her nose at me.

I just kept staring straight at them. The two of them pulled Cindy out of the bathroom. I knew she wanted to see the end of me, and I had no idea how I was going to stop her. All I had was the truth—with no evidence to back it up. And I didn't know if the fight was worth it anymore.

My phone buzzed. I took it out of my pocket and flipped it open. A new text message from John. I snapped my phone shut and rubbed my forehead with shaking fingers. I couldn't see how we could possibly make it. Everyone wanted us to fail. But he was wrong about me. At least I really hoped he was. I loved him so much. I couldn't imagine being without him. Then again, I hadn't really gotten to be with him all that much since all we did was fight. Maybe, sadly enough, he was right about me.

Of course, John and I had a fight about my encounter with the Tau Gamma Chi triplets. It seemed as if all John and I did anymore was fight. Sasha and her army were definitely winning in that respect. John and I came out of Starbucks together. We met there after class to talk. I told him about what happened that afternoon. He remained almost silent the whole time. Despite the previous night, or maybe because of it, I thought John wasn't trying hard enough. I was furious at him. Mostly because

I was afraid to be furious at anyone else—including myself. Even the thought made me feel frighteningly helpless and hopeless.

"What is it with you, John? Do you even care what happened?" I finally exploded after we reached his car.

"What do you want me to do, Denise? What do you want me to say? It's not like I can control them," John said with an exasperated sigh.

I rolled my eyes and put my hand on my hip. I stared at him, my mouth dropping open.

"What?"

"I am so tired of that line. You can't keep hiding behind that. You're not even going to take up for me? Sympathize with me?"

"I tell Sasha to stop. Apparently, it makes her worse. I've stopped trying. I try to calm you down and you yell at me for belittling you and not caring about your feelings. So I'm not really sure what I'm supposed to do here," John said. The tone of his voice was frustrated. Defeated. Tired. I refused to hear that at the time. I refused to hear anything coming out of his mouth.

"Well, you're just not doing enough."

"Fine. Blame me. Whatever. But I'm tired of hearing this. Can we just go home, go to bed, and start over tomorrow?"

"You don't even care. I could be out of school by tomorrow."

"I do. I'm sorry they hurt you. And I'm sorry it's because of me. But you can't just keep throwing this in my face, Denise," John said. Even in the scant light, the nearest streetlight being several yards away, I saw his jaw clench.

"What am I supposed to do? Your parents hate me. Your friends hate me—"

"I can't control my parents. How they feel has nothing to *do* with me. We've talked about the friend thing and why that's weak for you to say. And while we're talking about friends, how about that Astoria?"

"What about her? She was certainly right about you. You only care about what you can get out of me. If you cared about me, you wouldn't let those harpies do this."

"*Get* out of you? We hardly ever had sex! We don't anymore at all now. Look at yourself for a minute. You are being so selfish. I can't believe you are trying to put this all on me. I mean, I think I've been doing a pretty good job of taking your crap because I did feel like this was all my fault, but that stops now, Denise. You haven't once asked how I feel. How this might be hard on me. I haven't spoken to my parents in five weeks."

"Aha! I knew you cared more about them."

"They're my parents, Denise. Of course I miss them. That doesn't mean I agree with them. But you don't even care about anything going on in my life. About how I might feel. It's always gotta be about you."

"Well, you don't have—"

"What I don't have is the patience for this nonsense anymore!" John banged his hand down on the hood of his car. He hit it so forcefully, I was surprised he didn't leave a dent. For a moment, I was chilled, thinking that was how hard he wanted to hit me. But I quickly recovered.

"I'm doing the best I can here." I said.

"Well, obviously your best isn't good enough," John said. His tone had become dangerously low, his expression impassive. That stung. He was becoming closed off to me. I could almost feel it.

I knew then what was happening. Suddenly, my whole body went cold. And it had very little to do with the February night air. "So this is it? This is how we end?" I whispered. I could barely breathe.

John wouldn't look at me. He was staring down the street at nothing. "Yeah," he said quietly. "This isn't what I wanted, Denise. I know you think it is, but it's not."

I had nothing else to say. I couldn't even move. I watched. All I could do was watch. I wanted to respond to that asinine comment. Of course it was what he wanted. He was the one breaking up with me. I wanted to scream. I wanted to fight. I wanted to cry. But nothing would happen. I was useless. Vapid. I could do nothing. But watch.

John slowly shook his head. He looked at me one last time. Anger. Disgust. Was that pain? Did he have the nerve to have pain in his eyes? And then he turned his back to me. He walked slowly around his car. And I stood there, just watching. I didn't know what else to do. And even if I had, I'm not so sure I would have been capable of doing it.

Pain. It started in my chest. Ice slowly spreading to my stomach, and down, down until I was completely frozen. I heard the engine start. Saw John reversing out of his spot. All I could do was watch him drive away. I couldn't even wipe away the tears. I could only stare at the spot where John's car had been moments before.

I gasped. A sharp intake of breath. I suddenly became aware of the fact that I was still breathing. And then the ice shattered. I wrenched my bottom lip free of my teeth. I could taste the blood in my mouth as I filled my lungs with cold, unforgiving February night air. And I screamed with everything I had left inside of me. Anybody who heard me probably thought someone was being murdered. In a way, someone was. At first, I was surprised that no one called the cops. Then, I thought, the bitter truth was that was proof of just how truly inconsequential I was.

I knocked on Astoria's door. She opened it and just stood there with her arms crossed over her chest.

"You were right," I said, clutching a crumpled tissue in my hand.

"I'm sorry I was," she said, shaking her head. She opened her arms and I ran into them. All I could do was sob. Somehow, Astoria understood, and somehow, all the way to her place, I'd known she would. There was no "I told you so." Not even any berating John. Nothing. And that was exactly what I needed.

Astoria led me over to the couch. She sat me down and patted my back. I heard her walk away, and she came back with a glass of wine. I accepted it gratefully and gulped half of it down before she could even sit back down on the couch. I was also grateful to see she had thought to bring the rest of the bottle over with her.

I couldn't believe it was still the same day. The same day as the fight with those nasty Tau Gammas. It shouldn't have been the same day. I shouldn't have still been alive.

"Ugly little bastard. Inside and out. She can have him," I snapped. " 'Cause you know that's what's gonna happen. They're probably on the phone right now. Hell, she might be on the way to Virginia by now."

"Now, you know that boy is too pretty. That's the problem. He got you all caught up with those looks."

"Shut up, Stori. Let me have my moment."

"I don't get you sometimes, Denise. Are you crazy?" Astoria sounded both perplexed and a little pissed off.

"Huh?" I looked up at her, equally confused. She was supposed to be commiserating and comforting—not mean and confrontational.

"Why would you even want to be with someone like that? Why would you want to waste the talented, cultured, beautiful person you are on him?"

"Because I love him. I love him and it's Valentine's Day Friday and he's going to spend it with that skank. I just know it." I burst into fresh tears. Astoria sighed, taking the empty wine glass from me and refilling it. "I know I made one person happy tonight at least. That wench, Sasha."

"Don't worry about that right now. We have plenty of wine and all night. We're gonna forget about all about both of them. Okay?"

"Whatever," I spat, taking the wine glass from her. "You're right. They belong together. What the hell was I doing?"

"Being human. You loved him. In spite of everything, I could see that. And as much as it kills me to admit it, I think he did care about you."

"Oh, *please*! Why are you saying these things? You hate him."

"No, I don't," she said quietly, sinking into the couch next to me. "I think I hated that I was wrong more than anything."

"But you weren't. Look at me. He made a fool of me."

"Yes, I was, and no, he didn't."

"What? So I was wrong? You saying I was wrong?"

"No. Nobody was wrong. It was just a difficult situation. One neither of you should have been put in. And despite what you may think, I'm really sorry that both of you were," she said.

I just stared at her. It would be quite a while before I realized how true Astoria's words really were. I couldn't believe what I was hearing from her, though. Not ever before, and not until much later after, would she ever say anything so close to defending John. And so very close to the truth. That night, for once since the whole mess with John started, Astoria was the one making sense. Of course, I wanted none of it at the time.

"Whatever. Just give me more wine," I grumbled, holding out my glass.

And like magic, it was over. Not only my relationship with John, but the whole honor council debacle. The day after John ripped the heart from my chest, the day I was supposed to have the hearing, I was called in to talk to the honor council chief justice and the dean. I was told that it was all just a "terrible misunderstanding." Some miscreant, who—surprise, surprise—could not be found, had tampered with my thumb drive. The chief justice received an anonymous tip. Yeah, anonymous, alright. The only person who seemed disappointed by this news was Lindie.

So the sneaky bitches had kept their word. Big deal. I still felt dead inside. And they hadn't left me completely unscathed. My real note still hadn't shown up. All I had to work with was a very old, very rough draft saved on the school's network from the past semester that, like a fool, I never updated. My updated file on my hard drive had been corrupted. I had put too much stock in my thumb drive. Much as I had my ex-boyfriend—such empty, cruel, and cold words. So I practically had to start from scratch.

But I tried to find a bright side. I hoped burying myself in late nights of note writing would help dull the pain at least a little.

CHAPTER 18
BARRISTER'S BALL

I don't think I was ever as mad at John as when I found out he was taking Sasha to Barrister's. Up until that moment, I had been living in my own little world of denial. I pretended John wasn't seeing anyone. That John didn't matter to me. Deep down, I knew that neither of these things was true. But that denial let me keep myself from falling completely apart, from becoming nothing more than shards of a broken heart.

Astoria stood in front of me, waiting for my reaction after she dropped the bomb.

"What?" I dropped the garbage bag I'd been holding.

"Why are you surprised? He's gone to Boston almost every weekend since—well, for a while," Astoria said.

"I know he goes out of town. How am I supposed to know where he goes?" I picked the bag up and swiped a bunch of take-out containers off the kitchen table and into it. I was at the breaking point. I was actually cleaning up Tia's mess. Things were bad.

"You know he's with her, Denise. It's time to face that."

"Hmph," was my only reply as I furiously scrubbed at the countertop near the kitchen sink.

"So can I tell Erich we're on for Barrister's? You, me, Blue, Erich, Suse and Charles?" Astoria asked. Blue was yet another guy Astoria had picked up while clubbing. I scrubbed harder.

"Whatever. I already have my ticket," I said, trying not to remember how Suse had given me the ticket John had given her to give to me. We were on that level. He couldn't even hand me a ticket. And the fact that he was still trying to be decent burned me up, too. He might as well have kept the ticket for Sasha. "I might as well go."

"Great. Because I kinda already asked Erich to come with us."

I didn't say anything. I just stormed out of the house to take out the third bag of Tia's trash I had collected. I happened to look up as a red Mercedes sped by. Even though it was obviously not John's, that was it. I slumped down by the dumpsters and buried my face in my hands, drawing my knees up to my chest. My entire body was shaking.

He had gone right back to her. I would have been better off if he had never said the first word to me. All I had left was emptiness. Emptiness because he decided it would be fun to play with me for a few months. It hadn't been worth it; those few moments of happiness. Hours seemed like days. The few weeks since we had broken up seemed much longer than the months since that first evening at Barnes & Noble.

He should have just left me alone. He knew we could never work. Why hadn't he just left me alone?

But was it fair to say that? Had I been selfish by—

No. I wasn't going to allow myself to think that way. It would destroy me.

"Denise, don't do this to yourself."

I jumped, startled by the sound of Astoria's voice.

"That's enough out of you," I said.

"I just want you to listen—"

"No. I don't want to hear it. Stop pretending like you care how I feel. You're glad this happened. Because I'm that friend everybody wants around. The one you can always look to for reassurance that you're not a loser. The hopelessly, perpetually single friend. The one you can 'aw' over and feel bad for. But secretly be glad your life isn't that pathetic. And you know what? I am sick and tired of being that friend. So you're just going to have to get over yourself, as hard as that may be, and let me be."

"That's not it at all, Denise. You're not listening."

"I've listened to you too much. And I'm right where you wanted me because of that. Be happy. Gloat. Whatever. But leave me alone."

"You need to—"

"I don't have to do anything. I know you always think you know what's best for me. But spare me today. I just need to be alone right now. What I don't need is for you to perpetually try to run my life. And for you to try to set me up with people you know I won't work with so you can always be in charge. Go run somebody else's life or whatever. But excuse me while I wallow in despair and disappointment," I said, pushing past her and leaving her staring stupidly after me.

I lay on the floor in Suse's room, wrapped around a box of her mom's oatmeal cookies. I was safe with her. Suse listened to me. She let me be sad. And most important of all, she let me believe I was right—even when I was dead wrong.

"So, she just sat there, rubbing it in. All smug. I know she hates John, but was that necessary?" I stuffed another cookie into my mouth.

"I'm sorry, Denise," she said. She was beginning to sound like a broken record.

"I don't understand," I wailed. My stomach was all knots. I pushed the cookies away. I'd made the mistake of driving the long way to Suse's so that I had just happened to go by John's house. And of course that thing's Range Rover had been parked out front. I didn't know why I loved to torture myself. It almost seemed I thought that if I hurt myself badly enough, it would make me stop loving him.

"I know it sucks. I know it hurts. But you have to know everything happens for a reason."

"How he gonna say he loved me? What kind of mess is that when he just went back to her? He made a fool of me and I let him," I said, ignoring Suse's words.

"Maybe he did."

"Huh?" Suse was finally saying something I was interested in. I turned my head to face her.

"Well, maybe it really was too hard for him."

"Hmph."

"Have you tried to talk to him since the breakup?"

"What would be the point? He made his choice," I said. I wasn't entirely sure that was true, though. In fact,

I knew it was false. I wanted to hear his voice even if he was an ass. I wanted to know he still knew I was alive. And for him to care about me. I at least wanted to know he missed me. That he was in at least half the pain I was in. I knew it was stupid, but it was also all I wanted. I refused to call him, though. I had at least that much going for me. For all he knew, I could be over him and doing just fine.

"Well, all you're doing is making yourself sick over this. I hate to see you so sad," Suse said. "Maybe this is for the best, you know? The two of you tried. But it's hard to make a relationship work even when both people are—"

"Are what, Suse?" I glared at her.

"You can get angry with me if you want to, Denise. But you know it's true. Different races? Different classes? Completely different backgrounds? It's a lot," Suse said.

I said nothing. I just turned away from her.

"Well, I'm going to Barrister's with regular, plain, black Erich. You and Astoria should be the happiest people on earth."

"I just want you to be happy, Denise. And if I thought John could provide you with that, I'd be all for the two of you. But it seems you've never been unhappier. Starting almost as soon as you two started dating. How am I supposed to want my best friend to be in a relationship that's destroying her?"

"Make up your mind. Stop saying two different things. Anyway, I wasn't always unhappy. Most of the time, I was happier than I've ever been. And it's destroying me more not to be with him."

"Are you sure about that? Ask yourself honestly. Don't answer for me or Astoria or anyone else. Just answer yourself that," Suse said.

I said nothing back. I just kept staring straight ahead. That was the very question I'd been trying to avoid asking myself since before John and I had broken up. Maybe it really was too hard. I knew one thing for sure. It was too hard to love him. But it was even harder to stop.

Astoria, Suse, and I all got ready for Barrister's together. Astoria was getting on my last nerve. She was convinced Erich and I were getting together because I'd agreed to go to Barrister's with him. She was planning out all this stuff we were all supposed to do together. And talking about how Erich's parents had a timeshare up north that he'd talked about wanting to take me to and a lot of other stuff I had no desire to hear.

My mind was on Sasha and John. I knew Sasha was in Richmond at that moment. Were they at dinner? Were they screwing? How much had they screwed since she'd gotten into town? I bet they laughed about me and John. That it was some giant joke between them. I knew her smug ass was eating it up that John and I hadn't lasted. I knew she was full of I-told-you-so's and I-always-knew's. And I couldn't stand it.

"C'mon, Denise. It's already six-thirty. Dinner's at eight," Astoria said.

I shrugged. I was still in jeans and a sweatshirt, staring forlornly at my dress. I'd had to exchange the dress I'd really wanted for that one because the first dress matched John's tux and I refused to wear a dress that matched his tux. I'd gotten a simple full-length black halter dress instead. It was fitting. I was in mourning. I didn't even really want to go anymore. But I knew Astoria would kill me if I didn't. And it also wouldn't have been fair to poor, innocent, caught-in-the-crossfire Erich.

"Yeah, Denise. Your hair isn't even finished. You have no makeup on. You haven't done a thing," Suse said with a sigh.

"Well, I thought Astoria was going to dress me. She does everything else for me. I'm so helpless. Apparently, I can't do anything for myself," I muttered angrily.

"I'm gonna let that go because I know this is hard for you," Astoria said lightly. Sure, she was happy. She finally had me on a date with Erich. I couldn't even look at her.

"I brought that necklace you wanted to borrow," Suse said, holding out a silver necklace with a black opal pendant along with matching earrings.

I didn't move to take them from her.

She put the necklace set on the desk in front of me and placed her hand on my back. "Are you sure you still want to go tonight?"

"Of course she does. What are you talking about?" Astoria quickly jumped in. No doubt to save her master plan.

I looked up sourly at them both. "I'm not going to back out now. Plus, the only thing worse than staring at them together all night is thinking about them together all night. I spend too many nights doing that already." I turned away from them and put my head in my hands.

"Don't let him have so much power over you," Astoria said.

I said nothing. All I could see, hear, feel, taste or smell was John. John kissing me. John laughing. John joking with my dad and uncle. Pulling me into his arms. Raising his eyebrows in that very John way when I said something that didn't make sense to him. Asleep next to me on the sofa during some movie I made him watch that he had no interest in. John taking up for me at his parents'. The John I had finally gotten. The John who apparently no longer existed, although I was not quite ready to believe that. I couldn't get him out of my head. And all *they* could do was to just keep insisting I do the impossible. Easy for them to say.

"Denise—"

"No, Suse, that's enough."

"Denise. Honey. I know what it's like to be completely in love with someone and have your heart broken. I thought Keith and I would last forever. I had started picking out my engagement ring and cutting out pictures of wedding dresses I liked and even bookmarking wedding web sites. But I had to cut him loose. He had too many problems that I couldn't help him fix. And now he's married to that woman. And it's nobody's fault." Astoria's voice was quieter than I'd ever heard it. "Sometimes . . . it's just nobody's fault no matter how badly you want to have someone to blame."

I looked up, stunned. I knew how hard it was for her to talk about Keith. She really did want to help. I walked over and put my arms around her. She hugged me back fiercely.

"Okay, I guess it's time to grab that shower," I said with a tried, tired smile. I pulled back from Astoria and grabbed my robe from the back of the desk chair. I was dying inside, but I had to try. I had to attempt to come out of this thing. If not for myself, for Astoria and Suse. They were trying so hard to bring me back to life. I could at least pretend they had succeeded for their sakes.

Barrister's was held at a hotel downtown. We arrived about an hour after the dance started. That was at least one less hour I had to pretend with Erich and secretly torture myself with stolen glances at John. I walked into the room, pretending that I didn't even see John looking as good as he wanted to look. But of course I had searched him out as soon as we came into the room. And of course that skank was hanging off of him.

Erich was a good guy. And he looked good in his tux. But I had no desire to be there with him, and I only paid attention to him when I knew John was looking at me. For instance, as soon as I saw John noticing me after I walked into the room, I turned to Erich immediately. From the corner of my eye, I saw John tap Ral on the shoulder and start talking to him.

I could tell as the night wore on that John was pretty drunk. And I had seen him and some of the other guys surreptitiously pull out flasks more than once that night. Ral seemed to be getting pretty fed up with it all. He and his date moved to the outer edge of the group. Sasha spent most of the night huddled around with those horrible cookie-cutter Tau Gamma Chi girls. They seemed really excited about something. I had no doubt it had something to do with John. Sasha was certainly the center of their attention.

As the night wore on, I wanted to be there less and less. Especially once when John looked dead at me. My heart pounded as his eyes burned into mine. For a moment I was crazy enough to think he was coming over. Then he chose a seat at his table that put his back completely to me.

"Want to dance?" I said to Erich shortly after John decided all I would see was his back for the rest of the night.

Erich looked shocked, and I couldn't blame him. I'd made every excuse possible to avoid dancing with him until he'd just stopped asking. Eventually, he nodded.

I led Erich out on the dance floor. Out of the corner of my eye, I saw John and Sasha already out there. I pulled Erich to me by his hips and started grinding my body against his.

"What's going on with you?" Erich asked, seeming bewildered yet pleased.

"Do you really care?" I grinned, wrapping my arms around him.

"I just hope whatever it is doesn't get out anytime soon."

I smiled. But inside, I was seething with rage. I wanted to tear John apart. And his little Sasha, too.

Erich and I danced too closely and slowly for the beat. We danced for most of the rest of the night. I was surprised Astoria could keep herself from leaping around the room with joy. And I was surprised the rage burning me up inside didn't show on the outside; that I could focus it all on my efforts to make myself want to be with Erich. That I could turn it into way more dancing than I had endurance for, especially wearing stilettos.

I continued to watch John from across the room whether I was dancing or sitting, even though he went to great lengths to avoid looking my way. I stole a glance whenever I could in a way that wouldn't provoke a kick under the table or an elbow from Astoria. And whenever she caught me, Sasha would bore her eyes into me, no doubt willing me to drop dead on the spot. I hadn't been in the same room with John much since our breakup. We didn't have any classes together that semester and we made a point of avoiding each other.

Once or twice I caught his eye that night. When I did, he would glare at me and I glared right back. Then, he would then turn completely away from me and pull Sasha close to him. Not that she was ever that far from him at any point in the night. I was enjoying hating them, loathing them. It was all I really had left. Besides Astoria annoying the hell out of me and a date I didn't really want.

By the end of the night, Astoria was wrapped up in Blue, Suse in Charles, and I was trying to wrap myself up in Erich. But it was hard when my eyes kept traveling across the room to where John was. I didn't want anything to do with Erich; at least not in the way he and Astoria wanted me to. I was so angry and disappointed that I was quite surprised I could keep a smile plastered on my face all night.

My stomach was killing me. One good thing, if you could call it that, was that I'd lost about ten pounds since John and I had broken up. I was so disgusted with him—and myself—I couldn't even eat. My head hurt. My eyes hurt. All I really wanted to do was go home and cry.

I watched a few straggling couples drag themselves across the dance floor. The DJ looked like she wanted to go home worse than I did. Erich tapped me on the arm and I looked up at him.

"You want to go?" Erich put his hand on my back. "Get ready for the party?"

"Sure," I said. I knew he was probably tired of me staring across the room. I'd caught him catching me staring a few times. I turned to the rest of the table. "You guys ready to change and head over to the party?" I didn't really want to go to the party, but I felt obliged to keep up my act.

Everyone agreed that it was time to leave. Erich got up. I followed quickly behind. I had spotted John disappearing out of the door. I didn't give Astoria or Suse a chance to object.

I saw John outside. Erich was getting the car. I walked up to him and he turned to me, his face blank. I couldn't help it. I didn't want to walk up to him. I didn't want to talk to him. But I couldn't stop myself.

"Why?" I asked, choking back tears.

"We're engaged," John said bluntly, slurring his words a little. The bottom dropped out of my stomach. Okay. That, I really hadn't needed to know. I gasped audibly despite my efforts not to react. I clenched my purse tightly in my hands to keep from screaming.

"You're what?"

"It's not like we were ever going to make it, Denise. It was just never going to work out for us. Because you're determined it's not," John said.

"You're what?"

"I mean, what do you want me to do? What can I say? I tried. You were working against us the whole time."

"You're the one with the racist parents."

"That's my parents' problem. Not mine."

"Yeah, like you're going to go against them for me forever."

"See? There you go. We never had a chance because you never let us have a chance. You were defeatist from the beginning."

"So you're marrying her?"

"Well, if I'm not going to be with you, I might as well be with her."

"Excuses. Lies. You never loved me!"

"I love the hell out of you. Don't you even start with that tonight. You don't love me enough, or yourself enough, or whatever. But the point is, Denise, you wouldn't let us happen. You did this to us. And I will not carry that blame around for you," John said. And before I could say another word, he stormed off to an Escalade full of his jackass friends.

I was fuming at the after-party. John was engaged. So that was what the harpies had been so excited about at the dance. I was so angry, I didn't even want to drink. I was afraid of what I'd do if I drank. I sat in a corner by myself most of the time. Erich had given up on me almost immediately after we'd gotten to the party. He started talking to a group of girls once Astoria and Blue disappeared.

Not that there had been a real chance of me and John getting back together, but the news John had so callously given me had crushed any chance of a dream of a hope I might have ever had. He'd told me many times he'd never really loved Sasha. Not the way he'd loved me. And even that night, when he'd told me about the engagement, he hadn't mentioned loving her. It was beyond ridiculous that they were engaged. I couldn't stand the thought.

I had to stay angry. I had to stay outraged. If I didn't, I would dissolve into tears. And I was afraid that if I did that, I'd never be able to stop crying.

I pulled out my phone with a sigh once I felt it vibrate against me. I flipped it open. A new text message. From John?

Hey. I got a room downtown. Wanna come down here? It read.

Where's wifey? I texted back, sneering at my phone.

Not here. I left the party we were at early. I was bored. And I wanted to see you, he texted back.

My heart nearly stopped. *For what? You're getting married. Go find her.*

She's not you, Denise. Can I please see you tonight? I need to see you.

I sat there in silence, staring down at my phone, wondering what kind of games he was playing. And wondering if I wanted to get wrapped up in such games. I definitely knew it wasn't smart to get involved in such games. Well, objectively, I knew that. Another text. I opened the message. He'd texted me the hotel's address. I closed my eyes and sighed. Shaking my head, very disappointed with myself as I did it, I texted him back that I would be over soon.

I stood up and walked over to Erich slowly, wondering if there was even any point in telling him.

"What?" Erich looked up at me, eyes glazed. At least he was too drunk to care. Hopefully.

"I'm leaving. Tia just texted me. She's really sick and she asked me to come home. You gonna be okay getting home if I leave?" I couldn't believe how fluid the lie was. I was even more ashamed of myself than I'd been texting John. I had driven Erich and he'd left his car at his apartment since I hadn't planned to drink.

"Sure." He smiled.

I wondered why he wasn't pushing the issue, but I was glad that he wasn't. I assumed it had something to do with the girls surrounding him. I went to find Suse and feed her the same lie before heading out. I didn't know where Astoria was, but I knew she was too preoccupied with Blue to worry about where I was going and why Erich wasn't going with me. And I was afraid she would figure it out if I did talk to her. It was bad enough Suse was suspicious. But luckily, Suse didn't press me. I did my best not to give her time to, either.

John opened the door and grabbed my wrist. He pulled me in before I could say a word. It was dark, but I could feel his lecherous, alcohol-clouded eyes all over me.

"Wait a minute." I pulled away from him.

"Look. I didn't ask you to come over here to talk. Talking doesn't work for us," he said, already leading me from the front of the suite into the bedroom. I had a million questions. Whose suite was this? Did he get it for an after-party? If he had, why were we the only two there? Had he planned this? Had he planned to bring his future wife there originally?

"I don't want it to be like this."

"Look," John sighed angrily, letting go of me. He flipped on the light. My heart hurt. He was so gorgeous, standing there in just his boxers. My eyes raked over his abs. Those arms. I wanted those deep green eyes to look at me the way they had before everything had gone wrong. For just a moment, I thought I saw a flicker of—

"John—"

And it was gone. "No. You know I didn't invite you over here at four in the morning to watch television. You know what this is. And if you want to act like you don't, then you can leave. We had this discussion at the dance.

We're not having it again," John said. He closed those beautiful eyes to me completely. All I saw was coldness.

"Fine," I said, trying to make my voice steely. But it was hard enough just to keep it from shaking, and I wasn't sure that I had succeeded.

I walked out of the room, chest heaving. I had known, deep down, sure, but had he had to put it out there like that? And so harshly?

"Denise. Wait," John said.

Inwardly, I breathed a sigh of relief and stopped about halfway to the front door.

"I'm sorry. I didn't want that to come out so harshly."

I turned around, careful to avoid his eyes.

"Can't we just have a few hours? Not think about anything else? Things are the way they have to be. But I just want to forget that right now."

Stupid boy, I thought, but to him I said, "Whatever, John."

I walked back toward the bedroom. He followed me. John's arms wrapped around me from behind. I closed my eyes and sighed in resignation.

If that was all I could have, at least I could be near him. I loathed myself for that thought as soon as it crossed my mind. I sank back against him. There were so many things I wanted to say, but obviously if I said any of them, I'd be on my way out. Alone. And I didn't want that. Even if staying meant being shady and weak and the type of girl I didn't want to be. I wondered what he was thinking of me at that moment. Did he think I was a slut? Did he think I had no morals? Was he thinking at all?

I turned around to face him and he immediately buried my head in his shoulder. Had I seen sadness in his eyes?

I let him slip my shirt over my head, and then buried my face right back into his shoulder. I breathed in the fresh scent of soap and deodorant; nothing had ever smelled so good to me.

This is wrong, this is wrong, this is wrong, I thought as we fell onto the bed and I noticed his BlackBerry lying on the nightstand. I had a feeling it was turned off. But part of me didn't care. I wanted to be with him. It felt so good to have his skin on mine again. To feel his tongue against my tongue. To feel his fingers pressing softly in all the right places. It felt right—like things were the way they were supposed to be. We fit in every way. Physically. Mentally. Emotionally. I felt as if a part of me was inside of him. And whenever I was away from John, I was missing that part. I was the one who deserved to be with him anyway. I was entitled. Or so I told myself.

"I love you," he whispered.

I put my hand on his forehead and pushed him away from me. Hold on. That was not cool. He didn't get to say that.

"What?" I said, sitting up in the bed.

"I never said I didn't." John pushed away my hand and tried to pull me to him.

"No, John. You don't get to say that anymore. You don't get to throw a little fit like you just did, you don't get to be all up on Sasha all night, you don't get to ask her to marry you and then come out the mouth with something like that." I pushed him away again and sprang out of the bed.

"You're not going anywhere, Denise."

"The hell I'm not." I pulled my shirt back over my head.

"You came here because you want me."

"And that doesn't give you the right to treat me this way. Thank you, John, for bringing me back to my senses. I can't believe I was going to do that." I snatched my shoes from the floor. As I started to pull them on, he stood up. I tried to avoid looking at him. He was very right. I still wanted him. And I hated myself for it. And him.

"Denise, don't do this."

"No, John. How 'bout *you* not do this? All you have done is mess with my head since I met you. I'm tired of this. I'm tired of it always has to be John's way and John's always right. You're the selfish one. You think you can have everything you want? You don't get to have it both ways. You don't get to make me your whore and walk around with her in the light of day. You're getting married and you want to fuck me? What is wrong with you? What makes you think you have that right?" I screamed at him. I felt really good. For all of ten seconds.

John's face changed completely. "Whatever. Get out. I don't need this from you. Nobody made you come here, Denise. You're crazy," he said, turning his back to me. Had I really wanted to do that? I mean, he hadn't asked me there with the best intentions, but if there was ever to be a chance—

No. There are no more chances. He's engaged. *He thinks you're crazy and he only wants you for sex. Just get out!* I thought. So I said nothing. I grabbed my purse and walked toward the door.

"Oh, and Denise? Thanks for proving my point yet again that we'd never work." I froze at the sound of John's voice.

"You know what? Fuck you, dumb-ass frat boy." I slammed the door behind me before he could say another word or I could burst into tears.

I walked slowly back to my car, as if in a trance. I fell into the driver's seat. I don't even remember closing the door, but I must have. I fell across the console, my arms in the passenger seat, and just lay there.

I couldn't hold it back any longer. I filled my lungs with air. My eyes were stinging. My hands were shaking. Just when I thought my lungs would burst, I let out a long, trembling, screaming sob. My whole body convulsed with the force of my sobs. Tears poured down my face.

John was gone. No more green eyes. No more touches. No more kisses. All gone. Lost to Sasha. He had told me so many times he didn't love her. And I wasn't just imagining things. I had never seen him look at Sasha the way he looked at me. Even that night, when he'd told me he loved me, the way he had looked at me . . .

I don't know exactly when I fell asleep. I just know I opened my eyes and the first thing I saw was the door to my glove compartment sometime later that morning. I picked myself up, my side aching from being slumped over sideways for hours. My head hurt, and so did my throat. I turned the engine over, rested my forehead against the steering wheel, and waited for the car to warm up.

"Erich, you have it all wrong," I rasped. My voice was almost gone.

"Save it. I always knew you were still hung up on him. I just have proof now," Erich said quietly.

I felt like the horrible, nasty thing I'd become. I had no romantic interest in Erich, but I still had no desire to hurt him. Erich told me he'd seen my car outside of the hotel on his way home that morning. And that he'd seen me texting John at the after-party but hadn't said anything. I didn't think there was any way he could know that and he was just trying to save face. I let him. I didn't call him on it. After seeing my car, he'd made a U-turn and come to my apartment to wait for me.

"Nothing happened." I struggled to find my voice. I was fully aware of how stupid and cliché that sounded.

Erich raised his hands in front of him, palm side up. "Denise. What's the big deal? You never wanted me anyway. I was stupid to let Astoria fool me into thinking you did. I kept lettin' her put me on you, and listening to John both before when he said nothing was going on and after y'all broke up when he said it was over. But I knew better. I did," Erich said, looking away.

I reached out to touch his arm and he backed up, pulling away from me.

"You don't understand. Just let me explain."

"I don't have to understand. You know why? Because I'm done, Denise. I am *done*."

"Nothing—"

"Happened. I know. That's why you're wearing the same clothes you wore to the party last night. And why your car was still there at ten this morning. Really, Denise. Did you even shower? You smell like him."

"I fell asleep in my car."

"Hm. You can't even lie right. You slept in your car in a hotel parking lot? I could see right through you last night. I let you go without saying anything because I wanted you to set your own trap. Not because I believed you. Please," Erich said. I had never seen him so angry. Actually, I had never seen him angry at all.

I shook my head sadly. "It doesn't matter. Believe what you want." I sank down into my couch.

"I feel sorry for you, Denise. I really do. All wrapped up in this boy, and everybody in the world can see he doesn't want you except for you," Erich said. The disgust in his voice stung.

I nodded. I could see it. That didn't change the fact that I couldn't let go.

"You really messed up. I was ready to treat you like a queen. But it's good that you did. Because you deserve to be treated like crap. If that's all you want for yourself. Which apparently it is."

"I thought you were leaving." I forced the words out of my swollen throat while staring down at my hands.

"Oh, I am. Don't worry. I can't believe I let Astoria get me caught up in your crazy. But let me let you know. You don't have to worry about seeing me ever again."

"That's for the best."

"Believe me. I know."

"Look, I never pretended anything was there that wasn't."

"You know, before last night, I could have agreed with that. But now, I can't even say that much is true. I can't even say that for you." Erich grabbed his coat, stormed out and slammed the door behind him. I just sat there, blankly staring at the door.

My heart jumped when my phone buzzed. Even though it was insanely stupid to do so, I hoped I would see John's number on the caller ID. I took it out, saw Astoria's number and let out a hoarse scream of frustration, throwing the phone across the room. Tia was just emerging from her room, surprise written across her face.

"Dang. I think maybe you broke that thing," she said.

"Good. I hope I did. There's no one I wanna talk to anyway," I snarled, jumping up.

"What's wrong with you?" She looked puzzled.

I needed someone to take it out on. And I was quickly running out of people brave or stupid enough to cross my path. "Nothing. And clean up your mess sometimes. Can't you see I just cleaned in here? What is wrong with you?" I threw a pair of her jeans across the room. She ducked just in time and they sailed over her head.

As I stormed off to my room, I heard her mutter, "bitch" under her breath; but from that day on, the apartment was definitely cleaner.

That evening, with the day I was having, of course I ran into John's roommates while picking up a few things at Wal-Mart. And they actually had the nerve to stop me. They'd barely said two words to me the whole time John and I were together. Shawn James and Tyler Ross. Shawn was blond, and the dark-haired Tyler stood next to him.

"What do you want? Sasha set you two on me, too?" I asked. I didn't want to see anybody at that moment; least of all them. Then I heard some of the most shocking words I had ever heard in my life.

"No. Um, I just wanted to say I'm sorry," Tyler said. Shawn rolled his eyes. He kept looking at his watch and staring impatiently toward the front of the store. He obviously didn't want to be there.

"Really?" I was truly confused.

"Yeah. It was so stupid of us to act dumb, like when you came over. The way we acted while you were with John was not cool. I just wanted to say it's gonna be different now," Tyler said.

"Okay," was all I could think of to say. Tyler looked around and then he leaned in close.

"So. I was thinking maybe you could come over tonight. You know, after Sasha leaves. I know you wouldn't want to be there while she is. But I could give you a call later. If you give me your number. I heard you know how to have fun," Tyler said quietly.

My mouth dropped open. I was furious. The fact that I actually considered it for a minute pissed me off even more. After all, he was hot and it would have been great revenge.

"I don't know what John's been telling you, but I'm not like that." I drew away from him.

"Whatever you say," Tyler said with an amused grin.

"No. I mean it. Get out of here," I said, glaring at him. Shawn was suddenly interested in our conversation again. He snickered. Their maturity level was astounding.

"Well, I've heard about you, no matter what you say. And I like what I hear. So you take this. Just in case," Tyler said, writing his number on the back of a receipt he'd taken out of his wallet while he was talking. He had the nerve to stick it down the front pocket of my jeans. And he was in no hurry to remove his hand when he was done. He grinned, winking at me. I angrily pulled his hand out of my jeans and pushed him away.

"You nasty little fool!" I cried.

"Oh, you want me. So, so bad." He and Shawn laughed.

I stomped off, leaving them laughing behind me. I was fuming over what John might have been telling people. And wondering how many people he'd told.

The week after Barrister's, I was walking down the street from the law school to Astoria's apartment at the undergrad dorms. She worked in residence life and was a head resident for one of the dorms. We were on the phone, talking about our spring break plans, or lack thereof. I was going home for the week and Astoria was going on a mission trip with a group of people from her church. We had carefully avoided talking about anything that had to do with Erich, John, or anything related to that whole mess since the night of the dance. We had come to an unspoken truce.

Suddenly, I felt a hard tap on my shoulder; almost a punch. I whirled around, annoyed, and came face-to-face with *her*.

"Sasha," I said blankly, wondering where she had come from and what she wanted.

"Yeah. I've been followin' you. Trying to decide whether to come up to you or not. But I have to say this," Sasha said, out of breath. Her face was red and it starkly contrasted with the platinum blonde hair swirling around her head.

"Yes?" I said coolly.

"You need to stay the hell away from John!" she snarled. My heart was pounding, but I was trying my hardest to keep my face impassive.

"John and I broke up. I don't see him except for around school," I said, hoping my voice didn't expose my lie.

"Yeah? Well, I saw you two talking after Barrister's. And I heard you two were at a hotel together that night."

What? I thought, but I said, "I don't know what you're talking about. And please stop screaming in my face right now."

"Stop lying to me. You slept with my fiancé, didn't you?"

"I never spent that night at any hotel with John," I said. That much was true.

Sasha glared at me, nostrils flaring. I was still holding my cellphone in my hand. I absently put it in my purse, not knowing if Astoria was still there or not.

"If you don't tell me the truth right now—"

"What? What, huh? You already have the man I want. You're engaged to him. You won, okay? You and those harpies you set on me. What else do you want from me? I don't have anything else for you."

"Tell me the truth, you liar."

"I was there, okay? But I left before anything happened. That's it."

Her chest heaved. And, if it was possible, she was getting even redder. I wanted her to make a move. I couldn't wait to pop her in the face.

"I don't want to ever hear you've been near him ever again," she said in a somewhat normal voice. She'd stopped yelling anyway.

"Then you better stop having your little crew spy on me."

"Whore."

I was ready for that first punch. I had never hit anyone in my life, but I was ready. It couldn't be but so hard to make a fist and punch someone. I wasn't going to back down from her. Not after she had taken everything from me. And every time I saw that ring flash, it made me want to hit her even more.

"You don't know anything about me. And it's not my fault he can't stay away from me."

She screamed and drew back a tiny, white fist. A dark hand wrapped around that fist.

"*Oh,* no. I don't think so," Astoria said. "I heard you two on the phone. And I ran down here." Astoria let go of Sasha's hand.

Sasha's face was contorted with disgust and anger. "We're not finished. This isn't over!"

"Yeah. Okay. Get out of my face."

"You just wait. You got lucky!"

"No, you did. Go!" I roared.

She elbowed me aside and stalked up the sidewalk, toward the law school parking lot. I glared after her, shaking my head.

"That girl is not right," Astoria said. "That's why you shouldn't have been fooling around with those white people."

I whirled around, turning my anger on her, "You really think that's what I want to hear right now? Really? Do you? Astoria, can you just be a friend now? John's gone. You should be happy. I don't wanna hear it anymore."

Astoria shrugged, looking a little put off, but she knew she couldn't say anything. She knew she was wrong.

"So you still want to come over?" Astoria asked.

"As long as I'm not going to hear another word about this," I warned. She looked down at the gold bracelets on her wrist. "Astoria."

"No. Okay?" she said, shifting her weight to one of her yellow pumps.

"Let's go," I said, walking off. She fell in step beside me silently.

"So I guess you don't want to hear about what Erich—"

"Astoria," I said through clenched teeth, "I thought we were past this. No, I don't want to hear anything about Erich ever again."

"Just wanted to let you know he says he's sorry for being so mean to you," Astoria said.

I said nothing. I guess she took that as approval to continue.

"I mean, he meant what he said. And he knows you two would never work. He just said he shouldn't have been so harsh. That it's obvious he's not what you wanted and that's not your fault."

"Okay," I replied stonily, still staring straight ahead.

"And I guess—the same goes for me. I'll leave you alone about this relationship stuff. I guess you just need time to heal and figure out what you want. Not someone trying to force what she wants for you on you. Even if she means well," Astoria said.

I nodded. That was a start at least. If she meant it.

CHAPTER 19

I'M STILL IN LOVE WITH YOU

Well, it turned out John wasn't spreading rumors about me. The roommates had just figured out John and I had met up after Barrister's. And Sasha had found out because of her spies. But it didn't make me feel much better to know either of those things.

I tried my hardest to put it all behind me. I fell to my old defenses with a renewed vigor. I put so much into school, activities, and friends that I passed out every night from exhaustion for the few hours I set aside for sleep.

Astoria, Suse, and I had joined an amateur roller derby league because we got bored easily with the gym and we wanted something we could all do together. Also, I thought it might help Astoria get some of her aggression out. Well, that spring, it was helping me with the aggression. The team had been pushing me to be more aggressive since I joined, and I was finally getting the hang of it. We'd won two games in a row and I was a local hero. They'd let me play a lot more after seeing me at practices after Barrister's Ball.

One afternoon in March, Astoria, Suse, and I skated over to the side of the rink after practice. Our teammates slapped us on the shoulder as they passed by on their way to the locker room. I pressed my hand gingerly against the top and then the side of my thigh, wondering if I'd have any bruises from my particularly firm hip-checks that day. I was learning how to be a back-up jammer. The jammer is the point scorer. The jammer's job is to bull her way through a pack of girls during a two-minute jam without getting knocked out. Fun, but a little hard on the body. All three of us were regularly blockers, which meant it was our job to block the other team's jammer and help our jammer get through the pack.

"Denise, you were really killing it out there," Astoria said. Suse agreed. Another thing that was funny to me about Suse. You'd never know she was aggressive until it came to contact sports and killing defenseless animals in the woods.

"Yeah, well, I think I'm getting the hang of this roller derby thing," I said. I'd been the most reluctant to join the team out of the three of us, but that spring, it seemed I had become the one having the most fun.

After showering and changing, we walked outside into a roaring March wind. It was still early March, just before spring break, which was the second week of the month, and so spring hadn't really kicked in yet and probably wouldn't until some time in April.

"That was our last practice before spring break," Suse said.

"Yeah," I said. Spring break meant little to me. It was just an opportunity to put the finishing touches on my note before the deadline for consideration of publication.

The law review board would choose which of the staff's notes would be published in our school's law review shortly after spring break. I didn't have high hopes with Lindie behind it all, but I was going to try anyway.

"I can't wait. Charles, Daddy, and I are going on a fishing trip," Suse said. She was gushing. It was a big deal for her that her dad no longer wished Charles would drop dead. Her dad should have trusted his first instinct.

"I can't wait to get back to New York, man. I don't know how being out in the country like this doesn't bother you two," Astoria said. "Denise, I wish you would just come with me. You could work on your note up there."

"Nope. I'll get more done at home, in the country, with no distractions," I said, affecting a deep Southern drawl. We laughed.

"Anyway, I have to come back early for dress rehearsals. When are you coming back to town?" Astoria said. We stopped in the parking lot by her car.

"I can come back early and meet you. Let me know when you get back. Oh, yeah. How is your play going?"

Astoria shrugged. "Okay. I mean, the leads can sing."

"Why didn't you audition for anything?" I asked. Astoria was part of the stage crew and she was helping out with costumes.

"A musical?" Astoria snorted.

"What? You can sing."

"In a church choir surrounded by people."

"Maybe next year," I said as they three of us got into Astoria's car.

"Maybe. I'm trying to convince them to pick something that's not a musical for the fall. I dunno, though. Our self-proclaimed de facto leader loves those things."

"Okay." I grinned, strapping on my seatbelt. Things were much better. I had my friends, my life, and everything else that mattered back. I was finding my way back to the old me and wondering why I'd ever thought deviating from that was a good idea.

I plotted my way through O'Hare, weaving my way through streams of impatient bodies, each rushing off in a different direction. My plane from Richmond had arrived an hour late and, in theory, my next plane would leave Chicago in a half hour. I wondered why they were all hurrying—O'Hare having a plane on time is almost newsworthy—but I was doing it, too. I guess airports just give you that feeling. Like you should rush.

I was on my way to a trial team competition in New York, and the flight the law school booked for me had me connecting through Chicago. My teammates were already in New York. I'd had to catch a later flight because of another obligation. I'd had to see the speaker I'd booked for a lecture the day before off to his train. I'd organized a lecture series for the International Law Society. I'd basically put together the whole lecture series, and so it was a duty I had no desire to delegate to make sure our speakers got to the law school and on their way home smoothly.

I was driven. On a mission. My head was full of points I wanted to make in my opening statement. I even tuned out the neon lights in the ceiling of the tunnel I had to pass through to get between concourses A and B of the United terminal. I tuned out the new age space music as well. No time for errant thoughts or even for the outside world. My life was all about focus and moving forward.

My phone vibrated in my bag. I answered it without looking at the caller ID. It didn't matter who it was because I planned to get rid of the caller in as few words as possible regardless. I was already in a sour mood. My eyes hurt, I couldn't find my eye drops, and I hadn't eaten in hours since nobody wants to feed you on a plane anymore and I had accidentally packed my wallet in my big suitcase, which was hopefully on its way to Flight 494.

"Hello," I said, maneuvering around a mother and her large stroller.

"Denise." The voice that came through my phone was flat and obnoxious.

"Lindie. What do you want?" I said. I hadn't had much to say to her since the honor council mess.

"Just because your note is being published doesn't mean you don't answer to me anymore. I'm still in charge for now. I asked to meet with you before you left for the airport." Her voice became even tighter. I think it almost killed her that my note was chosen for publication even after all that had happened.

"I couldn't risk missing my plane."

"The school is not that far from the airport, Denise. You wouldn't have missed anything."

"Look, Lindie, I don't have time for this right now. I have to catch my connecting flight, and my plane from Richmond was late. I haven't been able to get any information about my flight to New York yet. And this is a pointless conversation anyway. Whatever it is can wait until I get back."

"There's no need to attack me, Denise. I just wanted to let you know that you've been selected as next year's editor-in-chief for law review."

I stopped by the escalator leading up to the concourse and stumbled backward a bit. "What? Really?"

"Congratulations." Her voice was stiff.

"Thank you," I murmured, a grin spreading slowly over my face. Warmth chased by chills raced over my body. We said our goodbyes and I slipped my phone back into my purse. I couldn't stop smiling until I got to the gate my flight was supposed to leave out of. I knew there was a problem when I saw that there was not one available chair at my gate, or any of those nearby. People lounged on the floor. Bored-looking teenagers sat in the aisles and toyed with laptops, cellphones, and MP3 players. I looked up at the nearest flight board just then and my heart sank. My flight was canceled.

"What?" I dropped my carry-on to the floor and glared at the flight board.

Someone tapped my shoulder and I jumped. I turned to see Donnovan smiling at me.

I smiled back. It was catching. "Shouldn't you already be in New York?" He was on my competition team, and the only other person connecting through Chicago. The other three members of our team had all gotten a flight together with a different connection.

He sighed and scratched the back of his neck. "Yeah. About that. Neither one of us are going anywhere tonight, Denise. They've grounded some of the planes and cancelled the rest of the night's flights. Something about safety checks."

I'd rushed to the gate for nothing. I tapped a finger against the boarding pass I'd printed out from the self check-in machine and scrunched my lips up in disappointment.

"I have some good news," Donnovan said. He leaned in closer to me with a conspiratorial grin.

"Oh, yeah?"

He held up two small pieces of paper. "I managed to wrangle two hotel vouchers."

"Oh, yeah? How'd you do that?"

"A little bit of flirting. I little bit of lying."

We laughed. I kept smiling afterward. Donnovan had broad lips that looked soft to the touch. His dark brown hair was cut close and he had round, dark brown eyes to match. There was a shadow of a beard across his long jaw line. He was about my height and a few shades darker than me.

I realized he was asking me something and I had to ask him to repeat it, the blood rushing into my face.

He chuckled. "I asked if you wanted to go over to the hotel and grab a drink at the bar there before bed."

"Um, sure," I said. I smoothed a few stray hairs back down, attempting to tidy my ponytail. I wished for the second time that day that I'd taken time to iron my gray pants and burgundy blouse that morning, but at least I wasn't wearing the sweats I'd contemplated changing into for the duration of the trip.

We took the shuttle to the airport Sheraton and sat at the bar. We called our coach and teammates on the way to the hotel to let them know what was going on. I was glad I always packed a change of clothes in my carry-on in case my luggage was lost. And that I wasn't stranded alone at the airport, curled up in some corner at the gate. The night could have been worse. And I could have had worse company.

Once we were seated at the bar and had ordered our drinks, we started chatting about the competition and about school. We were both on law review and he congratulated me when I told him about editor-in-chief.

To break a lull in the conversation, Donnovan said, "I heard about what happened between you and John."

I forced the start of a grimace to finish in a smile. I didn't even like hearing that name. "It's okay."

"That wasn't cool at all what he did. He really lost out, and you can do better."

I nodded away his concern and flashed another forced smile. "So, speaking of relationships, how's Sandy?" Sandy was his girlfriend. She was in grad school at a college in North Dakota.

He turned back to his rum and Coke and twisted the stirrer between his fingers. "We broke up a little while ago."

"Wow. It must be in the water or something," I said with a nervous laugh.

"Well, here's to us doing better and showing them, right?" Donnovan said with a wink, raising his glass.

"Right." I clinked my glass to his. Taking a long sip of my chardonnay, I let my mind wander for a moment, wondering if Donnovan and I would work and if I should initiate giving it a try.

Chalking it up to rebound fantasies, I pushed the thought aside.

We won the competition, and Donnovan and I joked that we carried it for the team thanks to the adrenaline surge we were given by making it to the conference center just hours before the competition began. After that trip, Donnovan and I spent a lot of time together. He even came to my last roller derby game of the season. When I was around him, my heart felt a little lighter. Every time Astoria tried to label it, I gave her a look that shut her up. And shutting Astoria up isn't easy to do.

Life was almost back to normal. I was doing pretty okay until one Saturday night in early April when I was rudely awakened by my cellphone's ring. There's always something.

"What?" I mumbled, barely holding the phone up to my ear.

"Denise," a voice I hadn't expected said.

"Thom?" I said, shocked completely out of my sleep, wondering why John's brother was calling me. Why, why,

why, when I'd been doing such a good job of pulling myself back together?

"John doesn't know I'm doing this. And he would kill me if he knew, but this is for his own good," Thom said in lieu of a greeting.

"Huh?" I was still trying to figure out why I was talking to Thom.

"He won't listen to a word I say, and someone's got to stop him from flying down this path of destruction he's on. My brother is an ass. He's a confused ass. I know he asked her to marry him, but that doesn't make any sense. He's still in love with you."

"Yeah. Your brother's good at that. Not making any sense," I said, rubbing my eyes and fumbling for my alarm clock, wondering what in the world time it was.

"But he told me he still loves you."

"Yeah. He tells me all the time. Still marrying that bitch."

"But he told me the night before he asked her to marry him. He just didn't tell me his plans at the time. He told me he loves you more than he could ever love Sasha."

I dropped my alarm clock.

"I can't take any more of this, Thom. The disappointment. The anger. The hurt. It's over. I've moved on. And that's the way it has to be. Let him marry her. I don't care."

"Yes, you do. It hurts you as much as it hurts everyone else involved."

"Oh, I don't know. It doesn't seem to be hurting John or Sasha very much," I said. "And I'm sure it's not hurting your parents, either."

"John is hurting more than you think. He's gotten very good at covering up pain, disappointment, and anger over the years. Just trust me. There's a lot you don't know about growing up in this house. There's a lot money can't buy. What he said at dinner that day you were here—that doesn't even begin to cover it all," Thom said.

I remained quiet. I didn't like it him pointing out John might have a side in all this.

"Denise?"

"What do you expect me to do? Huh? They're getting married. That's perfectly clear. There's nothing I can do to stop it. So what does it matter? Even if he cares about me, which I doubt he does."

"I don't think you believe that any more than I do," Thom said. His voice was quiet, yet firm. "John was never so happy about being with anyone before. I know there were problems. Massive ones. But you should have heard how he talked about you to me. I know it's out of line for me to call you, and I wouldn't if I didn't think it was really important and I didn't know what I know. I just didn't know what else to do. If only you knew what he was going to—if only you knew. I don't think it's too late. And I think you'd be making a huge mistake to just let go. And not try."

"He's not trying."

"I love my brother, but he doesn't always do what's best for him. I was hoping you'd see things more clearly than him. For both of your sakes."

"Well, us being apart is really what's best for both of us."

"So letting everybody else tell the two of you what's best for you is what's best? Really?"

"Thom, you don't know what it's been like."

"I know I've seen John go through changes over the past few months. And even at his most miserable with you? He was happier than he is now. I mean, like I said, he's good at putting up fronts. But I know him. I know John well. And he's really dying inside. And I'd be pretty willing to bet you are, too," Thom said. "Even for that short time I saw you two together, I could tell that you two were for real. That you really had something that's still worth saving."

I said nothing. I couldn't. I didn't know how to respond to that without breaking down. John was probably off somewhere with Sasha at the very moment I was talking to Thom. I wished he was dying inside, but he couldn't have been. I refused to believe it.

"Denise? All I know is Sasha being in my brother's life is no good for anybody. And don't even bring up my parents. But you? You in his life? I think you could change everything for the better. You were already working on that before everything went wrong. And you were doing a great job."

"Thom, I can't talk about this, okay? Stop—just stop. Okay?"

"I just want you to think about it, okay? For both of your sakes."

"You don't know, Thom. You just don't know."

"Neither do you, Denise."

"Bye, Thom."

"Please, Denise. Just please—"

"Bye, Thom."

"Think about it. Bye, Denise," Thom said.

I switched the phone off and let it fall out of my hands. I took deep, gasping breaths as I fended off the body-quaking sobs I felt rising in my chest.

Almost involuntarily, I called Astoria and told her to get over to my place at two in the morning. She came, no doubt cussing me the whole way. I told her all about my conversation with Thom. She sat on my bed, cross-legged, listening to the whole thing, nodding and not interrupting. For one, brief moment, I thought she was going to be a good listener and just commiserate with me.

Then she opened her mouth. "Well, that just goes to show you. You should have never gotten involved with this fool. Now his brother is trying to draw you back in. I hope you're not thinking about it," Astoria said obtusely as soon as I was done telling the story.

"You know, Astoria, it would be nice if you could just be on my side sometimes," I sighed.

"You kiddin', right? I'm always on your side. That's why I'm trying to get you to see the light, as always."

"Sometimes I just need an ear, and not a mouthful."

"If you ask me, you should just go ahead and ask Donnovan out. If you had sense, you would do that."

"Well, I guess it's a good thing I didn't ask you, then, huh?"

"Well, well, well . . . I—"

"Well, well, you what? Huh?"

"You asked *me* over here and you have the nerve—"

"No. You have the nerve. A good friend knows when to shut up and just be there for her friend."

"No, Denise. I'll tell you what a good friend does. A good friend gets her ass up at two in the morning and comes to her crazy friend's house because her crazy friend is doing something crazy again. A good friend tries to help her crazy friend see what's best for her. A good friend doesn't let her crazy friend make the same old mistakes over and over!" Astoria shouted back.

"What mistakes? I haven't gone near him since—"

"Since when, huh? Since Barrister's? Since when, exactly? I know you weren't going to say since you two broke up. You can't leave that boy alone, Denise!"

"That's not true. I haven't even talked about him in weeks."

"You almost hooked up with his roommate just to get back at him."

"That's not how it happened at all!"

"Denise, I am not having this fight again," Astoria said, jumping up. And she was gone before I could say another word.

The day after my "heart to heart" with Astoria, I went to Apryl's and sprawled out on the couch. The best thing about my cousin is she always seems to understand me without words. She just let me lay there, watching her premium cable with glazed-over eyes. Astoria and I only had basic cable, and we often came to Apryl's to watch our favorite shows on HBO, Showtime and the rest of those channels.

But that day I couldn't concentrate on the television, and I should have been studying for finals anyway. But all I wanted to do was lie on Apryl's couch, being mostly left alone. I was only interrupted from doing that when Taye pounced on me occasionally and told me some inane fact or asked me a slew of questions. Once I acted enlightened by his fact or answered his stream of questions, he was off again, leaving me wishing I was that easy to make content.

When Astoria walked in, I barely looked up at her.

She sat on the arm of the couch nearest my feet. "I thought you'd probably be here. I called Apryl and she told me you were."

I shifted to a more comfortable position, but remained on my side, watching the television.

"Suse is here, too. She's out in the car, talking to Charles. She'll be in here in a minute."

"I thought she was going to see him this weekend," I said, sitting up on the couch.

Astoria slid over next to me. "That's what they're screaming about on the phone right now. I told her about last night and she said there was no way she was abandoning you."

I snorted. "Abandoning me? What did you tell her? That I was drowning?"

"Would I be wrong to tell her that? Seems pretty true to me." She looked down at her hands and then back up at me. "Denise, why do you let him affect you like this?"

"What do you want me to say? You've already heard me say it all."

"I can't believe it after all of this. Crazy Sasha following you around. The way he's treated you. And nice, good-looking Donnovan always hanging around, wanting to spend time with you? After all this, you would still be caught up and over that wh—"

"Don't you start. I'll leave right now," I cut her off. Astoria and I sat there, glowering at each other.

"I don't even understand why you put yourself in this position. Why do you let that idiot affect you like this?"

"You act like you don't know me. Like you don't know I don't always make the smart decisions."

"One thing I do know is that you need to start taking responsibility for the things that happen in your life."

"Don't worry about the things that happen in my life. No one's asking you to pick up after me. I'm not your child, your project, or anything else."

It got quiet again.

"I'm just trying to look out for you," Astoria finally said. "Friends do that for each other."

"I know. But you have to stop. We are never going to see eye-to-eye on this. And I really don't want us to lose our friendship over this, but I can feel it slipping away if you keep this up," I said.

Astoria stared down at her hands.

"Astoria, think about it. Every time we have this conversation, it ends up exactly like this. You can't save me from everything. I appreciate you trying. I know you're just trying to be a good friend. But all you're doing is making me resent you. And I don't want to resent you. I love you, Astoria. But I need to get through this on my own. In my own way. I need you to understand and respect that," I said.

Astoria continued staring down, not saying a word. "I just—I wanted to save you from some of the pain I went through." When she did look up, her eyes were full of sadness.

I moved closer and put my arm around her.

"I know. But that's not what I need right now. I need you to step back. I just need to work through this," I said.

"I'll back down. Our friendship means more to me than proving that I'm right. Even though I know I am."

I laughed. That was the best I was going to get, and I knew it. "Good." I hugged her. However, I had the feeling that she was already formulating a new plan of attack as we sat there.

CHAPTER 20
SOFTBALL BATTLE

The last day of the law school's annual softball tournament was a turning point. One of those "that's it" moments. Everybody had been drinking beer and playing all day. We were pretty drunk by the time we ended up at some guy's house afterward. And of course, John and his team ended up at the same party Astoria, Suse, and I did. Of course this meant Tyler and Shawn were there. Thankfully, Sasha wasn't in town that weekend. Apparently, she'd had to go to the Hamptons with her family for some social engagement. John had refused to miss the tournament. Sasha wasn't happy about it, but she'd been unable to get out of the Hamptons thing, and so they had to spend their first weekend apart since Barrister's. I overheard some people talking about it, shocked that she'd torn herself away from John for a weekend.

Suse and Astoria wanted me to leave as soon as we got there and realized John was there as well. I refused to leave. I baby-sat the keg and flirted with Donnovan, who'd been with us all day. He was on our softball team.

Once they realized I wasn't going to leave, Suse tried to make the best of it at first, breaking out into choruses of the school fight school with Donnovan and I occasionally. She and I would then burst into giggles. Astoria split her time between "checking on me" (translation: making sure I was nowhere near John) and flirting with this guy she'd met at the game. He was a grad student from another program, but he was friends with a lot of the law school guys at the party.

Suse clapped a hand on my shoulder. "Denise, you were so funny. I've never seen anyone run from the ball before."

I laughed. I had struck out, but I'd done it with flair. "Hey, that's why I like roller derby. No ball involved."

"Denise, you are too much," Donnovan said with a chuckle, putting his arm around my waist.

I put mine around him and caught his eye, realizing my flirting had gone too far. He leaned in close and his lips almost brushed mine. I turned my head at the last minute and reached down to pour myself another cup of beer. Things got strange between us after that, and we drifted off in opposite directions. I didn't see him for the rest of the time I was at the party.

Later that evening, a lot of people headed downtown for the bars. Most of the people left had migrated to the living room. Astoria and Suse wanted to go. Astoria was bored. Her crush had moved on with the downtown crowd, and she wanted to follow him to the Bottom. And neither of them liked me and John being in the same room. Astoria hadn't said anything about John since our little talk at Apryl's, but I could constantly see it in her face that it took effort for her not to mention him. She still wanted to play protector.

"Why can't we just go?" Astoria sighed yet again. I felt as if she was asking that every single minute.

"You can. I'm not ready." I answered with the same reply I'd given her countless times, my eyes trained on John and some of his cronies across the room, a faint sneer on my lips.

"Is it really fun for you to sit in this little corner and stare at him? Is that just making your night?" Suse snapped. I was surprised by her sudden change in tone and attitude, but I kept my eyes focused forward. I said nothing. She sighed, throwing her hands up in frustration. "You guys can find a ride home if I leave?"

"Yeah. Sure," Astoria said.

"Bye," Suse said, grabbing her purse. Astoria said bye to her. I gave a half wave in her direction, my eyes still focused forward. I think maybe I was trying to burn a hole into John with my eyes. Suse walked off with a little cry of frustration.

"Hey. You never called me." I finally looked away from John, startled by the sound of Tyler's voice.

"Tyler. Hi," I said, leaning back against the wall. John finally looked in my direction. I saw him over Tyler's shoulder. Was his jaw clenched? Or was it just a combination of alcohol and wishful thinking that made me see that?

"So. I've been thinkin' about ya," Tyler said as he set his beer down on a nearby table.

"Really?" I let Tyler put his arms around me and draw me closer.

Astoria uttered a cry of disgust and walked off. John took a few steps in our direction.

"Oh, yeah," Tyler said, lowering his lips to mine. I barely felt the tip of Tyler's tongue on my lips before he was pulled away from me so abruptly that I almost fell forward.

"What the fuck are you doing?" John roared, pushing Tyler backward.

"Just gettin' a taste, man. What do you care?" Tyler laughed.

John roared another string of choice words before punching Tyler in the face.

"What the hell's wrong with you, John?"

"No! What's wrong with you? You don't touch her!" John shouted. A couple of guys grabbed him. Shawn pushed Tyler backward, away from John.

"Man. You have lost your mind. What do you care about her? What anybody does with her? You had your jungle fever moment. Let somebody else take a turn."

"Let me go. I'll fuck him up!" John bellowed, trying to pull away from the guys holding him back.

"Oh, so you ain't done with her? I don't think Sasha would like you still mixin' it up like that," Tyler said, laughing even harder.

"C'mon, man. Let's just go," Shawn urged, still pushing Tyler toward the patio door.

"Fuck Sasha! You, too!" John shouted, still trying to pull free.

"Bye, Johnny boy. I'll see you at home. You looking for Denise later, why don't you check my room first?" Tyler was still laughing as Shawn pushed him out of the door. John finally pushed the other guys away from him.

And before I could say or do anything, John was gone out of the front door. I wanted so badly to run after him. But I knew that would be the completely wrong thing to do.

So I just sank to the floor, holding my head, trying to wrap my mind around the fact that John had just stood up for me.

For a moment, I had wanted to hook up with Tyler. Just to get some reaction out of John. Honestly, because I hoped it would hurt him. But after the scene that had just played out before me, all I felt was sick.

Later that night, I still hadn't learned my lesson. That included the fact that I still hadn't stopped drinking. I was so out of it, I didn't know how I'd gotten downtown, what had happened to the people I'd come there with, and whether or not Astoria had been among those people. I forgot Suse hadn't even come with us. I kept asking people where she and Astoria were. I was giving new meaning to getting my freak on out on the dance floor. Somehow, my softball shirt had gotten ripped off at the bottom so that it covered little more than my bra.

I was watching two guys approach me when I caught sight of him. If he was in a room, I was going to know it. No matter how drunk I was, how dark it was, no matter what.

Of all the people I expected to see in the Bottom that night, John wasn't one of them. I had never seen or heard of John going to a club before. But he made it downtown that night, too. And we ended up in the same place again. I didn't recognize the people he was with, but all of them were wild and at least as drunk as I was.

I absently pushed away the two men who had been trying to make a sandwich out of me. One of them had been waiting for me to act out the song blaring out of the speakers. He was more than a little disappointed when he lost my attention. He kept insisting I was going to dance with him. When I pushed him away again, he tried to pull me against him by grabbing my hips from behind.

"No," I snapped, pulling away from him and then pushing him away.

"Man, you a'ight. Can't dance anyway," he said, sneering at me. He then walked off.

I rolled my eyes, and made my way over to the bar. After what I had seen, it was time for another shot. Especially if I was going to be in the same place with John.

"Grey Goose. Tab's under Rich," I slurred to the bartender. She nodded. It wasn't like she needed my name. All the bartenders had to know me by that point. My tab was going to put somebody's child through college. Even if it caused my tuition check to bounce. That was probably why I wasn't getting cut off.

"So, you want my roommate now? Donnovan not enough?" I jumped at the sound of John's voice in my ear. So many emotions flooded through me at once. I hadn't been that close to him since the night of indiscretion after Barrister's. And he hadn't murmured in my ear like that since—whoa. That was a dangerous memory to have. I immediately tensed up just thinking about the possibility of thinking about it.

"Donnovan and I are friends, your roommate wants me, not the other way around, and what does any of it matter to you?" I slammed down my shot before turning to him. Big mistake. Just seeing him did something to me. Especially looking into those eyes . . .

"Yeah I do. And you want me, too," he said.

I glared at him. I was determined that there wouldn't be a repeat of Barrister's.

I tried to ignore my thoughts. Because none of them involved anything I should be doing. I tried hard to concentrate on how hurt and angry I was. But with him so close, that was more than difficult.

"Yeah, whatever," was all I trusted myself to say. I tried to push past him, even though all I wanted was to stay where I was. I was annoyed with myself for almost feeling relieved when he pushed me back and blocked me from leaving the bar. I couldn't trust myself to look at him. It was going to be way too easy for him if I did.

"Are you sure you don't want me?" he whispered, letting his hand slip down to the small of my back.

"Yeah. No. I don't," I said breathily. We both knew that was a bold faced lie.

He pulled me closer. "Really?" he murmured, his lips brushing my ears.

"Really," I moaned, my eyes rolling back in my head with pleasure as he kissed the top of my ear.

"I don't believe you," he said, kissing the corner of my mouth.

"You better stop before somebody sees us," I said while slipping my hands up the back of his shirt.

"Yeah. Like that's gonna happen. And like you want it to," he said. My body was now so tightly pressed against his that I could feel every breath he took.

"I hate you," I murmured.

"You love me and you want me."

"That's why I hate you," I said, eyes closed, as he trailed kisses down my throat. It was crazy. Everybody could see. And I didn't care. All I wanted was for John to touch me. And for me to taste him—his warm, salty skin—beneath my tongue as I licked the corner of his mouth between kisses. I was in my own, little world with him at that moment.

And suddenly I was rudely brought back to reality by the raking of perfectly manicured nails down my back. Screeching in my ears. A slap across my face. Flying hair and screams. And the next thing I knew, I had two fists full of blonde hair. And I was screaming, mad as hell that this shit always happened to me.

One of Sasha's spies had attacked me. My old friend, Cindy. She was Sasha's second in command. I think I would have tried my best to kill that girl, had I been given the chance. I don't think I ever stopped screaming as I did the best to beat the plastic surgery off her face.

I had never been more full of rage in my life. It scared me a little, but I also felt more free than I had in a long time. I barely noticed her feeble attempts to push me off. All I knew was that I wanted to give her all the pain and hurt I had inside. I felt that if I could beat it all into her, I wouldn't have to feel it anymore. After all, it was all her fault that I was in that pain anyway. At least the way I saw it.

I don't know who finally pulled me off of her. I have no idea who dragged me outside of the club. All I could think was that I didn't see John anywhere and that I hoped I had killed that whore. Somebody was screaming at me how stupid I was and that I had better hope she didn't press charges. Asking me how I would explain that to the Bar. I vaguely remember telling that person I didn't care what the skank did.

I gotta get outta here. Out of this club. Away from this school. Outta this town, was the next predominate thought in my mind. And suddenly, I knew I was going to be sick. It had nothing to do with the alcohol. I couldn't believe what had just happened. Least of all, what I had been about to do. I needed to get John out of my head. For good.

He was ruining everything without even really being in my life. Well, I reminded myself, he was always in my life whether he was physically around me or not. I didn't know how much longer I could stand my life the way it was.

There was a trial team party on the last day of classes. Suse and I went together. Donnovan was there, too, but we avoided each other for most of the night. I didn't know what to say to him, knowing he'd heard about my latest John run-in at the club. Suse and I spent most of the night talking to Melissa, another trial team member and my friend Lindie stole editor-in-chief from, and our friend Inez, who was also on the team.

While everyone else talked about their summer plans, I let my eyes wander around the room. Our coach had reserved a dining room in a Cuban restaurant for us. It was a nice place. Lots of red and yellow and well-polished wood. The music was festive and some people were dancing. I felt like an impostor in the cheery room. Especially when it came my turn to talk about my upcoming summer.

Inez combed an olive-toned hand through her dark hair and looked at me with large, dark eyes. "So, Denise. Dettweiler, huh? That's not an easy one to pull off."

I forced a smile. "Yeah, well, it's a job."

Suse put a hand on my back and shook her head. "Don't you be modest about this." She then turned to the rest of the group and gushed over my summer associate position at the big, fancy firm with the other girls.

I didn't really care about it one way or the other anymore. I didn't feel the same passion for law school as I once had. The more the semester dragged on, ever since the law review debacle, the more I began to wonder what the point of it all was. From school to the golden handcuffs—chained to a high-paying job I was certain I'd have no passion for—to what? What was the point?

I came back to the conversation, curious as to why everyone had stopped talking. Until I saw that Donnovan was walking our way. Suse exchanged glances with Inez and Melissa.

One side of Donnovan's mouth moved up in a tentative half smile. "Denise? Can I talk to you for a minute?"

"Sure." I turned to tell Suse and the others I'd be right back, but they practically shooed me off before I could. Donnovan and I walked out to the patio that was behind the dining room we were in to escape our nosy classmates.

He took a deep breath and laughed nervously. "Why is it so hard to talk to you all of a sudden?"

I laughed back, hoping it would help break the tension. "Yeah, it shouldn't feel this strange."

"Denise, about you and John . . ."

"John and I are through."

He nodded and licked his lips. "So I hear. I just wanted to let you know that whatever happened between you two after the softball game—that's your business and his. Certainly not mine. I mean, we've always been just friends, right?"

"Right." My knees went weak with relief at hearing him say that. If only I could have been with someone sane like him. But I knew it wouldn't work. My heart couldn't be in it. I still needed time to heal. The softball nightmare proved that.

"I mean, it's probably obvious I think you're attractive and I wouldn't mind giving it a shot under different circumstances. But the heart wants what it wants. I get that."

"Yeah, I wish my heart had as much sense as you do," I said. We both laughed too loud, trying to compensate for the things we both avoided mentioning.

"Good. Now I don't have to avoid your eyes and feel stupid all the time," he said.

"Yeah, that is good." I smiled.

He hugged me and said, "So, good luck with all that's going on—well, good luck."

"Thanks, Donnovan." I pulled back from him, plans already formulating in my mind to set him up with Astoria. No point in letting a good man go to waste.

Not long after Donnovan and I went back inside, the party started breaking up. People floated off to start studying for finals, to get some sleep before diving into books and note outlines, or to enjoy one last night of freedom. Inez, Suse, and Melissa left, but I stayed to help clean up. I made them go ahead despite their reluctance to leave me. I wanted some time to myself, and I was looking forward to my walk home after helping our coach collect the decorations and other things she'd brought in from home.

The coach and I were the last ones of our party to leave. We said goodbye to each other and turned in opposite directions to head home outside of the restaurant. That's when I bumped against a man in a tan jacket.

"Excuse me," I said, moving to go around the man.

He didn't move. "Denise?"

I looked up and saw that it was Ral I'd run into. "Hi, Ral. How are you?" I hadn't seen much of him since the breakup.

"I'm good, Denise. How are you?" The way he asked the question connoted that he actually cared about the answer.

"Great. We're almost third years," I said, my fake smile still in place.

He saw right through me. "I'm sorry he's such a jerk. If it makes you feel any better, he's lying to everyone. Including himself."

My smile fell. "It doesn't."

"I didn't think it would. But it was worth a try," Ral said, patting my shoulder. "I just feel so bad about everything that happened."

"Don't, Ral. Because I'm going to be okay. I'm moving on, life goes on, insert your favorite cliché here . . ." I said.

He laughed. "You really are a great person. And he might be my friend, but he's also a real idiot."

"When you're right, you're right."

"I think it's so stupid that we can't hang out anymore because the two of you broke up. Who made that stupid rule up, anyway?"

"Who says we can't?"

"Call me sometime, okay?"

"Sure," I said, although I had no intention of doing it. Ral was fun to be around, but too close to the source for that. I'd just see John the whole time.

"Well, I'd better get going. I'm meeting someone for drinks."

"Someone?" I gestured with my hands, wanting him to elaborate.

Ral grinned, shaking his head. "You wouldn't know her. She goes to University of Richmond."

"Okay, Ral, have fun."

"See you around."

"See you," I said. He continued down the street and I turned and headed in the direction of my apartment complex.

I dragged my feet down the sidewalk, trying to block out the phantom thoughts that were always hovering too close to the surface. Talking to Ral had triggered them again. Between Thom's words and John practically jumping on me at the club, I was having a lot of trouble thinking straight. I was glad finals were starting soon. I wouldn't have much time to think such dangerous thoughts.

CHAPTER 21
FINALITY AND FINALS

My flight was boarding. Finally. I needed to get the hell out. I had decided to abandon everything. I called Dettweiler, the law firm that I was supposed to work for that summer, and told them I wasn't coming. I wrote my mother a letter because I was too weak to face her and tell her the truth. I wrote Suse and Astoria emails for the same reason. My lease with Tia was up. I was running away. I didn't want any of it anymore. Law school seemed so unimportant. Everything in my life seemed badly constructed and wrong.

John had mended my heart, shattered it, and then shattered it even more. Every time I thought about him was another stab to my heart. The more I tried not to think about every time he'd made me laugh, held me, touched me, told me he loved me . . . the more those thoughts filled me up so that I could see, hear, think nothing else. The more I remembered our brief—very brief—time together. We started dating a little before Thanksgiving. It ended a little before Valentines Day. It didn't seem right. We'd deserved more time together. Every memory hurt. And then there were Thom's words still scorching my head and heart.

I fought my way through finals even though my heart wasn't in law school anymore. My heart wasn't in anything anymore. My life just felt kind of stale.

I'd given it my best shot, but finally realized there was no salvaging my old life. It was a complete mystery how I'd gotten through finals, but I was done. I resigned from my position as editor-in-chief on the law review board for the upcoming year. What was the point? I wasn't going back. Not that they knew it yet, but I wasn't. I was done. I decided that as I turned in my last final. I had thought, what was I doing there? That I didn't want to be there. And there was no reason for me to stay. I didn't want law school or anything else in Virginia. I didn't stop to think about how selfish that might be to my friends and family.

Time to walk away. Nothing had turned out right. My plan had failed in every way possible. I had to leave my painful, old life behind.

The night after my last final, while watching a reality show set in Vegas, I started wondering about how great it would be if I could just go to Vegas. Start over. Then I asked myself why not? Why couldn't I? Couldn't I at least get a fresh start? Didn't I deserve that much?

John, as always, had had perfect timing. And so he picked that night to show up on my doorstep. I don't know what possessed him to come over that night. I just knew that he had some nerve after everything that had happened. He showed up right as I had been in the midst of my dreams of starting over. He came in without a word and went straight to my room. I followed, making faces at his back the whole way.

"Come on in," I said sarcastically as I shut my door. He didn't say a word. I crossed the room, glaring at him, and sat on my bed.

John sat next to me with a sigh. He put his head in his hands. His shoulders slumped forward. I continued to stare straight ahead, my arms folded over my chest.

"I don't know what else to say. I've told you I'm sorry, like, six hundred times," he said hollowly. Mechanically. As if he was just saying what he thought he ought to say.

"You've said enough. You've said way too much," I said quietly, my heart beating rapidly. I tried not to let myself think about the possibility that he had come over to tell me he wanted to be with me. "I don't even know why you're here."

"I'm trying to get you to stop hating me. But that seems pretty futile," John said softly.

I finally turned to face him, my mouth hanging open in disbelief. "You the one been actin' hateful. How you gonna say something like that? All you do is come around here, trying to make me feel guilty for just trying to get through life the best way I can. It's hard right now, you know."

"It's hard for me, too."

"Bull."

"Whatever. I should have known better than to try to have a real conversation with you. To try and reason with you."

"Yeah. Whatever you say. You're always right. I don't know shit."

"I didn't say that," John said with an impatient sigh. He ran his hands over his head and clasped them behind his neck, his head lowering slightly further.

"Why did I let you in? Why did you even come over? No, why did you ever even kiss me? Why'd you ever even talk to me? If it was just going to lead to this? I wish you and her were just married and out of my life already!"

"I don't think you do," John said quietly. "I also don't think you have ever tried to see it from my side."

"And what's your side? Huh? What could possibly be so wrong in your perfect little life? Especially since you got rid of me?" I snapped.

"Like you give a damn. All you want is to hear yourself ranting, Denise. That's all you've ever done since this whole mess started back in January," he said, still not looking up. Hands still clasped over his neck. I glared at the top of his head, but I was still curious. Especially thinking back to my phone conversation with Thom.

"C'mon. I'm giving you your chance. You're always giving me that same, tired line about me not letting you speak. So go on."

"What's the point if you never listen to what I have to say?"

"Well, you're the one who came over here. I didn't ask you to. If you have something to say, say it. I'm listening."

"Yeah right."

"I am," I said in a less harsh tone.

"It's funny that you just assume I have everything because my family has money. I mean, you really think money means a person has no problems? Denise, I wish you knew what it was like to be a commodity to your parents instead of a son. And all of those people? I feel more alone around them than when I'm anywhere else. You think I'm a spoiled frat boy, huh? Well, you're always accusing people of stereotyping you, but you were happy enough to stick that label on *me* without looking deeper."

I said nothing. I could think of nothing to say. I knew I had to hold onto my anger, though. It was all I had left. It was holding me together.

"Denise, you were one of the few people in my life that I felt more than nothing with. You made me warm inside. I don't know exactly what it was about you, but I just felt like everything was going to be okay when I was with you. But our love maybe scared me. I dunno. I'd never been in love before. I didn't know what to do. And I don't think you knew, either. We were both fumbling in the dark. We were playing a dangerous game. And we had no idea what the rules were."

"I never—you can't speak for me—I . . ." But the right words just wouldn't come to me. He finally looked up, smiling sadly at me. His liquid green eyes shone with unshed tears. I hadn't known it was possible for my heart to break even more until that moment. He gently put his hand to my mouth.

"It's the way it has to be now. I'm sorry I hurt you. I'm sorry we hurt each other. But I'm not sorry I talked to you. I'm not sorry I kissed you. And even though it didn't work out, I will never be sorry I fell in love with you. And I'm glad, I'm so glad that I love you and I'll always love you. Because I haven't felt such a real, raw emotion in

NICOLE GREEN

maybe . . . ever. And it makes me feel alive. Even now. When almost everything else inside of me is dead."

"John, what are you saying? Where is all this coming from?" I mumbled over his hand. I took it away from my lips and placed it over my heart.

"I know you think I'm full of it. I know you probably hate me for what I've done and even more for what I'm saying. But I can't help it. It's how I feel," John said, tears silently falling down his cheeks. I saw red. My teeth clenched. I pushed his hand away from me.

"Out." I shrank away as he reached for me.

"Denise—"

"Just get out of here," I said, my voice rising an octave with every syllable.

"I was just trying to explain everything to you." John rose to his feet.

"Out of here now. With your doubletalk and your lies. I don't want to hear it anymore. You get out and don't you ever come back. Let Sasha put up with your nonsense!" I followed him all the way to the front door, screaming at him.

"Denise, why don't you understand—"

"What? That you're a nut case? I understand that fine!" I slammed the door in his face.

Time to make a change.

Immediately after John left, I started looking up flights. The next morning, I packed up a couple of suitcases and took the rest of my stuff to the Salvation Army. I mailed the letters that I had written to my parents and sent the emails I had saved as drafts the night before to

Suse and Astoria. Those were the only people who needed to know. But I didn't want to see any of them.

As I got on the plane, I started mentally going over my plan again. I would live in a hotel until I could find an apartment. I would look for work in the casinos as soon as I got there. I had looked online briefly after buying my ticket. I decided I wanted to try to find work as a blackjack dealer. I just liked the sound of it. All a part of my new "on a whim" lifestyle. I decided to bluff experience if it was required. I had played blackjack before. How hard could it be? I could probably figure it out. Besides, options were limited. It wasn't like I could be a showgirl with my lack of coordination.

I sat in my seat with a sigh and closed my eyes, hoping some loud, obnoxious woman wouldn't come sit next to me and tell me her life story. Knowing I was going to get somebody as it was a full flight, I hoped it would be someone quiet. And small. Who wouldn't fight me for the armrest. But when I saw the screaming kid followed by the stressed-out, yelling mom heading for my row, I rolled my eyes, took out my sleep mask, and put my headphones on.

Why should things start going my way now? I thought with a heavy sigh.

CHAPTER 22
TWENTY-ONE

That Thursday, I opened my front door as I was buttoning the vest of my dealer's uniform, expecting room service. I was a blackjack dealer-in-training. I looked up, readying myself to tell the waiter yet another lie about why he would get no tip and stopped in mid-button as I saw Suse and Astoria and two of the fakest smiles I'd ever seen in my life. I didn't so much as attempt a fake smile of my own.

"What are you doing here?" I asked flatly. They walked in uninvited, rolling their suitcases along.

"We could ask the same question of you," Suse asked as their eyes traveled around my suite. It was pretty nice. Lots of large, expensive furniture, a gigantic flat-screen television, a bar, and all the other usual suite perks. Since Visa was footing the bill for at least a while. But I knew my days were numbered and that I'd soon be heading to some disgusting roach haven.

"Obviously you got my email," I sighed, closing the door. I turned to face them, arms crossed over my chest.

"Yeah, but it didn't make much sense. I mean, did you really think that we would let you run all the way across the country and—" Astoria started.

"What Astoria is trying to say—" Suse broke in.

"I don't need rescuing," I cut Suse off. Period. End of story. Except it wasn't going to be so easy with those two. I should have known better, and was silently cursing myself for sending them emails at all.

"Well, apparently you do. How else do you explain this?" Astoria muttered.

Suse threw her a scathing glance. Astoria smirked at her, but said nothing. There was a very distinct change between the two of them, but I was too busy being angry at them to fully pick up on what it was at the time.

"Look. If my parents aren't even out here, what makes you two think you can do this?" I snapped.

"They're only not here because we told them not to worry and that we'd bring your craz—that we'd bring you back. You really freaked 'em out," Astoria said.

I just kept staring at them with iced-over eyes, but inside, I winced at that comment.

"Well, you wasted your time," I said.

"Oh, no, you don't. You had all us driving all across the country—"

"You drove? What were you thinking?"

"I know you didn't just ask what *we* were thinking." Astoria dropped her suitcase and threw her hands up in a gesture connoting disbelief.

"I want to be left alone. How many times do I have to say that? How many ways do I have to say that?"

"If that was true, why did you email us?"

"I didn't want anybody to worry."

"Then you shouldn't have run off to Vegas like you did. I can't believe how selfish you are. Whose problems did you solve? Not even yours! Think about it!" Astoria screamed.

I stood there in stunned silence. There was that word again. Selfish. Was I? Wasn't I entitled to be? It was my life. Didn't I get to decide what happened in my own life?

But how much control did I have over my own life if I was doing crazy things like running off to Vegas? And how much had it helped? I'd cried myself to sleep every night since arriving. And I had a photo of John and myself tucked under my pillow at that very moment. On top of that, I'd never felt more lonely and sad than when I'd stepped off of the plane a few days earlier. And wasn't I fighting at that very moment not to feel relief that Suse and Astoria were there—to feel anger instead? Hadn't I been fighting to feel anger for so very long?

"So this is you two knowing what's best for me again?" I asked, stubbornly holding onto my self-right-eousness.

"No. This is us trying to be your friends. This is us determined to help. Friends don't let friends run off to Sin City and—and—please tell me you're wearing that ridiculous outfit for some reason other than you're a blackjack dealer," Suse said.

I laughed, unbuttoning my vest and tossing it onto the back of the couch.

"Okay, okay. Let me call in to the casino and tell them I'm not coming tonight. This thing with us is going to take a while, I guess. And yes, I am. A very good one,"

I said, turning away from them and finally allowing a smile to spread across my face.

⌒⁓

Later that night, we were all sitting around with a bottle of wine, laughing. And I was extremely happy they had followed me. I begrudgingly realized I hadn't been as ready to run away as I'd thought I was.

"Remember how we used to talk all the time about how we were going to take a trip to Vegas before we graduated?" I asked.

Astoria and Suse laughed.

"Oh, yeah. Well, this definitely isn't how we planned it, huh?" Suse said with a lazy grin.

"Guess not," I said, squinting at the wine bottle. "Okay. I'm going to get the other one out of the fridge."

"Wow. I think this should be it," Astoria mumbled, face down on the floor. She had the lowest tolerance of all of us and was just about done in.

Suse, Astoria, and I discussed a lot that evening. I could tell they were treading lightly, especially Astoria, and I appreciated it. They were really trying. I decided to put forth effort, too. I needed to do better than I was doing. I had never looked at the situation in a light that put me at fault. I tried to make everyone else the villain. To some extent, maybe they were. But I wasn't completely helpless and hapless. And I definitely needed to accept that maybe running away would accomplish nothing. But for that night, I was working mainly on accepting the idea that it was possible for me to be wrong. Baby steps.

Little did I know at the time that their sneaky asses had gone behind my back and called that fool up. Apparently, John hadn't been happy at all since our breakup and especially since Barrister's. And the more wedding plans Sasha and Elizabeth made, the more miserable John became.

John, by nature a party boy, had really been screwing his life and liver up since Barrister's. Apparently, he'd been out drinking with Tyler and Shawn every night after finals had ended. Sasha didn't care because she was wrapped up in visions of white and wedding bells. His parents didn't care, either. All they knew was that he had "regained his senses." Nobody was there to watch him spin down, down, down. But Suse and Astoria had noticed. And they put every feeling they had about the situation aside except for their concern for me.

So once they found me in Vegas, they gave Mr. John Archer a call. They waited until I went to work the next night. They didn't waste any time.

"What?" he slurred into the phone.

Astoria put him on speaker phone. "Listen, drunk ass, it's Astoria and Suse."

"What do you want? You ain't done enough yet?" John belched loudly into the phone.

What does she see in this fool? Astoria mouthed to Suse. Suse shrugged.

"I never did anything to you," Astoria snapped.

"You put ideas in Denise's head."

"I was just trying to warn her about guys like you. And you did just what I said you would, didn't you?"

"Okay, I'm hanging up now."

"Wait!" Suse cried, giving Astoria a dirty look and mouthing, *This is for Denise. Stop.*

"I'm waiting," John slurred in a sing-song voice.

Astoria rolled her eyes. She sat back on the bed.

"We're with Denise. In Vegas. And we think you should come here," Suse said with a sigh. There was a long pause on the other end. "John?"

"What are you doing in *Vegas*?"

"We found her here. She's got a job as a blackjack dealer, she claims she's dropping out of law school and she's never coming back," Astoria said and mouthed, *And it's all your fault!*

"She doesn't want me there," John said.

Astoria threw herself back on the bed with an exasperated sigh. Suse gave her a disapproving look and leaned in closer to the phone.

"She's sick over you, John. And I think you're sick over her, too," Suse said.

"I'm engaged," John countered quietly.

"Do you love Sasha?"

"I'm marrying Sasha. That's the way it's gotta be," John said.

Astoria stood up, shaking her head and went into the bathroom.

"And you don't want Denise anymore? You don't even want to be her friend? You don't want to stop her from throwing her life away?" Suse asked gently. "Because at this point, I think you're the only one who can."

"No, I can't," John said.

"John, what is *wrong* with you?" Suse said. "My best friend can't get over you, you can't get over her, and you really want to keep pretending she doesn't matter to you and marry someone you can't stand?"

"You don't know anything about me and Sasha."

"I know you haven't looked any happier than Denise has since the two of you broke up," Suse said.

"Well, she's impossible. She's the one who pushed me away."

"It wasn't easy for her—"

"For *her*? I was almost disowned!"

"John, think how she felt. She never thought you'd choose her over your family. She doesn't trust easily and she has trouble letting people in. Whatever. We all have flaws. But she had all that stuff with the Tau Gammas going on and everything. You could have tried to see it from her side a little more," Suse said.

John was quiet again.

Astoria burst back into the room and stormed over to where her phone lay on the bed. She shouted down at it, "You have no idea what she's even been through, do you? You know who Joe is?"

"Who?" John had obviously never heard of Joe.

"Astoria, no. Denise wouldn't want us—" Suse started.

Astoria shushed her impatiently. "No. He needs to hear this. And he will."

"Hear what?" John spoke up.

Astoria flopped down on the bed next to the phone. "Joe was Denise's boyfriend in college. Her first and only boyfriend before your lame—"

"Astoria! What did we talk about?"

"Okay, Suse. Calm down. Anyway, she met Joe in her last year of undergrad at a party. She was really in love with this guy. And he treated her right and said all the right things for a while. Then, one day, somebody new caught his eye and he was gone. Just like that. No explanation. Just a text message saying he didn't want to see her anymore. He wouldn't answer her calls, emails, texts, anything.

"Denise thought she would never be able to love anyone again. She had gotten it in her head in those few months they were together that he was the only one for her. He told her some stupid lie about wanting to marry her and she believed it. She just knew that they would get married after graduation and she had already started planning her life around him.

"When he left her, it destroyed her. I mean, completely destroyed her. It even broke her body down. She was so sick that the doctor almost misdiagnosed her with mono. She lay in bed for weeks, missing most of her classes. Her GPA plummeted. She shut everyone out. She lost most of her friends from undergrad that year because of it. And after that, she convinced herself that if he could say all those things and not mean them—if he could seem that sincere and be lying the whole time—that it was impossible to find true love.

"Just thought you should know all of that. Since you're so ready to blame her for everything," Astoria said.

I was furious when I first heard that Astoria had told him about Joe, but ironically, Joe probably helped bring us back together. Joe was a part of the darkest days of my past. Losing your first love is never easy. But when you're stressed out anyway in your last year of school and not knowing where your life is headed, and you're emotionally fragile to begin with, it can be devastating.

"You shouldn't have done that. Denise wouldn't have wanted him to find out like that," Suse hissed.

"He needed to hear it," Astoria said firmly.

Unable to argue with that, Suse turned her attention back to the phone. "John?"

Suse thought he'd hung up when he said, "Suse?"

"Yeah?"

"I know. I know we both messed up. And I do want to try to make this work. I want that more than anything. What I'm really afraid of is she won't give me another chance. I've already screwed up so much with her," John's voice cracked. "Especially considering what Astoria just said."

"John, she ran away from home over you. This thing between you two is not beyond repair. You still have her heart. You just have to be more careful with it. Really. If you break it again, I'll break your neck," Suse said.

John laughed. "Suse . . . I really hope you're not wrong about this."

"I'm not."

"I'm going to buy my ticket tonight. Don't tell her I'm coming, okay?"

"Are you kidding? So she can run away again?"

"I thought you said this is what she wants."

"Yeah, but she doesn't know that yet," Suse said with a sly grin. John laughed again. Suse heard the clicking of a keyboard in the background from John's end. He asked for the hotel's address and she gave it to him.

"Okay, I'm looking up flights right now. See you tomorrow, Suse."

"All right. Bye." Suse hit the "end" button on her phone, feeling pretty pleased with herself.

"So you talked him into it." Astoria looked shocked out of her mind.

Suse shrugged. "Yeah, with your help. As unbelievable as that is. Denise may kill you for what you just did."

"Whatever. He's coming. That's the important thing."

"Just don't break them up again. I can't keep going through this." Suse stood up and pulled her travel bag onto the bed.

"I didn't break them up before. Stop saying that."

"Just kidding," Suse said, walking toward the bathroom with her bag. "Sort of," she muttered under her breath.

"I heard that!" Astoria called after her.

Suse laughed as a flip-flop went sailing past her head, way to her left.

CHAPTER 23

JOHN ARCHER

I think I had a small heart attack when I opened the door and John was standing on the other side.

"You're being really stupid. How could you blow off your job like that?" Not the greeting I had expected. And it automatically put me on the defensive, of course.

"You're engaged to someone you don't love. I'm stupid?" I snapped.

"You gonna let me in?"

"I'm thinking about it," I said, crossing my arms over my chest. Inside, I'd never been happier to see someone in my life. But I didn't move. Because inside, I was also furious.

"Why did you do this?" John asked.

"That's not any of your business," I said shortly. I started to close the door. He pushed it open and pushed me backward into the room. He shut the door behind him and went into the living area of my suite. He sat on the sofa and looked up at me as if he was waiting for me to come over and sit. I stayed exactly where I was. He'd already pushed his way into the room. He wasn't going to command me around it, too.

I stared at him angrily, at a loss for words. Where did he get off? Where had he even come from?

"How'd you know I was here?" I asked, still making no moves.

"How do you think?" he asked in a tone matching mine in nastiness. "How many people know you're here, Denise?"

I rolled my eyes. "Astoria and Suse."

"You have some nosy friends. But that's a good thing this time."

"So I guess they talked you into coming here to talk me out of dropping out of school and talk me into coming back. Which is pointless," I said, biting my lip, tears threatening to fall. So many emotions were flooding through me for him at that moment. And almost all of them involved running over to him and jumping into his arms and pretending none of the last few months had happened. But there was just so much hurt inside of me.

"I'm not here to save the day," he said quietly. I couldn't look into those eyes. I looked over the top of his head. I hated him. I loved him. I never wanted to see him again, but I'd die if he ever left that suite. "I'm here for you and only you. I love you. And I'm not leaving without you."

"What are you talking about? You stop it right now. Your mom and Sasha are picking out china patterns. I've been down this road with you too many times, and I'm sick of it. You're not doing this to me again. I refuse to let you." I pounded my thigh with my fist for emphasis. "You told me love wasn't enough. Remember?" And I couldn't hold back the tears anymore. My whole body shook. I turned away from him. I was sobbing so hard I could barely breathe. But when I could catch my breath between sobs, all I could do was scream.

"I was wrong," he said quietly. I could hear him walking toward me. I ran out onto the balcony. But before I could get the door shut, he was out there, too. And blocking my way back inside. Nowhere to hide. "Love is enough. It's all that matters."

I sank down to the cement floor of the balcony and hugged my knees to my chest. I rested my head against my knees. I was still sobbing—only a little quieter.

"Do you—know how much it hurt—to hear you were marrying her? Do you— know how much it hurt—to lose you? Do you *know*—how much it *hurt*—to try to hate you? Do you know how much it hurt to think I would never see you again?" I said, almost over my sobs. I burst into fresh tears after I got my last word out.

"I'm never going to hurt you again," he said solemnly. I shrank from his touch, forcing myself as far into the corner I was sitting in as I could manage.

"You're right. Because you're not going to get the chance," I said.

John sighed, lowering himself to the floor of the balcony and sitting right in front of me.

I put my head back down on my knees.

"I messed up big time. Huge. I could make a lot of excuses you don't want to hear. But they're all true. I was scared. Okay, I'm a punk. But this is hard for me. It's taken a lot of adjusting. And trying to figure out what I really wanted. And I mean, you just made it so easy for me. When you picked that fight, I took the loser's way out. But I'm not taking it out again," John said softly.

I still wouldn't look at him. "I bet you didn't even call the engagement off yet."

"I just got here. I'll do it right now. Right here in front of you if you want," John said.

I looked up. He had his phone in his hand.

"Why are you doing this to me?" I asked. "I'm tired of being hurt. Please stop," I said.

"Denise, all I want is you."

"You're engaged."

"I want you. Whatever you want. I'd get engaged to you today. I'd marry you right now. This is Vegas. There's probably a wedding chapel in the lobby," John said.

I laughed reluctantly.

John smiled, looking a little relieved. "Can I at least hug you?" John asked. I didn't say anything. John stood up. He took my hands in his and pulled me to my feet.

It was all over. His touch. Those perfectly green eyes. I couldn't stop him from pulling me to him and I didn't want to. I wrapped my arms around him and squeezed his shoulders. He felt like John. He smelled like John.

It all came rushing back in on me so quickly that I would have lost my footing if he hadn't been holding me so tightly. He was really holding me. I felt his phone vibrate against his thigh. He took it out with one hand, still holding me with the other arm. He groaned. I knew he was rolling his eyes even though I kept my face tightly pressed into his T-shirt.

"It's Sasha, isn't it?" I mumbled into his shirt.

"Yeah," John sighed.

"Answer it. Tell her," I said suddenly, looking up. He smiled. He took my hand in his and led me back inside as he answered his phone. He put it on speaker.

"Hey Sasha," he said, setting the phone on the coffee table and sitting on the sofa. He pulled me onto his lap. I smiled, burying my head in his shirt again. I'd missed his smell so much. I'd missed his everything so much.

"Where have you been? You haven't returned any of my messages. I called you like, five times," she snapped.

John put his arm around me, squeezing my shoulder. "Sorry. I've had a busy morning."

"What? Where are you? You're supposed to be on your way to Boston. We have our engagement pictures tomorrow."

"I'm in Vegas," John said.

"Vegas? What the hell are you doing in Vegas?"

"I'm with Denise. It's over, Sasha. For real this time."

Sasha let out a shrill, piercing sound I can only describe as a howl. "Enough of this nonsense, John. I have your grandmother's ring. And I've booked the cathedral. You know how hard it is to get that reservation? And you just can't do this. I'm coming to get you right now!"

"Good luck finding me," John said. "This is Vegas. There are a lot of places I could be."

"I'm calling your mother right now. I'm going to put her on three-way right now!"

"Go ahead. She needs to hear this, too. Thanks," John said.

I looked up at him. He kissed my forehead. I rested my head on his shoulder, smiling. I couldn't remember the last time I'd felt so happy.

"Archer residence," John's mom's shrill voice came through.

"Liz! He's in Vegas! With Denise!" Sasha roared.

"John! John!" Elizabeth sounded hysterical.

"Hi, Mom. Say hi, Denise," John said, grinning.

"Hi," I said.

"Denise and I wanted you to be the first two to know. We're engaged," John said. I stared at him wordlessly. He whispered to me, "If you'll have my stupid ass."

"You can't be engaged to her. You're engaged to me!" Sasha screamed at the same time John's mother screamed something similar.

"Not anymore," John said. "Mom, it's between you and Sasha how you're getting Grandma's ring back. It's not my concern anymore. I wouldn't want to give it to Denise even if you'd let me. And I'm sure she wouldn't want it, anyway," John said.

I turned around to face him, my knees straddled on either side of him. I pulled him to me in a fierce kiss.

"John. We have discussed this," his mom said.

"No, John! You get your butt back here right now!"

I couldn't tell you how long they screamed into that phone or anything else they said. John and I had stopped paying attention to them. He was my world and I was his. And we also had a lot of kissing to catch up on.

Later that evening, John and I were still on the sofa. Suse and Astoria had insisted on getting their own room, at least for that night. We were just lying there together. I had never been happier to do anything than to just lie in his arms. The only thing we'd done since breaking the news to Sasha and Elizabeth was take a nap. We hadn't even moved from that spot. That evening was delicious.

I watched the sun sink lower in the sky, so satisfied with everything.

"I got you something for Valentine's Day. Obviously, I never got to give it to you. I brought it with me," John said.

"What is it?" I asked, pulling his arms tighter around me.

"First, you never answered my question earlier."

"You never asked properly," I said, knowing exactly what he was referring to.

John smiled, getting up from behind me. "Fair enough." He went over to his bag and pulled out a small, black box. He turned back to me. My eyes went wide. My mouth went dry. "You're the one I really wanted to ask."

"Huh?" I said weakly.

"Now, I wanted a romantic dinner. I had rented a tux. I was going to go all out. And I want you to remember that when you tell people about this. But I can't wait anymore."

"Huh?" I stared down at the black velvet.

John dropped to one knee in front of me. He opened the box. Even in the dim light of the room, that thing was sparkling. It was the biggest rock I'd ever seen in real life. I couldn't take my eyes off it. John gently lifted my chin, bringing my eyes back to his.

"So. I already gave you my huge speech on why you make my life worthwhile earlier today. And you do. You really do. And I want you to keep doing that forever. Will you marry me?" John was grinning.

I thought my face would crack with the smile spreading over it as I nodded vigorously. I couldn't make words come out. I didn't even try. He took the ring out of the box. My heart was pounded as he took my left hand in his.

As he slid the ring onto my finger, I finally found my voice again. "So you were going to ask me then?"

"Yeah."

"But you barely knew me."

"I knew that I couldn't get enough of you."

"And you asked Sasha instead," I said, my anger flaring a little; I forced myself to not give into it. That was the past.

"I know. It wasn't smart. I was a moron."

"Yep."

"All I can say is I'm sorry. I mean, I can't go back in time. I wish I could. There's so much time I wouldn't waste not being with you if I could," John said quietly, earnestly. I just sat there, staring at him, trying to take it all in. "So?"

"I think I deserve another big speech," I finally responded.

"I think you do, too. I think you deserve anything you want that I can possibly give to you," John said, kissing my hand gently. I held it up to my face, inches from it. Wow. Was that really mine?

"Okay, so big speech," I grinned, admiring my hand.

He took my hand down from my face, kissing it again. He nodded. "Denise, I can't believe how lucky I am. I thought my dumb ass had ruined everything between us. It killed me to see you with Erich at Barrister's. It killed me to see you and not be with you. I hated to see Donnovan near you. I wanted to kill Tyler when he touched you. I think I tried to.

"I thought I had ruined everything. And I almost did. But then, this miracle happened today. You decided to give me a second chance. Not that I deserve it. And I don't know what I can ever do to make things up to you. But I'm going to try my hardest to do that.

"I was so stupid. I had the most wonderful thing I'd ever seen or known in my life. And I did worse than let it go. I pushed it away. And I would have hated myself for that for the rest of my life, but you rescued me from myself yet again by forgiving me. You are a beautiful person. I'm better because you love me. My life has worth—meaning—because you want to be in it. And all I could think of from the moment I was stupid enough to drive off and leave you standing there that day was how all the light was gone from my life because I was dumb enough to let it go. No. To make it go.

"And all this time, it seemed like the more I tried to tell myself I was doing the right thing, the more I realized just how wrong I was. I was crazy to do what I did. And I drove myself even crazier after I did it. I was hurting, Denise. I know I hurt you and it kills me that I did. But I was hurting, too. And knowing what I was doing to you made it even worse.

"But tonight, you healed me. Tonight, you changed everything. For the better. I'm never going to be the same John again. And I don't want to be. I want to be better. I want to be the man you deserve. And I want us to have a great life together. I want to marry you. And for us to have a family. And I want us to raise our kids to be just like you. Because you are the best, most golden person I know in this world.

"And I don't care what my parents or anyone else thinks. Our life—our love has nothing to do with them. They don't have anything I need. Because all I need is you. And if they can't accept you, then they can't accept me. You're a part of me. You always will be. The very best part of me. I love them, but they're stupid. And if I never talk to them again, it won't be because of anything I did wrong, and definitely not because of anything you did wrong. And so I'm okay with that. They either accept all of me, which includes you, or they accept none of me.

"And so, all this love I have for you. This love is so big, so deep, I can't—I don't know how to explain it. I can't put it into words. All this love is all that matters. That's all I know. That and I want to be close to you forever. Because you bring me a joy. A joy and a peace that I've never known before. I just feel like things are so natural when I'm with you. They are the way they should be. I just—love you so much. You're all that's best about me. And all I can do is say that I love you, I never stopped loving you, and I will always love you so much that I just—I feel like my heart isn't even big enough to hold it all," John said.

I couldn't think of a word to say. I suddenly became aware of the fact that I had been crying as he gently wiped tears of joy, anger, and frustration from my face. I gave him a watery smile. He kissed me gently. I sighed happily against his lips as he pulled me to him.

CHAPTER 24

THIS ISN'T WHAT
THEY WANTED

John and I never stopped kissing all the way to the bedroom. Our lips only broke contact as we hastily removed our shirts. I couldn't believe that any of it was real. As we fell back onto the bed, I pressed my body into John's. I wanted to be surrounded by him. I fully enjoyed his hands, lips and tongue all over my skin. He filled up my world in a way I had longed for ever since he'd lost his mind and left me. Especially since the night of Barrister's. He was the world to me and I never wanted anything else to exist ever again.

"I wanted you so much that night in the hotel room," I whispered in his ear.

"I know. I don't blame you for leaving, though. I was such an ass," he whispered back, gently biting at my earlobe.

"Yeah, well, that's the past now. I'm so glad that's the past."

"What's this?" John asked with an amused grin. He was holding the picture that had been beneath the pillow. I tried to grab it, but he moved away from me. "Oh, I think somebody likes me," he said, moving to the edge of the bed.

"You are such a jerk," I said, laughing. I reached for him again, and he fell off the bed in the process of trying to get away from me. I laughed even harder. "See? That's what you get!"

"Denise, you're a strange person," John laughed, fending off the pillow I was attempting to beat him with as he jumped back onto the bed.

"Yeah?" I said.

He threw the pillow back to the head of the bed. "Oh, yeah," he said as he gently slid one of my bra straps down and kissed my shoulder. "You uh—run away from me, but you still keep a picture of me under your pillow."

"Who says I was running away from you?" I asked breathily as he laughed into my other shoulder. He dropped my bra to the floor. "I never said why I left."

"Well, how many law-students-turned-blackjack-dealers do you know? You had a burning passion suddenly so intense, it compelled you to come out to Vegas and pursue your true calling?"

"Something like that." I grinned, watching my pants sail across the room. They were soon followed by John's jeans.

He laughed softly in my ear before kissing it, pushing me gently back onto the bed. He suddenly stopped, giving me a look that was too close to sadness to fit with the moment we were sharing. "What?"

"That thing Astoria said before. About you crying yourself to sleep every night. Was it true?"

I looked away from him. I didn't want to talk or think about that. I had him back and that's all that mattered.

"Denise, it hurts me that I hurt you," John said thickly.

I put my hand to his cheek, shaking my head. I'd missed him so much. I couldn't believe I was finally getting what I wanted. I didn't want to think about those things.

"It doesn't matter now. All that matters is you're here."

He kissed my forehead. "I know about Joe."

"You what?" I pulled away from him, sitting up in the bed.

"Astoria told me."

"She what?" I was furious. It hadn't been Astoria's place to say anything about Joe, or anything else. John sat back on his heels, looking at me with doleful eyes. I felt too betrayed and exposed to say anything. "Is that why you're here? You feel sorry for me?"

"I'm here because I love you. No other reason," he said solemnly, moving over to sit next to me. I let him take my hand in his, but I didn't say anything. "But I can't stand that he did what he did to you. And that I did what I did after what you'd been through."

"John, it doesn't matter anymore," I said, while trying to ignore the pain the memories brought to me. I just wanted John. I didn't want to fight. And I wanted to believe his words whether or not they were true. He hugged me to his side.

"Yes, it does. I want you to know I'll never be like him. I never want you to cry yourself to sleep over me again. I'm going to try—I'm going to try so hard—to make sure it doesn't happen, okay?" John whispered to me.

I nodded, and then I felt him kiss the top of my head.

"I'm tired." I really was despite the long nap we'd had earlier. The day had been draining and John had completely killed the mood. He stood and helped me to my feet. I walked to the bathroom to get ready for bed, making it clear that I needed some time alone. He respected that.

Joe was from a part of me that I didn't like to visit. Astoria had nearly ruined everything again by trying to help. I didn't want to feel as if he had interrupted my life yet again. I really tried to believe that John had come back because of me and not because of guilt. And on top of that, I hadn't wanted John to know yet. That I had nearly lost my mind once. I wasn't sure that I had ever wanted him to know.

When I came out of the bathroom, he was watching television in the living area of the suite. I went into the bedroom and lay down. I pretended to be asleep when I felt him climb into bed an hour or so later. I couldn't fight the warmth I felt, however, when he put his arm around me and drew me close to him.

"I love you," he whispered as he curled his body around mine.

I hope so. Because I love you so much it scares me, I thought.

The next morning, I grumbled, pushing John away and rolling over as he teased my neck with his tongue.

"It's too early," I complained as his hand traveled slowly down my back, caressing me as it went. His hand did feel good against my skin, but eight in the morning was definitely too early.

"I've been thinking about this for a long time, Denise. I can't wait any longer. Besides, it's never too early for a good morning."

"A good morning, huh?" I asked as he trailed soft, slow kisses across my neck.

"A *good* morning." He threw the blanket back and pulled me close to him. He whispered against my ear, tickling it softly. I giggled and shivered all at once. He held my eyes with his as he pulled my panties down to my knees. He then watched with greedy anticipation as I wriggled the rest of the way out of them, tossing them off of my foot. He slid his hand slowly up my thigh, pushing my nightshirt up and over my hips. My breathing quickened as his eyes devoured the flesh he had exposed. He bit his lower lip, a hint of white gleaming as he pulled his upper lip up slightly. Warmth radiated from my center as I watched desire consume his face.

He moved between my legs, pushing his shoulders under my thighs. My calves rested lightly on his back. He teased my outer opening with his index finger as he looked up at me with liquid green eyes.

"Still mad I woke you up this morning?" he asked as his finger slipped inside and started making circular motions against a very sensitive area of my body. I couldn't respond. I fell back against my pillows with a deep moan. I felt his mouth press against me in a slow, teasing kiss before his tongue took the place of his finger and his finger slipped inside of me. His tongue flicked insistently against me, bringing me wicked amounts of pleasure. He moaned shakily as he slid in a second finger. I twisted the sheets in my hands as the lower half of my body rocked and writhed in sweet, hot ecstasy. He pressed his lips close, kissing and sucking. My eyes rolled back in my head as I held him tightly to me. The pleasure was relentless. I could hardly breathe as he commanded my body's attention.

"I'm coming," I whispered, barely aware of my words. He mumbled something without his mouth ever leaving its very important work. The vibrations of his mumbling did it. Waves of pleasure took over my body. My breath came in short gasps. My body throbbed against his fingers. He continued to hold that part of me between his teeth even as I shuddered with the last, passing waves of pleasure.

He trailed kisses up from my lower abdomen to my belly button and further upward between my breasts. Up to my chin. He then lay with his body pressed against mine, his face inches from mine.

"Did you like that?" he whispered.

"I know you don't have to ask," I whispered back. We grinned at each other as he gently traced his fingers along my hairline and forehead. "I guess I have to do you now, huh?"

"Not unless you want to. And I think it'd be all over if you did anyway. That made me really—uh—ready to go," he said before kissing my closed lips. That made me want him even more. He had only whetted my appetite for him, and his words were making it worse. "I want you to put the condom on, though. I want you to touch me."

For some reason, that drove me wild. I took the green, square packet from him while kissing him deeply. He groaned as I sucked on his tongue for a moment. I ran my hand up and down his hard length once. He gave a long, drawn-out sigh, putting his hand over mine.

"I'm serious. It'll be done," he said.

I became even wetter for him. I tore the package open with my teeth while giving him what I hoped was a sexy look. I squeezed the tip and slid the latex slowly down and into place while still looking him in the eye.

"John," I murmured as he pulled me close to him. "I need you inside me," I whispered to him as I sat on his stomach, rubbing eagerly against his flesh. He put his hands on my hips, his fingers kneading the flesh there.

"Denise . . ." his voice trailed off as he pushed slightly against my hips. I needed very little prodding. I lifted myself up slightly and we both feverishly guided him into me. He groaned richly as his hands traveled up to my breasts.

I gasped as mind-numbing pleasure took over once he filled me. I lowered myself over him, my elbows digging into the mattress. My hips smacked into his over and over with need and desire.

I looked into his eyes as I felt the sweat beading on my forehead and upper lip. His eyes were so full of desire and love that they made me want him more than I had thought possible. I bent to kiss him and as his tongue slowly pushed over mine; he rolled over so that he was on top without ever separating our lips. He pushed my legs further apart and pressed his thumb to the area he exposed, gently teasing me with it as he thrust feverishly against me.

"I can't—I'm gonna—" I couldn't finish my thought as unreal amounts of pleasure began building inside of me again. I wrapped my legs around him, locking my ankles. My heels rested lightly against his rear.

My breathing became light and shallow and I trembled in anticipation of that final burst of pleasure. John's breathing was ragged in my ear. He pressed his forehead to my cheek for a moment. His thumb stopped moving against me. He put his arms under me and grasped the tops of my shoulders tightly. He pushed himself deeper inside of me. He tried to kiss me, but neither of us could concentrate on our mouths at the moment.

I cried out, pushing my body tightly to his as the waves of pleasure hit again. Just moments later, I felt him pulsing inside of me, which intensified my own peak of satisfaction. I moaned his name over and over as we came down from our sexual highs together.

John lay on top of me for a moment, propped up on his elbows, smiling down at me. I looked up, returning his smile.

"Good morning," he said, kissing my damp cheek.

"Good morning," I said, laughing softly as I reached up and wrapped my arms around his neck. He chuckled before burying his head in my neck.

CHAPTER 25

BUT IT IS WHAT WE NEEDED

Needless to say, I was no favorite of the Archers. When John, Astoria, Suse, and I returned to Virginia, John was faced with a very nasty note telling him of the storage facility where he could find all of his things from Connecticut, quite a few choice words about him and me, and no Kompressor. They had gone as far as sending Alex to the airport to pick it up while we'd still been in Vegas. Not to mention news that he'd have to find his own way to finance his last year of law school, that he had no summer job—he had been lined up to work with his dad in New York—that his trust fund had been revoked, and of course that he'd been written out of the will.

But John took it all in stride. He pointed out that he'd have more time to spend with me since he wouldn't be spending the summer in New York. And we decided to move into my new place together. After a lot of begging, explaining, compromising, and a little lying, I was able to get my landlord to let me have the apartment I'd run out on and I was able to get my summer job back. Considering I had been gone less than two weeks, it wasn't that bad to get things set straight again.

My mom yelled at me and John. A lot. Especially me. But then she got more excited for the wedding than I could have ever hoped for. And my dad gave his blessing almost immediately. He said that anybody who could make me as happy as John had was all right with him, and that what had happened between us was our business. Ah, that's why I love my dad.

Suse seemed genuinely happy for me. And Astoria was biting her tongue better than I'd ever seen before in my life. Suse had made herself my wedding planner almost immediately. The extent of Astoria's input was reminding me of how hideous she looked in baby blue. I immediately told Suse that her and Astoria's dresses had to be baby blue.

The night that John and I moved the last of our stuff into the apartment, we sat on the floor with our Chinese takeout. Most of the furniture from my old apartment had been Tia's, and John's furniture had been shipped back to Connecticut. His parents were determined he wouldn't have it because they paid for it even though they had no use for it.

John was singing, quite horribly, to me songs he thought we should have at our reception. While I was laughing at him and really enjoying just how bad he was, I was also wondering if we would be able to afford a formal ceremony, let alone a reception. Not that it mattered. I already had what I wanted out of the deal. I'd be happy at city hall. I just wanted to be married to John. Part of me was even wishing we'd just done it in Vegas.

"So, you regretting any of this yet?" John asked with a wink. I shook my head vigorously as I swallowed a mouthful of orange chicken.

"Are you? You jobless, carless bum?" I asked, laughing.

"Oh, no. Not one bit. In fact, I'm loving it more every moment." He grinned. "And besides, we have a car. The Sentra is better than that piece of crap I had." He laughed, catching the fortune cookie I'd thrown at his head.

"You know, I'm surprised they didn't take the ring," I said, looking down at my hand and the sparkling rock.

"They couldn't. I bought that with cash back in January. They don't even know about it," John said, putting down his plate and moving over next to me.

"Clever." I grinned.

"I try to be," he said, kissing the tip of my nose.

"Hm. I just hope you never stop loving me."

"Impossible," he said before kissing my ear.

"You think Sasha will ever recover?" I asked.

He laughed into my neck. Sasha had gotten into Central's law school and actually decided to come. Apparently, she was determined to get John back. John had changed his number and not given it out to anyone who talked to Sasha. Not even his parents—not that they wanted it. She kept threatening me. And she routinely sent John emails alternating between threatening and obsessively passionate. And they occasionally contained the tactless nude pic. He showed me every email.

Sasha wasn't a big deal to me anymore. I felt a love from John that I hadn't even known could exist. And the feeling was mutual.

"Ask me if I care." He put his arm around my waist.

"Do you?"

"No."

"You better not," I said, pressing my nose to his. He kissed my closed lips.

"Face it. You're never going to be able to get rid of me now."

"Good. 'Cause the plan is to keep you," I said, pushing John back onto the floor and jumping on top of him.

I was finally happy. I was never letting John Archer go again. For anything or anyone in the world.

ABOUT THE AUTHOR

Nicole Green received a Bachelor of Arts in English from the University of Virginia and she currently attends law school at the College of William and Mary in Williamsburg, Virginia. When she's not studying the law, she returns to Tappahannock, Virginia, where her parents and younger sister live. She enjoys reading, writing and spending time with her hilarious and wonderful friends and family. They inspire her to be a better writer and add to her enjoyment of life every day. You can visit her online at her website at *www.nicolegreen.webs.com*. She would love to hear from you.

2010 Mass Market Titles

January

Show Me The Sun
Miriam Shumba
ISBN: 978-158571-405-6
$6.99

Promises of Forever
Celya Bowers
ISBN: 978-1-58571-380-6
$6.99

February

Love Out Of Order
Nicole Green
ISBN: 978-1-58571-381-3
$6.99

Unclear and Present Danger
Michele Cameron
ISBN: 978-158571-408-7
$6.99

March

Stolen Jewels
Michele Sudler
ISBN: 978-158571-409-4
$6.99

Not Quite Right
Tammy Williams
ISBN: 978-158571-410-0
$6.99

April

Oak Bluffs
Joan Early
ISBN: 978-1-58571-379-0
$6.99

Crossing The Line
Bernice Layton
ISBN: 978-158571-412-4
$6.99

How To Kill Your Husband
Keith Walker
ISBN: 978-158571-421-6
$6.99

May

The Business of Love
Cheris F. Hodges
ISBN: 978-158571-373-8
$6.99

Wayward Dreams
Gail McFarland
ISBN: 978-158571-422-3
$6.99

June

The Doctor's Wife
Mildred Riley
ISBN: 978-158571-424-7
$6.99

Mixed Reality
Chamein Canton
ISBN: 978-158571-423-0
$6.99

2010 Mass Market Titles (continued)
July

Blue Interlude
Keisha Mennefee
ISBN: 978-158571-378-3
$6.99

Always You
Crystal Hubbard
ISBN: 978-158571-371-4
$6.99

Unbeweavable
Katrina Spencer
ISBN: 978-158571-426-1
$6.99

August

Small Sensations
Crystal V. Rhodes
ISBN: 978-158571-376-9
$6.99

Let's Get It On
Dyanne Davis
ISBN: 978-158571-416-2
$6.99

September

Unconditional
A.C. Arthur
ISBN: 978-158571-413-1
$6.99

Swan
Africa Fine
ISBN: 978-158571-377-6
$6.99$6.99

October

Friends in Need
Joan Early
ISBN:978-1-58571-428-5
$6.99

Against the Wind
Gwynne Forster
ISBN:978-158571-429-2
$6.99

That Which Has Horns
Miriam Shumba
ISBN:978-1-58571-430-8
$6.99

November

A Good Dude
Keith Walker
ISBN:978-1-58571-431-5
$6.99

Reye's Gold
Ruthie Robinson
ISBN:978-1-58571-432-2
$6.99

December

Still Waters...
Crystal V. Rhodes
ISBN:978-1-58571-433-9
$6.99

Burn
Crystal Hubbard
ISBN: 978-1-58571-406-3
$6.99

Other Genesis Press, Inc. Titles

Other Genesis Press, Inc. Titles (continued)

Other Genesis Press, Inc. Titles (continued)

Eve's Prescription	Edwina Martin Arnold	$8.95
Everlastin' Love	Gay G. Gunn	$8.95
Everlasting Moments	Dorothy Elizabeth Love	$8.95
Everything and More	Sinclair Lebeau	$8.95
Everything But Love	Natalie Dunbar	$8.95
Falling	Natalie Dunbar	$9.95
Fate	Pamela Leigh Starr	$8.95
Finding Isabella	A.J. Garrotto	$8.95
Fireflies	Joan Early	$6.99
Fixin' Tyrone	Keith Walker	$6.99
Forbidden Quest	Dar Tomlinson	$10.95
Forever Love	Wanda Y. Thomas	$8.95
From the Ashes	Kathleen Suzanne Jeanne Sumerix	$8.95
Frost On My Window	Angela Weaver	$6.99
Gentle Yearning	Rochelle Alers	$10.95
Glory of Love	Sinclair LeBeau	$10.95
Go Gentle Into That Good Night	Malcom Boyd	$12.95
Goldengroove	Mary Beth Craft	$16.95
Groove, Bang, and Jive	Steve Cannon	$8.99
Hand in Glove	Andrea Jackson	$9.95
Hard to Love	Kimberley White	$9.95
Hart & Soul	Angie Daniels	$8.95
Heart of the Phoenix	A.C. Arthur	$9.95
Heartbeat	Stephanie Bedwell-Grime	$8.95
Hearts Remember	M. Loui Quezada	$8.95
Hidden Memories	Robin Allen	$10.95
Higher Ground	Leah Latimer	$19.95
Hitler, the War, and the Pope	Ronald Rychiak	$26.95
How to Write a Romance	Kathryn Falk	$18.95
I Married a Reclining Chair	Lisa M. Fuhs	$8.95
I'll Be Your Shelter	Giselle Carmichael	$8.95
I'll Paint a Sun	A.J. Garrotto	$9.95
Icie	Pamela Leigh Starr	$8.95
If I Were Your Woman	LaConnie Taylor-Jones	$6.99
Illusions	Pamela Leigh Starr	$8.95
Indigo After Dark Vol. I	Nia Dixon/Angelique	$10.95
Indigo After Dark Vol. II	Dolores Bundy/ Cole Riley	$10.95
Indigo After Dark Vol. III	Montana Blue/ Coco Morena	$10.95

Other Genesis Press, Inc. Titles (continued)

Other Genesis Press, Inc. Titles (continued)

Other Genesis Press, Inc. Titles (continued)

Other Genesis Press, Inc. Titles (continued)

Order Form

Mail to: Genesis Press, Inc.
P.O. Box 101
Columbus, MS 39703

Name _____
Address _____
City/State _____ Zip _____
Telephone _____

Ship to (if different from above)
Name _____
Address _____
City/State _____ Zip _____
Telephone _____

Credit Card Information
Credit Card # _____ ☐ Visa ☐ Mastercard
Expiration Date (mm/yy) _____ ☐ AmEx ☐ Discover

Qty.	Author	Title	Price	Total

Use this order form, or call 1-888-INDIGO-1

Total for books	
Shipping and handling:	
$5 first two books,	
$1 each additional book	
Total S & H	
Total amount enclosed	

Mississippi residents add 7% sales tax